Bargai

b

"Adam," G
was my idea, but I suddenly don't
know what to do next."

"We do what we planned to do. We make a child together."

"Right. I mean, that *is* what this is all about. So," she said, looking up at him, "no point wasting time, is there?"

He held her tight, his right hand sliding up her thigh. "Once I make a deal, I stick with it."

His heartbeat thudded beneath her hand and she knew he wasn't as calm as he pretended. "And so do I."

"Good to know. Now, how about we start taking care of business?"

The Wealthy Frenchman's Proposition

by Katherine Garbera

�10᛫᛫᛫᛫0

"I want you to be my fiancée."

"What?" Sheri was sure she'd misunderstood, because she knew Tristan wasn't the marrying kind. She thought he'd said…

"I want you to be my fiancée for the time being. Just until the furore of the press dies down."

She felt the blood rush from her face, and she closed her eyes. Of course it would be temporary.

But, sitting there, she felt a sense of rightness all the way to her soul, and she knew she'd say yes to his outrageous proposal for one reason. She was going to find a way to make Tristan Sabina fall in love with her.

Bargaining for King's Baby
MAUREEN CHILD

The Wealthy Frenchman's Proposition
KATHERINE GARBERA

MILLS & BOON®

Pure reading pleasure™

*First published in Great Britain 2009
by Harlequin Mills & Boon Limited,
Eton House, 18-24 Paradise Road, Richmond, Surrey TW9 1SR*

The publisher acknowledges the copyright holders of the
individual works as follows:

Bargaining for King's Baby © Maureen Child 2008
The Wealthy Frenchman's Proposition © Katherine Garbera 2008

ISBN: 978 0 263 87089 3

51-0209

*Printed and bound in Spain
by Litografia Rosés S.A., Barcelona*

BARGAINING FOR KING'S BABY

by
Maureen Child

Dear Reader,

The KINGS OF CALIFORNIA came about because I was thinking of writing about royalty. My mind whirling around with different ideas, I suddenly thought, what about men who aren't royal, only *think* they are?

The King brothers are arrogant, bossy, sure of their own place in the world and utterly gorgeous. Needless to say, I fell in love with all three of them.

In this book, you'll meet the oldest of the King brothers, Adam. He's been burned by love and has lived to tell the tale. Now he concentrates on the family ranch, building it into the biggest holding in the state. Until, of course, his neighbour Gina Torino comes to him with an offer he can't refuse.

I hope you fall in love with the King family, too. And I'd love to hear from you!

Happy reading,

Maureen

MAUREEN CHILD

is a California native who loves to travel. Every chance they get, she and her husband are taking off on another research trip. An author of more than sixty books, Maureen loves a happy ending and still swears that she has the best job in the world. She lives in Southern California with her husband, two children and a golden retriever with delusions of grandeur.

You can contact Maureen via her website: www.maureenchild.com.

To Carter, for bringing so much love into our lives. We wish for you all the good things life holds, and we're grateful to be able to watch you discover the world around you.

One

"You're obsessed." Travis King looked at his older brother and smiled. "And not in a good way."

"I agree," Jackson King said, with a shake of his head. "Why is this so important to you anyway?"

Adam King looked from one of his brothers to the other and paused for a few seconds before answering them. When he did, he used the tone he usually reserved for his employees—the tone that precluded arguments. "We agreed when we took over the reins of the family businesses from Dad that we'd each be in charge of our own areas."

Then he waited, because Adam knew his brothers weren't finished. Every month, the King brothers held a meeting. They'd get together either here at the family ranch, at the vineyard Travis operated or on one of the executive jets Jackson owned and leased to the mega-wealthy of the world.

The King family had holdings in so many different areas, the monthly meetings helped the brothers keep up with what the tangled lines of the King dynasty were up to at any given moment. But it also gave the brothers a chance to catch up on each other's lives. Even if sometimes, Adam thought, that meant putting up with interference—no matter how well meant.

Picking up his Waterford crystal tumbler of brandy, he swirled the amber liquid in the bottom of the glass and watched the firelight from the hearth wink in its depths. He knew it wouldn't take long to get a comment from his brothers and he silently bet himself that it would be Travis who spoke first. A moment later, he was proven right.

"Yeah, Adam, we each run our own areas," Travis said, taking a deep sip of a King Vineyard Merlot. Travis preferred drinking the wines his vineyard produced to the brandy Adam enjoyed. He shot a look at Jackson, who nodded at him. "That doesn't mean we won't have a question or two."

"Have all the questions you like," Adam told him. He stood up, walked to the massive stone hearth and stared down into the crackling fire. "Just don't expect me to answer them."

Jackson spoke up as if to head off a budding confrontation. Holding his glass of Irish whiskey, he said, "We're not saying that the ranch isn't yours to do with as you want, Adam. We're only trying to figure out why it means so damn much to you to get back every inch of land we used to hold."

Adam turned his back on the fireplace, looked at his brothers and felt that tight bond they'd always shared. Only a year separated each of them and the friendship they'd formed when they were kids was every bit as strong now. But that didn't mean he was going to explain his every move to them. He was still the oldest, and Adam King didn't *do* explanations.

"The ranch is mine," he said simply. "If I want to make it whole again, why should you care?"

"We don't," Travis said, speaking up before Jackson could. Leaning back in the maroon leather chair, he kicked his feet out in front of him, balanced the fragile wineglass on his flat stomach and looked at Adam through slitted eyes. "I just want to know why *you* care. Hell, Adam, Great-Grandpa King sold off that twenty-acre parcel to the Torinos nearly sixty years ago. We already own nearly half the county. Why's that twenty acre plot so important?"

Because he'd set out to do this and Adam had never given up on anything. Once he'd made up his mind to do something, it got done, come hell or high water. He glanced from his brothers to the wide front windows overlooking a stretch of neatly tended lawn and garden that stretched for almost a quarter of a mile before feeding into the road.

This ranch had always been important to him. But in the last five years, it had become everything to him and damned if he'd stop before it was complete again.

Outside, the night was thick and black, broken only by tiny puddles of decorative lights positioned along the wide, curved driveway. This was his home. *Their* home. And he was going to see to it that it was once again completely in King hands.

"Because it's the last missing piece," Adam said, thinking of the last five years. Years that he'd spent buying back every piece of land that had been in the original King land grant more than a hundred and fifty years ago.

The King family had been in central California since before the gold rush. They'd been miners and ranchers and farmers and ship builders. Over the years, the family had changed with the times, moving into different fields, expanding their dynasty. Generations of them had worked to broaden the family's holdings. To grow and build on the previous generations—with one exception.

Their great-grandfather, Simon King, had been more of a gambler than a family scion. And to support his gambling habits, he'd sold off pieces of his heritage. Thankfully the Kings who'd come after Simon had held on to their family history with both hands.

Adam didn't know if he could make his brothers understand—didn't know that he cared to try. All he knew was that he'd devoted the last five years to putting the jigsaw pieces of this ranch back together and he wasn't going to stop until he'd completed the task.

"Fine," Jackson said, shooting Travis a quick *shut-up* look. "If it's that important to you, go ahead."

Adam snorted. "Your permission isn't necessary. But thanks."

Jackson smiled. As always, the youngest of the King boys was almost impossible to rile. "Good luck getting that land away from the Torinos, though," he added, taking a sip of his whiskey and giving a dramatic sigh. "That old man holds on to everything that's his with both hands." His mouth twisted into a smile. "Like you, big brother. Sal's not going to just up and sell it to you."

Adam smiled now, and lifted his brandy snifter in a salute. "What was Dad's favorite saying?"

"Every man's got his price," Travis said, and lifted his glass, too, as he finished their father's quote, *"the trick is to find it the quickest way you can."*

Jackson shook his head, but lifted his glass to his brothers. "Salvatore Torino may be the exception to that rule."

"Not a chance," Adam said and he could already taste the victory he'd worked five years for. He wasn't about to let one stubborn neighbor stand in the way of success. "Sal's got a price. *Somewhere.*"

Gina Torino hooked the heel of her scuffed boot on the bottom rung of the weathered wooden fence. She crossed her arms on the top rail and looked out at the field in front of her. The sun was shining out of a clear blue sky, the grass was thick and green and a brand-new baby was trotting alongside his mother.

"See, Shadow?" she whispered to the contented mare, "I told you he'd be fine."

Of course, last night Gina hadn't been so sure. Playing midwife to a Gypsy horse she'd raised from infancy had absolutely terrified her. But today, she could smile and enjoy the moment.

Her gaze followed the black-and-white mare as she moved lazily around the enclosure, new baby at her feathered heels. The Gypsies were the most beautiful horses Gina had ever seen. Their broad shoulders, proud neck and the "feathers," or long, delicate hairs flying around their feet, looked exquisite. Most people, of course, took one look at the breed and thought…miniature Clydesdales. But the Gypsy horses were something else entirely.

Relatively small, but sturdy, the Gypsies had at first been bred by the roaming people who gave them their name. They were bred to be strong enough to pull loaded carts and wagons and gentle enough to be considered part of the family. They were exceptionally gentle with children and incredibly loyal to those they loved.

The horses, to Gina, were more than animals to be bred and sold…they were family.

"You baby them."

Gina didn't even turn when her mother spoke up from behind her. This was a long-standing argument—with her mother claiming that Gina spent too much time with the horses and too little time looking for a husband. "There's no harm in that."

"You need your *own* babies."

Gina rolled her eyes, grateful her mother couldn't see the action. Teresa Torino didn't care how old her children were. If they sassed, they were just as likely to get a swat on the back of the head as they had been when they were children. If she'd had any sense at all, Gina told herself, she'd have moved away like two of her three older brothers had.

"I know you're rolling your eyes...."

Grinning, Gina glanced back over her shoulder. Teresa Torino was short, curvy and opinionated. Her black hair was going gray and she didn't bother dyeing it, instead reminding everyone in the family that she'd *earned* those gray hairs. Her chin was stubborn and her brown eyes were sharp and didn't miss much.

"Would I roll my eyes at you, Mom?"

One dark eyebrow lifted. "If you thought you could get away with it, yes."

Gina lifted her face into a soft wind blowing in off the nearby ocean and changed the subject. Safer that way. "I heard you talking on the phone to Nick this morning. Everything all right?"

"Yes," Teresa said, walking up to join her daughter at the split rail fence. "Your brother Nickie's wife is pregnant again."

Ah. So this explained the *let's get Gina married and pregnant* theme of the morning. "That's great news."

"Yes. That will be three for Nick, two children for Tony and four for Peter."

Her brothers were really doing all they could to re-populate the world with Torinos, Gina thought with a smile. She loved being an aunt, of course. But she wished they all lived closer, so they could take more of the heat off of *her.* Yet of the three Torino sons, only Tony lived here on the ranch, working it with their father. Nick was in Colorado, coaching high school

football and Peter was in Southern California, install-
ing computer software for security companies.

"You're a lucky nana to have so many grandbabies
to spoil," Gina said, sliding a glance at her mother.

"Could be luckier," Teresa countered with a sniff.

"Mom…" Gina couldn't stop the sigh that slipped
from her. "You've got eight and a half grandchildren.
You don't need me to produce one."

Her mother had always dreamed of Gina's wedding
day. Of seeing her only daughter walk down the aisle
on her father's arm. The fact that Gina hadn't complied
didn't sit well with Teresa.

"It's not good for you to be alone, Gina," her mother
said, slapping one hand against a board hard enough to
make the fence rattle.

"I'm not alone," Gina argued. "I've got you and Papa,
my brothers, their wives, their kids. Who could ever be
alone in this family?"

Teresa, though, was on a roll. The music of her still-
thick Italian accent colored her words when she spoke
again. "A woman should have a man in her life, Gina.
A man to love and be loved by…"

Gina felt her back go up, even though a part of her
agreed with her mother. It wasn't as if she'd gone out
of her way to decide to *never* get married. To *never*
have children. It's just the way things had worked out.
And she wasn't going to spend the rest of her life being
miserable because of it.

"Just because I'm not married, Mom," Gina interrupted, "that doesn't mean I don't have men in my life."

Teresa sucked air in through her nose in a disapproving sniff that was so loud, one of the horses in the meadow turned its head to investigate. "I don't want to know about that."

Good, because Gina didn't really want to talk about her love life—or lack thereof—with her *mother*. She loved her parents dearly, she really did. Teresa had been born into a huge Sicilian family and had come to America more than forty years ago to marry Sal Torino. And despite the fact that Sal had been born and raised in America, he tended to side with his wife when she clung to Old World values—namely, that daughters who hadn't found husbands by their thirtieth birthday were destined to be old maids.

Sadly, Gina's thirtieth birthday had come and gone two months ago.

"Mom…" Gina took a breath, blew it out and prayed for patience. She'd hoped that having her own small house built on the family ranch would give her more privacy. Would make her parents think of her as a capable adult. She should have known better. Once a Torino child, *always* a Torino child.

Maybe she should have just moved away from the ranch entirely. But even if she had, she'd have been spending every day here anyway, since the Gypsy horses she raised and trained were her life. So she'd simply have to find a way to deal with being her mother's great disappointment.

"I know, I know," Teresa said, holding up one hand as if to stave off a familiar argument. "You are a grown woman. You don't need a man to complete you." She gave an impatient huff. "I should never have let you watch those talk shows when you were growing up. They fill your head with—"

"—sense?" Gina offered, smiling. She did love her mom, it was just so aggravating having to apologize for not being married and/or pregnant all the damn time.

"Sense. Is it sense to live alone? To not have love in your life? No," Teresa snapped, not waiting for an answer. "It is not."

It would be easier to argue with her mom if a part of Gina didn't agree. Okay, a small part. But a tiny voice in the back of her mind whispered that she wasn't getting any younger. That she should give up on old fantasies that should have died years ago.

Yet somehow…she couldn't quite manage it.

"I'm fine, Mom," she said, willing herself to believe it.

Teresa laid one hand on her daughter's forearm and gave her a pat. "Of course you are."

Okay, Gina was willing to accept that, even if her mom was placating her. At least it had stopped the conversation. "Where's Papa?" she asked. "He was going to come look over the new baby this morning."

Teresa waved one hand. "He has a 'meeting' he said. Very important."

"Yeah? With who?"

"You think he tells me?" Teresa huffed out a frustrated breath and Gina smiled.

Nothing her mother hated more than not knowing what was going on at all times.

"Well, while Papa's in his meeting, you can meet the new baby."

"Horses," Teresa muttered. "You and your horses."

Gina laughed and took her mother's hand. "Come on."

As they walked to the fence gate, a rumble of noise drifted to them and Gina turned to watch a car approach down the long driveway leading in from the main road. Dust billowed behind the black luxury SUV and Gina felt a stir of something deep inside her when she recognized the car. Despite trying to ignore that feeling, her breath caught and held in her chest and her mouth suddenly went dry.

She didn't even need to read the license plate… KING 1 to know without a doubt that Adam King was in that car. She felt it as surely as she felt the rocky ground beneath her feet. What was that, anyway? Some sort of inner radar that leaped into life whenever Adam got close?

"So, Adam King is the important meeting," her mother mused. "I wonder why."

Gina wondered, too. She knew she should just go about her business, but somehow, she couldn't make her feet move. She just stood there and watched as Adam parked his car and opened the door. When he stepped out and looked around, his dark-eyed gaze sliding across the ranch yard, something inside her jumped in reaction. Stupid, she told herself. Stupid to feel anything for a man who didn't even know you existed.

Adam's gaze kept moving, as if he were cataloging the Torino ranch and would be given a test on it later.

Finally, his gaze moved over Gina. She stiffened. Even from a distance she felt the power of his stare as if he'd reached out and touched her.

He nodded at her and her mother, and Gina forced herself to lift one hand in a halfhearted wave. Almost before her fingers had stopped moving, though, Adam had turned for the house.

"A cold man, that one," Teresa said in a quiet voice from right beside Gina. Crossing herself she added, "There is a darkness in him."

Gina had felt the darkness, too, so she couldn't really argue the point. But she'd known Adam and his brothers all of her life. And she'd always wanted to be the one to ease the darkness back for him.

Stupid, she supposed. What is it with women that we all want to be the one to "save" a guy? she wondered.

She was still standing there, watching after Adam, even though he'd already gone into the ranch house for his meeting with her father. And finally, Gina felt her mother watching her. "What?"

"I see something in your eyes, Gina," her mother whispered, worry tightening her mouth and flashing in her gaze.

Gina immediately turned away and started walking toward the horses in the meadow. She still felt a little shaky so she made sure her steps were long and steady. Lifting her chin, she whipped her hair back out of her eyes and said, "I don't know what you mean, Mom."

Teresa wasn't so easily put off, however. She hurried after her daughter, took hold of Gina's arm and dragged her to a stop. Looking into her eyes, Teresa said, "You cannot fool me. There is something there in you for Adam King. And you must not surrender to it."

Surprised, Gina laughed. "Excuse me? This from the woman who not five minutes ago was telling me to get married and start having babies?"

"Not with him," Teresa said. "Adam King is the one man I do not want for you."

Unfortunate.

Since Adam King was the only man Gina wanted.

Two

Adam knocked on the front door, waited impatiently and then jerked to attention when a shorter, older man opened it and smiled out at him.

"Adam," Sal Torino said, stepping back and waving him inside. "Right on time, as always."

"Sal. Thanks for seeing me." Adam stepped into the house and glanced around. It had been a long time since he was last here, but he noticed that the place hadn't changed much.

The entryway was wide and lit from above by a skylight that spilled sunshine in a wash of gold across the gleaming pine floors. The hall leading to the back of the house was covered in framed family photos of smiling kids and proud parents. The high, arched doorway that led into the living room where Sal gestured for Adam to follow had been unchanged, as well. The walls were still a soft, warm yellow, the furniture was oversize and comfortable, and a stone hearth, cold now, held a copper urn filled with fresh flowers. Sal took a seat on the sofa and reached for a coffeepot sitting on a tray atop a wide, scarred pine table.

While Sal poured coffee Adam didn't want, he wandered the room and stopped at the curved bay window. The glass gleamed in the morning light and provided a sweeping view of the neatly trimmed lawn ringed by ancient oak trees. Adam hardly noticed, though. His mind was already focused on the task at hand: How he would convince Sal to sell him the land he needed.

"So, what brings Adam King to my house first thing in the morning?"

Adam turned around to look at his neighbor. Sal stood about five foot eight, had thick black hair streaked with gray, skin as weathered and tanned as old leather and sharp brown eyes.

He walked over to take the coffee cup Sal offered him and then had a sip just to be polite. Sitting down opposite the other man, Adam cupped the heavy mug between his palms and said, "I want to talk to you about that twenty-acre parcel in your north pasture, Sal."

The older man's face split in an understanding smile as he leaned back into the sofa cushions. "Ah."

It wasn't good business to let your opponent know how badly you wanted something. But Sal Torino was no dummy. The King family had made offers for that

land several times over the last couple of decades and
Sal had always turned them down flat. So, he already
knew how important this was to Adam. No point in
trying to pretend otherwise.

"I want that land, Sal, and I'm willing to make you
a deal that'll give you a hell of a profit on it."

Shaking his head Sal took a gulp of coffee, swallowed and sighed. "Adam…"

"Hear me out." Adam leaned forward, set his coffee
cup down on the tray and sat back again, bracing his
forearms on his thighs. "You don't use that piece of
land for grazing or pasture. It's just sitting there."

Sal smiled and shook his head again. Fine. He was
stubborn. Adam could appreciate that. He bit down on the
impatience scratching at his insides and forced a con-
genial tone to his voice. "Think about this, Sal. I'm willing
to make you another substantial offer for the property."

"Why is this so important to you?"

Now we play the game. Adam wished this were all
somehow easier. Sal knew damn well about Adam's
quest to make the King ranch whole again, but clearly
he was going to have to spell it all out.

"It's the last piece of the original King family holdings," Adam said tightly. "Which you already know."

Sal smiled again and Adam thought the older man
sort of looked like a benevolent elf. Too bad he didn't
look like an elf who wanted to sell. "So let's get down
to business here. You don't need the land. I want the
land. Simple as that. So what do you say?"

"Adam," Sal started, pausing for another sip of

coffee, "I don't like selling land. What's mine is mine. You know that. You feel the same way I do."

"Yes, and that parcel is *mine,* Sal. Or it should be. It started out King land. It should be King land again."

"But it isn't."

Adam quietly seethed with frustration.

"I don't need your money." Sal sat forward, set his coffee cup down and then stood up to wander the room. "You know that, and yet, you come to me anyway, thinking to sway me with an argument for profit margins."

"Making a profit's not a sin, Sal," Adam countered.

"Money is not the only thing a man thinks about, though."

Sal stopped at the hearth, leaned one arm on the heavily carved mantel and looked down at Adam.

Adam wasn't used to being the one on the defensive in a negotiation. And looking up at Sal from the comfort of a too-soft chair made him feel at a disadvantage, so he stood up, too. Shoving both hands into the pockets of his jeans, he watched the older man and wondered what Sal was up to.

"I hear an implied 'but' in there somewhere," Adam said. "So why don't you just tell me what you've got in mind and we can decide if we're going to be able to make a deal."

"Ah," Sal said. "So impatient. You should learn to enjoy life more, Adam. It's not good to build a life solely on business."

"Works for me."

Adam wasn't interested in listening to advice. He

didn't want to hear about "enjoying" life. All he wanted was that last piece of land.

"There was a time when you didn't feel that way," Sal mused and the smile slipped off his features even as his dark eyes went soft and sympathetic.

Adam stiffened perceptibly. The worst part of living in a small town was having everyone for miles around knowing your personal business. Sal, he knew, was trying to be nice, so he kept a lid on the simmering knot of something ugly inside him. People thought they knew him. Thought they could understand what he was feeling, thinking. But they were wrong.

He wasn't interested in sympathy any more than he was looking for advice. He didn't *need* anyone's pity. Adam's life was just as he wanted it.

Except for owning that damned piece of land.

"Look, Sal," Adam said slowly, quietly, "I'm not here to talk about my life. I'm here to make a deal. So if you don't mind…"

Sal clucked his tongue in disapproval. "You are a single-minded man, Adam. And while I admire that, it can also make one's life harder than it has to be."

"Let me worry about my life, okay?" That sizzle of impatience he'd felt earlier had begun to bubble and froth in the pit of his stomach. "What do you say, Sal? Are we going to be able to come to an agreement?"

Sal braced his feet wide apart, folded his arms across his chest and tipped his head to one side, studying Adam as if looking for something in particular. After a long moment or two, he said, "We might be able to strike a deal. Though the terms I have in mind are somewhat different than you were expecting."

"What're you talking about?"

"Simple," Sal said with a shrug. "You want the land. I want something in return. And it's not your money."

"Then what?"

The older man nodded, walked back to the sofa and sat down again, getting comfortable. When he was settled, he looked up at Adam and said, "You know my Gina."

"Yeah…" Suspicion rattled through Adam.

"I want to see her happy," Sal said.

"I'm sure you do." And what the *hell* did Gina have to do with any of this?

"I want to see her married. Settled. With a family."

Everything in Adam went still and cold. He suddenly became hyperaware. He heard the ticking of the clock that hung over the fireplace. He heard a fly bumping against the bay window. He took a long, slow, deep breath and dragged in the enticing aroma of spaghetti sauce bubbling in the kitchen. Adam's skin felt too tight and every nerve ending in his body was standing straight up.

He took another breath, shook his head and stared at Sal, hardly able to believe what he'd just heard—realization at what Sal could be insinuating hitting him like a ton of bricks. But the older man was staring at him through steady, determined eyes, allowing Adam time to absorb what he'd said. But how could he possibly believe the old man was serious?

Adam had faced tough negotiators before and come out on top, though. Today would be no different.

"I don't see what Gina getting married has to do with me *or* this conversation."

"Don't you?" Sal smiled. "You're a man alone, Adam. Gina is alone, as well…"

This was *not* going the way he'd planned.

Gina?

Married?

To *him?*

No way. He looked into Sal's eyes and saw that the older man was absolutely sincere. No matter how whacked it sounded. Adam ground his back teeth together and took a couple of long, hopefully calming, breaths. Didn't help.

"Let me be clear," Sal said, shifting to rest one arm along the back of the sofa, like a man completely at ease with himself and his surroundings. "I offer you a deal, Adam. Marry my Gina. Make her happy. Give her one or two babies. And I give you the land."

Babies?

Fury erupted within and turned Adam's vision red at the edges. His lungs labored for air. His brain was covered in a mist of temper that made thinking nearly impossible. Which was probably for the best. Because if he took the time to actually consider what Sal was saying, who the hell knew what he might say?

He couldn't even remember being that angry before. Adam wasn't manipulated—he was the one who did the manipulating. *He* was the one who was a shark in negotiations. He didn't get surprised. He didn't feel at a loss. He was *never* at a loss for words, damn it.

And looking at Sal now, he could see the old guy was

really enjoying him being confounded, which only made Adam more furious.

"Forget it," Adam said, the words hardly more than a hiss of sound. Unable to stand still, he stalked over to the bay window, glared at the outside world for a second or two, then spun back around to face the man still seated on the couch. "What the hell's wrong with you, Sal? Are you delusional? People don't bargain their daughters for gain anymore. This isn't the middle ages, you know."

Slowly the older man stood up, narrowed his eyes on Adam and pointed his index finger, stabbing at the air with it. "This is not for my gain," Sal pointed out. "This is for *your* gain. You think I would accept *any* man for my Gina? You think I value her so lowly that I do this without thinking? Without considering?"

"I think you're *nuts*."

Sal snorted a laugh that had no humor in it. "You want the land so badly? Do this one thing and it's yours."

"Unbelievable." This was crazy. Plain and simple. He'd always liked Sal Torino, too. Who knew the old guy was off his rocker?

"Why does this seem so unreasonable to you?" Sal demanded, coming around the sofa to stand beside Adam at the window. Sunlight speared in through the leaded glass panes, dotting the two men and the wood floor with diamond-shaped splotches of gold. "Is it crazy for a father to look to his daughter's happiness? To the happiness of the son of a man I called friend? You're a good man, Adam. But you've been alone too long. Lost too much."

"Sal—" His tone filled with warning.

"Fine." He held up both hands. "We won't speak of the past, but of the future." Sal turned his head, looked out the window and stared into the distance. Nodding his head, he said, "My Gina needs more in her life than her beloved horses. You need more in your life than your ranch. Is it so crazy to think the two of you could build something together?"

Adam just stared at him. "You want your daughter to marry a man who doesn't love her?"

He shrugged. "Love can grow."

"Not for me."

"Never say never, Adam." Sal slid a glance at him. "A life is long and not meant to be lived alone."

Life wasn't always long and Adam had discovered that it was better lived alone. He had no one's interests but his own to look after. He lived the way he wanted and made no excuses or apologies for it. And he had no intention of changing any part of his life.

Irritation spiked inside him. He *did* want that damned land. It had become a Holy Grail of sorts for him. The last square to place in the King family quilt of holdings. He could almost taste the satisfaction of finishing the task he'd set for himself. But now…looked like he'd be tasting failure instead and that knowledge notched his irritation a little higher.

"Thanks, Sal. But I'm not interested." In any of it. He wanted the land, but he wasn't willing to marry again. He'd tried that once. And even before the crashing end, it hadn't worked out for him or for his wife. He just wasn't built to be a husband.

"Think about it," Sal said and pointed out the window.

Adam glanced in the direction indicated and saw Gina and her mother out in the pasture. While he stood there, Teresa walked off, leaving her daughter alone in the field, surrounded by small, sturdy horses.

Sunlight dropped down on Gina like a cloud of light. Her long, dark hair whipped around her shoulders and when she tipped her head back to laugh, she made such an intriguing picture Adam gritted his teeth even harder.

"My Gina's a wonderful woman. You could do worse."

Adam tore his gaze from the woman in the meadow, shook his head and looked at the older man beside him. "You can let this idea of yours go, Sal. So why don't you do some realistic thinking and come up with a price for the land that we can both live with?"

This whole situation had gotten way out of hand and Adam felt as if the walls were closing in on him. Looking at Sal, you'd never guess he was crazy as a loon. But clearly he was. Who the hell bartered their children these days?

Giving reasonable one last shot, Adam asked, "What the hell do you think Gina would say if she could hear you?"

Sal shrugged and smiled a little. "She doesn't have to know."

"You live dangerously, Sal."

The older man snorted. "I know what's good for my children. And, I know what's good for you. This is the best bargain you could ever make, Adam. So *you* are the one who should think carefully before you decide."

"Decision's already made," Adam assured him. "I'm not marrying Gina or anybody else for that matter. But if you change your mind and want to actually talk business, you give me a call."

Adam had to get out of there. His blood was buzzing in his veins and he felt like his skin was on fire. Damned old man, throwing something like this at him out of the blue. Turning for the foyer, Adam crossed the room in a few long strides and yanked open the front door just as Teresa Torino was stepping inside. She jolted.

"Adam."

"Teresa." He gave her a nod, shot another incredulous look at Sal, then walked outside, closing the door behind him.

Instantly he felt as if he could breathe again. The sharp, clear air carried the scent of horses and the far-off sea. A cool wind brushed past him and almost without thinking about it, Adam turned his head and thoughtfully looked at the meadow where Gina Torino was communing with her horses.

Even from a distance, he felt the tug of an attraction he hadn't felt in too long to count. The last time he'd seen Gina, it had been at his wife and son's funeral. He'd been too numb that day to notice and since then, he'd mostly spent his time working the ranch.

And rather than heading for his car, he surprised himself by heading toward the fenced meadow.

Gina watched Adam approach and told her hormones to take a nap. Apparently, though, they weren't listening. Nope, instead of lying down and keeping quiet, her hormones were instead tap dancing on every one of her nerve endings. Heck, she was surprised she wasn't actually *vibrating.*

"Oh, Shadow," she whispered, stroking the mare's velvety neck, "I am *such* an idiot."

"Morning, Gina."

She braced herself, turned to face him and with one look into Adam's dark eyes, Gina knew she could never be "braced" enough. Why was it this one man absolutely lit up her insides like a fireworks display on the Fourth of July? Why did it have to be Adam King her heart yearned for?

"Hello, Adam," she said and silently congratulated herself on keeping her voice so nice and steady. "You're out early this morning."

"Yeah." His features twisted briefly, then he made an obvious effort to ease them before saying, "Had a meeting with your father."

"About what?"

"Nothing," he said so quickly that Gina knew something was definitely going on. And knowing her father as she did, it could be *anything.*

Still, it was clear Adam wouldn't be talking about whatever it was, so she'd save her curiosity for later. When she could pry it out of her father. For now, it was all she could do to keep from gibbering like an idiot. Adam walked closer, leaned his forearms on the top rung of the fence and squinted into the morning light. And wouldn't you know it, the wind shifted directions, just so it could tease her by drifting the scent of him toward her.

Nothing so prosaic as aftershave, though. Nope, the only scent she picked up was soap and man. Which only made it harder to draw a breath. Oh, yeah. This was going really well.

"Looks like you've had a new addition to your herd," he said with a nod at the foal.

Instantly Gina grinned and looked at the sturdy baby nuzzling his mother. "He arrived last night. Well, the middle of the night, really. I was up until nearly four this morning—hence my close resemblance to Franken-stein's Bride."

God, idiot. Make sure you point out to the man how haggard and hideous you look. First time you've seen him since his family's funeral and you have to look like the wrath of God? Just fabulous.

"You look great," he said and almost sounded grudg-ing about it.

"Yeah. I'm sure." Gina laughed, gave Shadow one more caress, then climbed through the fence. She knew right away that she should have just taken a short walk and opened the gate. She was too tired and strung a little too tightly to gracefully maneuver slipping between the rungs of the fence.

The toe of her boot caught on the bottom slat and she only had a second to think, *This is perfect. I'm about to fall on my face in the dirt, right in front of Adam. Can this get any better?* Then Adam's hand curled around her upper arm and he held on to her until she found her balance again.

Flinging her hair back out of her face, she looked up into dark-chocolate eyes and said, "Thanks—" Whatever else she might have added died unspoken because her mouth dried up completely.

The heat in his gaze was nearly overpowering. She felt blasted by it, as if she were being hit by a flame-thrower. Blood sizzling, breath straining in her lungs, stomach spinning in wild circles, she could only stare at him. The feel of his hand on her skin only added to the sensation of heat pouring through her.

And just when she wondered what in the hell she could possibly say to explain why she had suddenly become dumb as a post, Adam said, "Have dinner with me."

Three

The words were out before he could stop himself and once they'd been said, Adam thought—*why the hell not?*

Yeah, he'd surprised himself and judging from the expression on her face, he'd surprised Gina, as well. But damned if he'd expected this rush of something hot and needy pulsing inside him. She'd caught him off guard, that was for sure.

Gina Torino was luscious. He hadn't noticed the last time he'd seen her. But now, just looking at her made him feel something he'd thought himself immune to. And he was male enough to enjoy the rush of lust crowding his system.

While she stared up at him out of golden eyes, he heard her father's offer repeat again and again in his mind. And as desire pumped fast and fiercely through his bloodstream, he told himself maybe he should re-think his instant rejection of her father's idea. It wouldn't be too much a hardship to make Gina Torino his wife.

And God knew he could hardly believe himself that he was considering this. But after all, it didn't have to be forever. There didn't have to be a baby. All he had to do was marry Gina and he'd get the land he wanted so badly. Then he'd divorce her with a good settlement and everybody's happy.

Was he as crazy as Sal? Possibly. On the other hand, Adam had always been able to look at a situation, see it from every angle and then make the moves neces-sary for him to come out on top. Why should this be any different?

It wasn't as if he was going into the deal with an idea to cheat Sal. The old man had come up with this bizarre plan all on his own. And Gina?

Well, hell. His gaze swept her up and down in a heart-beat of time. He took in her bright, golden eyes, her full mouth tipped into a smile, her lush breasts pressing against the faded fabric of a denim shirt and her rounded hips and long legs encased in worn jeans. She was enough to make any man's mouth water. And the fact that she was getting to him was enough to have him con-sidering Sal's proposal.

"You look surprised," he said when he realized that seconds of silence were ticking past.

"Well, I am." She brushed her palms against her thighs but it was clearly more about nerves than cleaning her hands off. "I haven't even spoken to you in the last five years, Adam."

True. He'd never been a social type, like his brothers were. And in the last few years, he'd cut himself off even further from his neighbors. "I've been busy."

She laughed and somehow the rollicking music of it seemed to slice through him, cutting him so deep his breath caught in his chest. What was this? Lust he could deal with. Use to his own advantage. But he wasn't looking to be intrigued or captivated by her.

Yet he wanted her. And after years of feeling *nothing,* this rush of lust felt damn good. All he had to do was remind himself why he was considering this. The land. Marry Gina, enjoy himself, and when he was finished with her, they'd divorce and then this *lust* would be over with and he would have the land he required.

"You've been busy." Nodding, she shot him a smile. "For five years."

He shrugged. "What about you?"

"What about me?"

"What've you been up to?"

Her eyebrows lifted and she tipped her head to one side to look at him. "Five years of news is going to take a little while to tell."

"So, do it at dinner."

"First a question."

"Of course." Women always had questions.

"Why?"

"Why what?"

"Why ask me to dinner?" She pushed her hands into the back pockets of her jeans, arching her back a little, making her breasts push against the fabric of her shirt. "Why now all of a sudden?"

Adam frowned a little. Figured she'd make him work for this. "Look, it's no big deal. I saw you, we talked, I asked. If you don't want to go, just say so."

She stared at him for a long moment or two, but Adam knew she wasn't going to turn him down. She was intrigued. She was interested. And more than that, she was feeling the same sort of physical buzz he was. He could see it in her eyes.

"I didn't say that," she said a moment later, proving that he could still read people pretty well. "I was just curious."

He gave her a casual shrug. "We both have to eat. Why not do it together?"

"Okay…where are you taking me?"

He offered the first place that came to him. It wasn't as if he'd planned this all out. He'd come to the Torino spread looking to make a deal. Now, it appeared that he was going to make that deal after all—just not the one he'd counted on.

Gina's insides were doing a happy skip and dance. She couldn't believe that Adam King had finally noticed her. And for a few minutes, that was the only thought she concentrated on. But finally, dumb ol' reality crashed in. Why now? She had to ask herself the question. She'd known Adam all her life and up until five minutes ago, he'd never acknowledged her existence beyond the occasional "hi."

Since the death of his family five years before, Adam had pretty much been a recluse. He'd shut himself away from everything but his ranch and his brothers. So why all of a sudden was he Mr. Charm? A tiny nugget of suspicion settled in the pit of her stomach, but it didn't do a thing to ease the thumping of her heart.

"What about Serenity?"

Ah. The almost impossible to get into place on the coast. He really was pulling out all the stops.

"Sounds good," she said, even though what she really meant was, *sounds fabulous, can't wait, what took you so long?*

"Tomorrow night? Seven?"

"Okay. Seven." The moment she agreed, she saw satisfaction glitter in his dark-chocolate eyes and the suspicion crowding her jumped up in her brain and started waving hands, trying to get her attention. Well, it worked. "Though I really would like to know what actually prompted this out-of-nowhere invitation."

His features tightened briefly, but a moment later, he gave her a small smile again. "If you're not interested, Gina, all you have to do is say no."

"I didn't say that." She pulled her hands from her pockets and folded her arms across her chest.

"Glad to hear it," he said and reached for one of her hands, holding it in his, smoothing his thumb gently across her skin. He looked into her eyes, gave her a small smile and said, "So, I'll pick you up at seven tomorrow? You can tell me all about what you've been up to for the last five years."

When he let go of her hand, Gina could have sworn she could actually *smell* her skin sizzling from the heat he'd generated. Oh, she was sliding into some seriously deep waters here.

Adam was charming. Friendly. Smiley. Flirty.

Something was definitely going on here. Something he wasn't telling her. And still, she wouldn't turn down this invitation for anything.

"I'll be ready."

"See you then." With one last smile, he turned around and walked with determined steps across the yard to the SUV he'd left parked near the house.

Gina stood stock-still to enjoy the view. His excellent butt looked great in the dark blue jeans. His long legs moved with a deceptively lazy stride and the sun hit his dark brown hair and gleamed in its depths.

Her heart actually *fluttered* in her chest. Weird sensation. And not a good sign. "Oh, Gina," she whispered, "you are in very deep trouble, here."

Just being that close to Adam, having him focusing his attention on her, had been enough to stir up all of the old fantasies and dreams. She felt shaky, like the time she'd had three espresso drinks in an hour. Only Adam King was a way bigger buzz than too much caffeine.

Her breath left her in a rush as Adam steered his car down the driveway and away from the ranch. She rubbed the spot on her hand where Adam had touched her. When the cloud of dust behind his car had settled back down onto the driveway, Gina thoughtfully turned her gaze on the house behind her. Adam might not be willing to tell her what was going on, but she had a bone-deep feeling that her father had the answers she needed.

"I can't believe it," Gina muttered, stalking around the perimeter of the great room. She must have made thirty circuits in the last twenty minutes. Ever since her father had confessed what his meeting with Adam King had really been about. Gina's temper spiked anew every time she thought about it. She couldn't seem to sit down. Couldn't keep still.

At every other clomp of her boots against the wood floor, she shot her father a look that should have frizzed his hair. When she thought she could speak without screaming, she asked, "You tried to *sell* me?"

"You make too much of this, Gina." Sal sat on the sofa, but his comfy, relaxed position was belied by the glitter of guilt and caution in his eyes.

"Too much?" She threw her hands high and let them slap to her thighs again. "What am I, a princess in a tower? Are you some feudal lord, Papa? God, this is like one of the historical romance novels I read." She stopped dead and stabbed her index finger at him. "Only difference is, this is the *twenty-first century!*"

"Women are too emotional," Sal muttered. "This is why men run the world."

"This is what you think?" Teresa Torino reached over and slapped her husband's upper arm. "Men run the world because *women* allow it."

Normally Gina would have smiled at that, but at the moment, she was just too furious to see the humor in anything about this situation. Oh, man, she wanted to open up a big, yawning hole in the earth and fall into it. What must Adam have been thinking when her father faced him with this "plan"?

God. Everything in her cringed away from *that* image. Could a person die of embarrassment?

"You said yourself Gina should get married and have babies," Sal told his wife.

"Yes, but not like this. Not with him."

"What's wrong with Adam?" Sal wanted to know.

Nothing, as far as Gina was concerned, but she wasn't about to say *that*.

"There is…*something,*" Teresa said with a sniff.

Gina nearly groaned.

"You don't know Adam well enough to think there's something wrong with him," Sal told his wife.

"Ah," Teresa argued. "But you know him well enough to *barter* your daughter's future with him?"

And the argument was off and running. Gina only half listened. In her family, yelling was as much a part of life as the constant hugs and laughter. Italians, her mother liked to say, lived life to the *fullest.* Of course, Gina's father liked to say that his wife lived life to the *loudest,* but basically, it was the same thing.

She and her brothers had grown up with laughter,

shouts, hugs, more shouts and the knowledge that they were all loved unconditionally.

Today, though…she could have cheerfully strangled the father she loved so much. Gina's gaze shifted around the room, picking out the framed family photos sprinkled across every flat surface. There were dozens of her brothers and their families. There were old, sepia prints of grandparents and great-grandparents, too. There were photos of children in Italy, cousins she'd never met. And there were pictures of Gina. With her first horse. As the winning pitcher on her high school softball team. Getting ready for her prom. Her graduation. And in all of the pictures of Gina, she was alone. There was no husband. No kids.

Just good ol' Aunt Gina.

Old maid.

The Torino clan was big on family. And she was no exception to that rule.

Gina had always wanted a family of her own. Had always expected that she would be a mother, once the time was right. But in the last couple of years, as she'd watched her brothers' families grow while she remained alone and single, she'd begun to accept that maybe her life wouldn't turn out the way she'd always hoped.

And on that depressing thought, she stopped walking crazily around the room, closed down her racing brain and focused her gaze on the slant of sunlight beaming in through the wide front windows and the dust motes dancing in the still air. The scent of her mother's sauce spilled from the kitchen and wrapped itself around Gina like a warm hug.

Sal scowled at his wife, shot his daughter a cautious look and said, "Besides, all of this is wasted effort. You're angry for nothing, Gina. Adam turned me down."

"He did?"

"Of *course* he did," Teresa said, reaching out to give her husband another smack.

"Hey!" Sal complained.

"Adam King is not a man to be trifled with this way," Teresa said, lifting one hand to wag a warning finger. "There is a darkness there...."

Sal rolled his eyes and even Gina had to stifle a snort. Any man who didn't like pasta wasn't to be trusted in Teresa Torino's world.

"There's nothing wrong with Adam," Sal argued. "He's a good businessman. He's steady. He's wealthy so we don't need to worry about a man marrying Gina for her money—"

"Oh," Gina snapped, feeling the insult jab its way home, "thanks very much for that!"

"*And,*" Sal continued before either his wife or his daughter could interrupt again, "he needs a wife."

"He had a wife," Teresa pointed out.

"She's dead," Sal argued.

"So you sign me up as a pinch hitter?" Gina demanded.

"It's not good to be alone," her father said.

"God." Gina slumped onto the arm of the closest sofa and stared at her father. "Did you and Mom rehearse that little ditty? Maybe we should put it to music!"

"There's no reason to be smart," Teresa said.

"No reason?" Gina slid her gaze to her mother in as-tonishment. Typical. A minute ago, Teresa had been furious with her husband. But the moment she felt he was the underdog, she jumped onto his side of the debate.

"Mom, I know Papa meant well, but this is…is…" She stopped and shook her head. "I don't even have a word for what this is. Beyond the usual. You know… humiliating. Embarrassing. Demeaning."

Teresa blew out a breath. "So dramatic."

Gina just goggled at her. How did a person argue with parents like this? And *why* was she still living on this ranch?

Oh, she wanted to scream. How mortifying was this? She was so pitiful, so unwanted that her father had to try to *buy* her a husband?

Her head was pounding and her chest felt tight. Vaguely she heard her mother's whispered mutterings as she continued her tirade. But Gina couldn't even think about her parents at the moment.

What must Adam have thought? Oh, God, she didn't want to know. Way better to just push that little question right out of her mind. How would she ever face him again? How would she be able to keep that dinner date with him tomorrow night?

And with that thought, everything inside her stopped.

He'd turned her father down.

He wasn't willing to marry her for the land he wanted so badly. So why, then, had he stepped outside and asked her to dinner? Was this a pity date? Poor little

Gina will never get married, why not toss her a bowl of soup and a nice night out?

No.

Adam wasn't the doing-good-deeds kind of guy. She didn't agree with her mother about the darkness in him, but he also wasn't the kind of guy who went out of his way for people.

So what did all of this mean?

Her headache erupted into migraine territory.

"So what?" Sal asked. "How long am I going to be in trouble?"

Gina glared at her father.

"Long time, I guess," he muttered.

"You want me to call and talk to Adam? Explain?" Teresa asked.

"Good God, no!" Gina hopped up off the arm of the couch. "What am I? In third grade?"

"Only to help," her mother soothed. "To tell him that your papa is crazy."

"I'm not crazy," Sal argued.

"Matter of debate," Gina said wryly and her father had the grace to flush.

"I meant no harm," Sal told her.

Gina's heart melted a little. No matter how furious he made her, she'd loved him too long to stay mad forever. "I know that, Papa. But *please* stay out of my love life."

"Yes, yes," he said.

When her parents started arguing again, Gina left them to it. She was just too tired to hold up her end of the battle. Walking across the ranch yard, she went straight to her own small house and stepped inside. It was quiet. Empty. She didn't even have a pet. Since she spent so much time with her horses, it seemed silly to have another animal around.

She stopped just inside the living room. Her gaze swept quickly around the familiar space but it was as if she were seeing it with new eyes.

Here, too, just like up at the main house, there were framed photos. Pictures of her nieces and nephews. Laughing kids with gap-toothed smiles. Snapshots of days spent at amusement parks, on the Gypsy horses, eating at her kitchen table. There were drawings taped to the wall, too, each signed by the young artist.

And there were toys. Some scattered across her coffee table, others in a chest she kept under her front window. Baby dolls and fire trucks. GameBoys and coloring books.

In a blink, Gina knew that this was the pattern of her life. As it was. As it would always be. She would forever be the favorite aunt. The children she loved would never be her own. And she would no doubt end up an old woman, alone, with a houseful of cats.

Tears stung the backs of her eyes as she imagined it, the years spilling out in front of her so clearly, it made her head spin. Her house wasn't a home. It was a place where she slept. It was a place that children visited and never stayed. It was a place that would forever be haunted by the ghosts of the children she *might* have had.

Unless she did something outrageous.
Something no one would expect.
Least of all Adam King.

Four

A dinner date with Adam King—especially this one—required nothing less than a new dress.

Turning in front of her mirror, Gina took a long, critical look and decided she looked pretty good. The black dress hit just above her knee and the full skirt swirled out when she turned. The bodice dipped low enough to give a peek at what was hidden beneath the silky fabric, and the sleeveless straps over her shoulders were narrow, delicate.

Her hair hung in a cascade of curls down her back and her new high-heeled sandals gave her an extra three inches of height.

"Okay," she said, smiling at the woman in the glass. "I can do this. Everything's gonna be great. I am sooooo ready."

Her reflection was not convinced. Frowning a little, Gina jolted at the knock on her front door. "Oh, yeah. You're ready."

Shaking her head, she snapped up her black clutch bag and headed for the front of the little house. When she opened the door, though, she found not Adam, but her brother Tony standing on the porch.

Hands on his hips, he said, "I just talked to Mom and thought I'd better come see you."

"No time," she said, looking past him at the driveway to the road.

"Why not?"

"I have a date." She waved one hand at him in a "shooing" motion. "Me. Going out. Thanks for stopping by. Bye now."

He paid no attention to that at all, just stalked past her into the house. Gina sighed at the dust his boots left on the floor, then she turned and said, "What're you doing here?"

"Mom told me what Pop did."

"Fabulous." Had her mom called Peter and Nicky, too, to bring them up to speed on the pitiful wasteland that was Gina's love life? Was she going to take out an ad in the Birkfield paper, too?

"I just want to say, Pop was out of line. You don't need him to find you a man."

"Thanks for the vote of confidence," she said and waved at the still open front door, trying to get her brother out of there before Adam showed up.

"Because, if you want a guy, I can find one for you."

"No."

Tony shrugged. "I'm just saying…Mike over at the bank? Great guy. Good job…"

"Did you learn *nothing* from Papa?"

"Pop's mistake was going for Adam. Adam's a bad bet," Tony said. "He's a good guy, but he's shut down emotionally."

"Huh?" Gina shook her head. "You've been reading Vickie's magazines again, haven't you?"

He grinned and the Torino golden eyes twinkled at her. "Gotta keep up. Don't want the wife thinking I'm just a dumb ranch hand."

"Uh-huh. How about you go home and tell her that?"

"What's the rush?" Then he seemed to notice her for the first time. He gave a long, slow whistle. "Wow. You look…did you say you have a *date?*"

Insulted, she demanded, "Why do you sound so surprised?"

"You never go out."

"Not true." Okay, semitrue. She wasn't a shy little wallflower virgin, but she wasn't exactly party central, either. And why couldn't she have had sisters instead of three well-meaning, but interfering older brothers?

"Who's this date with?"

"None of your business. Gee, look at the time."

"Why don't you want to tell me who this guy—"

"Hi, Tony."

They both turned at the sound of the deep voice. Adam stood on her porch, the wash of lamplight spilling out of the house to welcome him. He wore a well-tailored black suit with a dark red tie and he looked as at home in the elegantly cut suit as he did in his jeans and boots. As he looked from her to Tony and back again, his dark eyes shone with interest and what Gina suspected was humor.

So how long had he been standing there?

"Adam," Tony said with a nod, stepping out in front of his sister to hold out one hand.

Adam shook his hand, then shifted his gaze to Gina. The power of his stare was enough to make her head go light and her heart jitter in her chest.

"You look lovely," he said.

"Thanks. Um, Tony was just leaving."

"No, I wasn't."

"Well, we *are*," Adam countered and held out one hand to Gina.

The look on Tony's face was priceless. Gina smiled as she slipped past her brother to join Adam on the porch. Then she threw Tony a look over her shoulder. "Lock up when you leave, okay?"

The restaurant was amazing. Sitting atop a cliff overlooking the ocean, one entire wall of Serenity was glass, providing a breathtaking view of moonlight, waves crashing against the rocks below. Overhead lighting in the sprawling building was deliberately faint, as if each wall and ceiling sconce had been chosen to define the darkness rather than defeat it.

The musical clink of crystal and the whisper of muted conversations were flavored with soft jazz piping from the three piece band. Completing the atmosphere, each round table boasted a single votive candle and the effect of dozens of flickering flames was nearly magical.

All in all, it had been a perfect evening. Adam was considerate, charming and never even hinted at the deal her father had broached to him. And while Gina was enjoying herself, she'd been dealing with a twist of nerves in her stomach since the hostess had first seated them. Now that dinner was over and they were sipping a last cup of coffee before leaving, time was up.

She either faced Adam with her own deal—or came to her senses and forgot the whole thing. Gina stared out the glass wall beside their table and watched as waves rolled ceaselessly into shore, slamming into the rocks, sending white spray into the air.

"What're you thinking?"

"What?" She turned her head to find Adam watching her with a bemused smile on his face. "I'm sorry. Mind wandering."

"To where, exactly?"

Here it was, she told herself, fingers curling around the fragile handle of her coffee cup. Speak now or forever hold your peace. Funny *that* was the phrase that sprang to mind.

"Adam," she said before she could talk herself out of it, "I know what my father said to you."

His features tightened. "Excuse me?"

Now it was her turn to give him a small smile. Shaking her head, she said, "Forget it. Papa confessed all."

He shifted on his chair, scowled a little and picked

up his coffee cup. "Did he also mention that I turned him down?"

"Yeah, he did." Gina swiveled in her seat, turning her back on the wide vista of ocean and cliffs to face him. "And by the way, thanks."

"No problem." Sitting back in his chair, Adam watched her. Waiting.

"But," she said, "I had to wonder about you asking me out to dinner. I mean, if you weren't interested in buying a bride, why the invitation?"

His mouth flattened into a thin line. "One has nothing to do with the other."

"I don't know," Gina said softly, running the tip of her index finger around the outside rim of the cup. "See, I've had some time to think about all of this…"

"Gina."

"I think that when Papa first—" she paused as if looking for the right word before continuing "—*proposed*, if you'll pardon the pun, his little deal, your first reaction was no. Of course not."

"Exactly," Adam agreed.

"And then…" She smiled when he frowned. "You started thinking. You came outside. You saw Mom and I and you told yourself that maybe it wasn't such a bad idea after all."

Adam straightened in his chair, then leaned over the table, peering directly into her eyes with a hard stare. "I did *not* bring you here so that I could propose to you."

Gina actually laughed at that. "Oh, you wouldn't have done that. Not right away, anyway. You brought me here on a date." She stopped and grinned, looking around the restaurant in approval. "And it's been lovely, by the way. Anyway, after tonight, there would have been other dates. And after a couple of months, you would have proposed."

He stared at her for a long, silent minute and Gina knew that she was right. For whatever reason, Adam had reconsidered her father's offer. Which was good. In a way. Of course, she didn't like the idea that he'd been seriously willing to marry her for his own gain. Actually it made her heart hurt to think about that too long. After all, she'd been in love with Adam King since she was fourteen years old. But at least it made her own plan seem more reasonable.

"Okay, that's enough." He lifted one hand in a silent signal to their server, requesting their check. "I'm sorry you feel this way, but since you do, there's no point in continuing this. I'll take you home."

"Not ready to leave yet," she said, leaning back into her own chair to watch him. "I know you, Adam. And right now, you're a little embarrassed and a lot on the defensive."

"Gina, what I am is sorry that you misunderstood."

"But I didn't," she said. "In fact, I completely understand."

"Understand what?" His tone was clipped, impatient.

"Look, I know how much getting the King holdings back together means to you," Gina said and felt a tug of satisfaction when his eyes flashed at the thought. "I know that you would do just about anything to ensure that happens."

"Believe what you will," Adam said, then paused as the waiter delivered their bill in a sleek, black leather folder. Once the waiter was gone, he continued, "But there are limits to what I'm willing to do. Lines I won't cross."

"Well, if that's true, it's a shame."

He blinked at her. "I beg your pardon?"

"Adam, I know you want the land. I know you don't want to be married. And I know you don't like being manipulated any more than I do."

He nodded. "Go on."

"See, I've had a little time to think about this and I'm pretty sure I've come up with a solution that'll work for both of us."

Still scowling, he folded his arms across his chest. "Now, this I've got to hear."

She smiled and realized that the flutter of nerves that had been irritating her all night were suddenly gone. Because she'd finally brought everything into the light? Because she knew that what she was doing was the right thing? Or was it the wine they'd had with dinner?

Didn't matter now, she thought. She was in way too deep to quit at this point.

"Well," she said, letting the words tumble from her mouth in a rush, "the thing is, I'm willing to discuss my father's offer to you."

Adam was stunned. He couldn't believe she was saying any of this. First off, that she *knew* about Sal's offer was bad enough. The fact that she'd guessed Adam had reconsidered the deal was disquieting. Did she really know him as well as she seemed to? And why in the hell would a woman like Gina be willing to consider such an insulting bargain?

In the candlelight, Gina's eyes seemed to shine with the deep, rich glow of antique gold. Her skin was soft and smooth and lightly tanned. He'd hardly been able to look away from her all night. His gaze caught in the tumble of thick, dark curls that hung down her back in waves so silky they invited a man's hands to delve into them. Her black dress hugged every curve—and she had good ones—and her long, tanned legs looked amazing in high-heeled sandals that should have been impossible to walk in.

All night, she'd tormented him, simply by being Gina. How had he not noticed years ago just how beguiling she was? Had he really been blind enough to dismiss his little neighbor because he'd once known her as a pigtailed child? Well, she was all grown-up now and surprisingly enough, was damn calm and accepting about the bargain her father had offered.

And somehow, that worried him more than anything else.

"Why would you want to do that?" he asked and watched as something not quite identifiable flashed in her eyes.

"I have my reasons," she said, then smiled at him again.

Adam hissed in a breath. She really was beautiful—but it was more than that. It was something indefinable. Something that tugged at him. Prodded him. Why else would he have considered Sal's proposition for more than an instant?

"What are these reasons?" he asked.

"Mine," she said and didn't offer any more.

This wasn't going at all the way Adam had expected. What was it about the Torinos that could keep him off balance? First her father, now her. *He* was the one in charge of situations. On top of everything. He knew what the other guy was thinking, what his next move would be and exactly the right countermove to ensure that Adam King got exactly what he set out to get.

Having the tables turned on him wasn't something he appreciated. And it was damned uncomfortable to have someone know him as well as Gina seemed to. At the moment, she was watching him with patient understanding glimmering in her eyes and it irritated him that she was so damned complacent while he felt off balance.

Clearly then, it was time to take charge again. Time to let her know that he wouldn't be twisted around and made to feel as if he'd taken a wrong step. Time to let her know that this date was over.

"Gina…" He flipped open the check folder, tucked a credit card into the pocket, then closed the whole thing and set it on the edge of the table. Their waiter rushed by a moment later and took it away. "I don't know what you're getting at, but I won't be maneuvered. By you… or your father."

She laughed, damn it, and he was both annoyed and charmed. "I don't see what's so funny."

"Of course you don't," she said and reached across the table to pat his hand as she would have an excitable kid. "But come on, Adam. We've known each other way too long for you to put on the big crabby attitude and expect me to either salute or slink away!"

He ground his back teeth together and hissed in a breath. "Fine. Say what you want to say, then I'll take you home."

She shook her head and smiled again. "Charming to the last." Before he could say anything to that, she spoke up again, quickly. "Okay. To the point. I'll marry you, Adam, so you can get the land. But I have a condition."

"I can't wait to hear it."

"I want a child."

Adam felt the slam of those words crush into his chest and he could have sworn he felt his heart actually stop. Her eyes were clear and steady. Her features calm. Her manner at ease. All the while, his insides were churning and it felt as though the air was on fire. Otherwise, why would his lungs be burning with every breath?

"You can't be serious."

"Completely," she assured him and her face softened, her mouth curving gently. "I know what you went through with the loss of your son and—"

While he was reeling, the waiter brought their check back to be signed. Adam took it, glanced at it, added a hefty tip and signed his name. Taking his credit card and the receipt, he tucked them into his wallet and only when he was finished did he look up at Gina again.

"I don't discuss my son. Ever." His loss was just that. *His* loss. He'd survived. Put the past behind him and that was where he intended to keep it. Those memories, that pain had nothing to do with his life or his world today.

"Fine."

"And I'm not interested in being a father again."

"I don't need your help in parenting my child, Adam," she said and her voice went suddenly as chill as his own. "All I need from you is your sperm."

"Why are you doing this?"

"Because I want to be a mother." She leaned back in her chair, fiddled with the handle of her coffee cup and lowered her gaze to the tabletop. "My brothers' kids are beautiful and I love them with all my heart. But I don't want to spend the rest of my life being the favorite auntie. I want a child of my own. I don't want to be married any more than you do—don't worry about that. But I do want a baby. The way I see it—" she lifted her gaze to his "—this bargain satisfies both parties. You get your land. I get the baby I want."

He was already shaking his head. Instinct, he supposed, when she spoke again.

"Think about this before you turn me down. I'll marry you. Be your wife in every way. As soon as I'm pregnant, you get the land and we get a divorce. And I'll sign whatever you want me to sign, exempting you from any responsibility toward me or my child." Her gaze was steady on his as she added, "It's a good deal, Adam. For both of us."

She had him in a corner. He hadn't expected her to know about her father's proposition—let alone come up with one of her own. The tantalizing idea that he could, in a few short months, have the King family ranch whole and secure again was a tempting one.

He had to give Gina credit. She'd thought this out and had come up with a bargain sure to be tempting to him. And the fact that she, too, was getting something out of the deal made him feel less like some robber baron.

Yet the thought of fathering another child wasn't something he'd even considered. A pain he refused to recognize thrummed inside him for a long moment. Then it was gone, because he'd had years to learn how to distance himself from emotional distress.

Besides, it wasn't as if this would be a real marriage. A genuine family situation. This was something completely different and apart from the norm. Gina knew him. And she didn't want a husband any more than he wanted a wife. She wanted a child, he wanted his land. A win-win bargain. All it would take was being married to a desirable woman for a few months.

How bad could that be?

"Well, Adam," she said softly, her voice nearly lost in the quiet rhythm of the jazz spilling through the restaurant. "What do you say?"

He stood up and held out one hand to help her from her chair. When she was standing, too, he shook the hand she held out and said, "Gina, you've got yourself a bargain."

Five

Things happened pretty quickly after the proposal.

Within a few days, Adam had arranged for a marriage license—apparently it paid to be one of the wealthiest men in California. And, since Adam was anxious to get their bargain up and running, there was no time for the big, fancy wedding Gina's mom had always dreamed of.

Instead Adam, Gina and her parents took one of the King family jets to Vegas.

"Not exactly the wedding every little girl dreams of," Gina whispered to herself as she looked around the interior of the luxury garden the ceremony was taking place in.

The walls were painted a soft summer-blue, with white clouds sponge-painted on as accents. There were tall pedestals holding elegant sprays of silk flowers and the white carpeted main aisle still held the footprints of the couple who had been married before them. Classical music piped in from overhead speakers and Gina's fingers tightened on the handle of her complimentary bouquet.

Gina's heart did a bump and roll in her chest and she was very glad she'd insisted on doing some prewedding shopping in San Jose. The deep yellow dress she wore made her feel beautiful and Gina had known instinctively that she would need all the confidence she could find.

"You're sure about this, Gina?"

She turned her head to look at her father and swallowed hard before answering. "Yes, Papa. I'm sure."

Of course she was sure. She'd been in love with Adam King for what felt like forever. She'd dreamed of this day for years. Of course, in all of those dreams, Adam had loved *her,* too. Her dream groom was happy and smiling, surrounded by his brothers, looking at Gina with desire flashing in his eyes.

So okay, the reality was a little disappointing. Still, she thought, shifting her gaze to the head of the aisle where her groom waited. She was marrying Adam.

And Gina'd had a few days to completely rethink this bargain she'd made with her about-to-be husband. This was a business deal, certainly. Adam was getting what he wanted out of it and she would be getting the baby her heart craved.

But over the last couple of days, she'd begun to imagine a slightly different outcome to this bargain. If she were willing to take a chance, to risk her heart, she might find a way to get everything she'd ever wanted.

All she had to do was find a way to break Adam's defences. Her insides fisted and released at the daunting prospect. She'd come this far, why not take that extra step? She only needed time. Gina was sure that once Adam and she were married, he would see the truth she'd always known. That they could be a great couple.

She sucked in a deep breath as that thought shot through her brain and sent a current of adrenaline to the pit of her stomach.

"You don't look so good, honey," her father said.

"I'm fine, Papa. Really. It's all good. See?" She gave her father a wide, phony smile that, thankfully, he accepted at face value. "Let's get this done, okay?"

"Yes," he said. "Your mother looks anxious."

She did, Gina thought, sliding a quick look at her mom. Actually her mother looked as though she wanted to give Adam a stern lecture about how to treat her daughter. Best to head that off at the pass. Teresa Torino was already a little snippy about Gina marrying a man she didn't think loved her.

The string quartet suddenly began playing the solemn strains of the Wedding March. Gina's stomach lurched, but she fought down the last bits of hesitation she felt and started down the aisle on her father's arm.

Not a very long walk, really, but with every step, she moved further away from the life she knew and closer to the life she'd always wanted.

Adam's dark chocolate eyes were narrowed on her. His features were stiff and the smile she'd hoped to see didn't appear. But then, this wasn't a love match, was it? His gaze was steady, but blank, giving away no hint at all of what he was feeling, thinking. And Gina could only hope he wasn't able to read her emotions any better than she could his.

At the head of the aisle, Sal laid Gina's hand in Adam's and stepped back to join his wife.

Adam gave her a brief smile that didn't do a thing to ease the cool indifference on his features.

When the minister started talking, she found it hard to hear him over the thundering of her own heartbeat. She was only able to catch every other word, but they were the important ones. The ones that would change her life. At least for now.

"I will," Adam said and Gina swayed a little at the impact of two small words. And her heartbeat seemed to pound out, *if only.*

Then it was her turn. She felt Adam's big hand enveloping hers and focused on the minister. Here it was. Her last chance to back out. Or, she thought, the beginning of the biggest gamble she would ever make.

There was a long pause when the minister stopped speaking and the silence in the chapel was nearly deafening. She felt Adam watching her, waiting for her answer.

"I will," she said finally and it was as if the room took a relieved breath and let it out again.

Adam slipped a ring on her finger and as the short, round minister finished up the brief ceremony, Gina looked down at her hand. A wide, thick gold band glittered up at her. There were no stones set into the precious metal. No delicate carvings or etchings that proclaimed a deeply felt connection between two people.

It was plain.

Impersonal.

Much like her marriage.

Then Adam held her shoulders, pulled her in close and gave her a quick, hard kiss, sealing the bargain Gina really hoped wouldn't come back to haunt them both.

For the first time in far too long, Adam felt as though he'd somehow lost control of a situation. And he didn't like the sensation.

Yet somehow, he'd ended up here, in the Presidential Suite of Dreams, the newest, most opulent hotel yet to be built in Las Vegas, waiting for his bride to join him.

"Bride." He shook his head and poured himself a glass of the champagne chilling in a sterling silver ice bucket atop the table set up for them on the suite's private balcony. If ever a man needed a drink, it was now.

Taking a sip, he looked out over the view sprawling for miles. In the distance, he saw the purple smudge of mountains, crowned by the first stars blinking into life in the night sky. The setting sun still provided an orange glow on the horizon and in the streets far below him, other lights in dizzying colors and patterns glittered and shone like jewels in a treasure chest.

From thirty stories up, Las Vegas was beautiful. Up close and personal, Adam knew that the tattered edges of the city were much easier to spot. Much like his marriage, he thought wryly, taking a long sip of the cold, bubbly wine. From a distance, people would assume that he and Gina had been swept away by passion. Only they would ever know the cold, hard truth.

Which was what, exactly?

"That you're a hard ass," he muttered. "Willing to use a woman to get what you want. Ready to create a child and walk away from it without a second thought."

Surprisingly enough, that little jolt of reality bothered Adam more than he'd thought it would. He scrubbed one hand across his jaw, stared off into the night and reminded himself that this had been Gina's idea. She wasn't a victim in this but a willing conspirator.

When his cell phone rang, though, Adam grabbed it, grateful to have something besides his own thoughts to concentrate on. A glance at the screen had him sighing. Flipping the phone open, he asked, "What is it, Travis?"

"What is it?" his brother echoed. "You're not serious. I just talked to Esperanza and she told me you were in Las Vegas getting married."

Adam sighed. His housekeeper had a big mouth. "That's right."

"To *Gina*."

"That's right."

"So my invitation got lost in the mail?" Travis demanded.

Setting his champagne glass down on the stone balcony railing, Adam shoved his free hand into his pants pocket and tightened his grip on the phone. "It was a small ceremony."

"Yeah? I hear her parents were there."

"And now they're gone. The jet took them home this afternoon."

"Uh-huh. Any reason why you didn't want *your* family there?"

"It's not what you think."

"Really? Because what I think is you just married a kid we've known all our lives without bothering to tell your brothers."

"She's not a kid," Adam said tightly, his fingers clenching down hard on his phone. "Hasn't been one for a long time. And since when do I report to you and Jackson?"

"You don't," Travis countered. "But there's something fishy going on here, Adam. This 'marriage' of yours wouldn't have anything to do with getting that damned land, would it?"

There was a long, silent moment as Adam got a tight rein on the temper screaming inside, then Travis muttered, "You really are a son of a bitch, aren't you?"

"She knew what she was doing." Hadn't he told himself that over and over again since agreeing to the bargain Gina had offered him?

"I doubt it."

Shoving his free hand through his hair, Adam shot a look behind him to assure himself that Gina hadn't come out of the bathroom yet. Then he argued, "You know, Travis, you're not exactly the poster child for the better treatment of women."

"That's not the point," his brother snapped.

"It's exactly the point. I don't tell you to stop squiring bimbos around—or to avoid the damn paparazzi that follow you everywhere. So butt the hell out of my life, little brother."

"You screw with Gina and her father will make your life a living hell," Travis warned.

"Because my life now is just rainbows and kittens, right?"

"Damn, Adam," his brother said on a sigh. "When the hell did you get so cold?"

"When wasn't I?" Adam asked and snapped the phone closed before Travis could get started again. Then he turned the phone off before Jackson could call and have his say. He didn't need to hear his brothers' opinions. He knew going into this what they'd think. And it didn't matter a damn.

He and Gina were two consenting adults. Their marriage—such as it was—was nobody else's business.

"Well," Gina said from behind him. "You look like you want to take a bite out of somebody."

He turned, schooling his features into the calm, unreadable mask he used with everyone but his brothers. But even as he fought for distance, the sight of her had a hot ball of lust pooling in his belly.

In the pale wash of the soft balcony lights, she looked almost otherworldly. Her nightgown was short, stopping midthigh. A deep, rich red, the satin fabric clung to her skin, outlining every curve and exposing what looked like a mile of leg. The bodice was red lace and it cupped her breasts like a lover's hands. Her hair hung loose and thick over her shoulders, the untamed curls enticing him. She smelled like heaven—peaches and flowers and the smile she gave him was knowing and nervous at the same time.

"You look," he said, "beautiful."

Her smile brightened. "I feel silly." Then she smoothed one hand over her stomach as if trying to calm butterflies and he wondered if she was regretting making the offer that had brought them to this place.

Adam poured her a flute of champagne and when she took it from him, her fingertips grazed his skin and heat exploded. He ignored it for the moment. "Why silly?"

She waved a hand at her negligee and shrugged. "I went out and bought this, especially for tonight and I probably shouldn't have. It's not like this is an ordinary wedding night, is it?"

"No," he conceded and found he couldn't take his gaze from her. From the curve of her breasts. From the hard tips of her nipples, pressing against the dark red lace. "It's not. But it *is* the beginning of our bargain."

"True," she said and took a sip of champagne. Then she licked her bottom lip and everything in Adam tightened painfully.

"And," he said, taking a swallow himself, "for myself, I can tell you I appreciate your shopping talents."

Her eyes widened, then she smiled more easily. "Thanks." Stepping out onto the balcony, heedless of the negligee she wore, she looked out at the view and sighed. "It's gorgeous, isn't it?"

"Yeah, it is." But he wasn't looking at the neon-lit desert or the mountains beyond. He was staring at her. He took another drink of champagne, hoping the icy wine would spill into his blood and cool it off a little. No such luck.

She glanced at him over her shoulder. "Thanks for flying Mom and Dad here and home again."

He shrugged. He hadn't minded bringing Sal and Teresa along, though he also hadn't been sorry to see them go. Teresa especially. The woman had looked daggers at him all day. "Seemed important that they be there for you."

"But you didn't want your brothers?"

He leaned back against the stone railing. "I thought it would be easier all around if we kept it simple."

"Right," she said. "Simple. Do they know?"

"About us?" he asked. When she nodded he said, "They do now. Esperanza told them."

She smiled. "How'd they take it?"

He looked at her and lied. It didn't matter a damn to him what his brothers thought about this. "Fine. Talked to Travis a few minutes ago."

A desert wind sailed past them and Gina shivered.

"You're cold."

"A little."

He set his glass down on the table and went to her. A short walk and yet Adam felt as if each step were measured. He was about to seal their bargain. There would be no going back. And if he woke up tomorrow regretting what he'd done tonight, then he'd have to live with it.

But then, he'd had plenty of practice living with uncomfortable realities.

"Come here." Pulling her close, he wrapped both arms around her, drawing her in, her back to his front. Heat pooled between them, seeping into his bones, firing his blood. Adam felt that sweet rush of need fill him and he gritted his teeth to maintain control. He wouldn't be led around by his groin. This bargain was one thing.

Releasing control was something else. Something he wouldn't allow to happen.

"Adam," Gina said, her voice so soft, he almost missed it. "I know this was my idea, but I suddenly don't know what to do next."

"We do what we planned to do. We make a child together."

She shivered again and pressed harder against him. "Right. I mean, that is what this is all about. So," she said, turning in his arms to look up at him, "no point in wasting time, is there?"

She lifted her arms and hooked them behind his neck. Then she went up on her toes, tilted her head and kissed him. The soft, almost hesitant touch of her mouth to his lit up Adam's insides brighter than any of the neon stretching out across the desert beneath them.

He'd spent the last five years alone. Pushing aside wants and needs he didn't have the time or patience to deal with. Now, there was no reason to hold back. So he didn't. Wrapping his arms around her middle, he held her to him with a fierce grip and took her mouth with all the pent-up hunger he felt surging within.

She groaned a little as he parted her lips with his tongue

and tasted her warmth. She sighed and fed the fires racing through his blood. He held her tighter to him, grinding his hips against hers, needing that sweet pressure.

Again and again, his tongue delved inside, claiming her, taking all she had to give. He allowed his control to slip and he surrendered to the waves of desire crashing inside him. He slid his hands up and down her back, cupping her bottom, stroking her spine, threading through the thick mass of curls that fell in a dark curtain around her.

Her scent filled him. Her taste enflamed him. And his body physically ached to have her under him.

He tore his mouth from hers, like a man struggling for air before he drowned. Gina swayed unsteadily, but Adam's arms were like steel bands, supporting her, holding her. She tipped her head back to stare up at the desert sky while Adam's mouth moved up and down her neck, nibbling, licking, tasting. She felt like a banquet laid out before a starving man.

She felt needed. Wanted.

If only she also felt loved.

But when that thought appeared in her mind, she shut it off instantly. For now, it was enough that *she* loved. It was enough that she finally knew what it was to have Adam King's legendary focus directed at *her.* And she wanted more. She wanted it all. Tomorrow, she would begin the pretense of a marriage they'd decided on. But tonight was her wedding night and she wanted to remember every moment of it.

When Adam swept her up into his arms, she gasped.

Then she looked into his dark, dark eyes. She smiled at him, but there was no glint of humor or warmth in his gaze.

Only need.

A part of her saddened at that knowledge, but she fought that sensation back, cupped his face in her hands and said, "We can do this, right?"

His mouth quirked. "Oh, we're *going* to do this, Gina. Now."

A swirl of something delicious swept through her, heating her core, making her blood run thick. She took a deep breath as he started to carry her back into the suite. "I wasn't talking about sex, Adam. I was talking about our bargain."

He stopped dead just inside the French doors. Looking down at her, he asked, "Second thoughts?"

And thirds. And fourths, she thought, but didn't say. "No. Just making sure you're not having any."

He held her tighter, his right hand sliding up her thigh. "Once I make a deal, I stick with it."

"Of course you do," she said, nodding even as she let one hand slide from his neck, down his throat to his chest. His heartbeat thudded beneath her hand and she knew, whether his features were stoic or not, he wasn't as calm as he pretended. "And so do I," she added.

"Good to know. Now, how about we start taking care of business?"

"That might be easier for me if we didn't call it business," she pointed out, unbuttoning the front of his shirt.

He shook his head and his eyes seemed to swallow

her. "This is business, though, Gina. Nothing more. Don't fool yourself. Don't pretend that this is a real marriage. You'll only be hurt in the end."

Well, nothing like a cold flood of reality to warm you up for the night's festivities. He was making sure she didn't put too much of herself into this bargain they'd struck. And maybe assuring himself that there wouldn't be any hard feelings when it was done.

That was fine with Gina. He could think what he wanted. Her thoughts she would keep to herself. Her dreams would remain hidden and secret, locked away in her heart. For now, she had the man she'd always wanted and she wasn't going to let doubts or fears about the future ruin the night she'd been waiting for all of her life.

Six

His hands on her bare skin felt wicked. Felt…right. She felt as though she'd been waiting for this one particular moment all of her life. The moment when she would have Adam to herself. When she would take him into her body and hold him there.

Her stomach was spinning, a weird combination of nerves and champagne. Her brain was racing, alternately shouting out warnings and egging her on. But Gina didn't need urging. She unbuttoned his shirt and slid one hand across his bare chest. She felt his body jerk at the slight touch and knew that he wanted her as badly as she wanted him.

The plush, gigantic bedroom was dark, but for the desert moonlight streaming through the open balcony doors. The white sheers hanging there fluttered and swayed seductively in a soft wind and the scent of desert sage wafted into the room.

The bed was wide and high and covered in a luxurious white silk duvet that had already been turned down for the night. A mountain of pillows were stacked against the black iron headboard. Adam carried her with quick steps, right to the edge of the bed. Then he set her on her feet, grabbed the edge of the duvet and tossed it heedlessly to the foot of the mattress.

Gina's knees went a little wobbly, so she locked them just to make sure she didn't do anything totally stupid like topple over. In the semidarkness, Adam's chocolate-brown eyes looked nearly black as he stared down at her. His mouth was thin, tight, as if he were holding on to the ragged edge of control.

Well, she didn't want him controlled.

She wanted him wild and eager and spontaneous. Biting down on her bottom lip, Gina lifted her hands to the front of his shirt and undid the rest of the buttons. While he stood there, unmoving, she pushed the shirt off his shoulders and down his arms, to drop to the floor. Then she let her hands slide across his hard, warm chest. Felt the soft brush of the dark hair that whorled across his tanned skin. Felt him flinch when her thumbnail stroked the tip of one flat nipple.

He grabbed her waist, his hands big and hard and strong. Then he yanked her close, holding her to him so that she felt the thick ridge of his arousal. Looming over her, he stared into her eyes and Gina felt the heat of that gaze fire up her insides like a match to a pool of gasoline.

His mouth came down on hers with a fierceness she hadn't expected. His tongue parted her lips and she opened for him, inviting his exploration. Their tongues twisted together in a heated dance that was only a prelude of things to come. Gina's breath caught in her chest and her head began to swim.

Her body alive with sensation, she groaned from the back of her throat when Adam's hands slid up to cover her breasts. He stroked her, causing the lace to rub across her already sensitized nipples with a delicious friction that heated her core and drove her to the edge of madness. Each touch was a fire. Each touch only made her want the next. Each stroking caress tautened the tension already coiled inside her.

When he tore his mouth from hers to lick and nibble his way down the length of her throat, Gina tipped her head back to give him more access. His mouth was a wonder. His hands at her breasts a lovely torture.

Then he shifted position, lifting his hands to the thin, ribbonlike straps of her nightgown and he slid them down over her shoulders. Gina shivered a little at the cool glide of his fingertips against her skin, then shivered harder as he pushed the nightgown down and off to puddle at her feet.

The desert wind was cool as it brushed into the room and danced across her skin, but Adam's gaze kept her too warm to notice. He looked her up and down, then looking directly into her eyes, he lifted her again and dropped her onto the mattress.

She bounced once, then settled back against the backdrop of pillows, a lavender scent drifting to her like a lost memory of summer. Her center, hot and aching, had her shifting on the smooth, cool sheets, looking for the release her body already clamored for.

Gina watched as Adam stripped quickly out of his clothes. Her mouth went dry when he was naked and her gaze dropped down to the incredible, hard length of him.

Gina forced herself to relax, ordering her legs to loosen and the hard knot of worry to dissolve in the back of her mind. She'd known him her whole life practically. She knew he wouldn't hurt her. Knew that even if he didn't love her, he would take care of her.

Then he was moving over her and her brain shut down. All she had the strength to focus on were the sensations rippling through her body in relentless waves. His hands, his mouth, his body, lavished attention on her. Every inch of her felt alive and tingling.

He closed his mouth over one nipple and Gina nearly leaped off the bed. His lips and tongue and teeth tormented her until she whimpered and shifted beneath him, trying to get closer. Her hands slid up and down his broad, muscled back and her short, neat fingernails scraped over his skin.

He groaned against her and Gina's hips rocked into him. She lifted one leg, trailing the sole of her foot along his leg, desperate to touch him. To feel all of him.

"You smell incredible," he whispered, moving his mouth from one nipple to the other.

Gina made a mental note to buy more of the citrus/flowery body lotion she preferred.

She stared up at the moonlit ceiling above them and stared blindly as shadows shifted and waved against the pale lemon paint. Her breath struggled in and out of her lungs. Her body burned and when he moved lazily and she felt that hard, thick length of him rub her core, she gasped and arched higher. "Adam…"

"I know," he whispered, lifting his head to look into her eyes.

She met his gaze with a dazed look, and saw the wildness in his eyes. Gina took his face between her palms and drew his head to her. She wanted to kiss him. To feel that connection of want and desire build between them. To have his body atop hers, his heartbeat thundering in time with her own.

The kiss seared them both. Heat and passion trembled in the air and Gina put all she had into it. She gave him her heart in that kiss, whether he knew it or not. She poured the feelings she'd so carefully banked for years into that one instant of mouths and hearts blending and when she felt him shift, positioning himself between her legs, she kissed him even harder.

She wanted his mouth on hers when he entered her and so she moved with him, spreading her thighs, lifting her hips while at the same time keeping her lips firmly attached to his. His tongue swept across the inside of her mouth as he pushed his body into hers.

He lifted his head, looked down into her eyes and held perfectly still, allowing her body to adjust to the presence of his. Gina groaned, digging her head into the mound of pillows behind her. She wriggled her hips, lifting, shifting, feeling him slowly sink deeper within and as he claimed her, inch by inch, she felt her body stretching to accommodate him.

"Oh, my…" She let out a breath on a sigh and looked up at him smiling down at her.

She smiled, then gasped as he rocked his hips, pushing higher within.

He eased back, sitting on his haunches, scooping his hands under bottom, lifting her hips a little, pulling her body down harder on his. "We're just getting started."

"Oh, boy."

His thumb stroked the hard, hot nub of flesh at her center and Gina's back arched high off the mattress. Her hands scrabbled for something to hold on to and her fingers curled into the silken sheets beneath her. It didn't help; she still felt her world swaying and tilting weirdly around her as he moved, withdrawing only to plunge inside her again.

His fingers continued to rub and stroke her most sensitive spot, until Gina was writhing in his grasp, twisting her hips, unconsciously drawing his body deeper into hers. *Too much,* she thought. *It was all too much. She couldn't handle so many sensations. So much pleasure. Surely there was a saturation point where her body would simply dissolve and her mind become a puddle of goo.*

And then he showed her differently. Reaching for her,

he took hold of her waist and lifted her off the bed, settling her down on his lap, so that his length was deep inside her. Gina looked directly into his eyes as he guided her in an easy rhythm that had her rocking on him, tantalizing them both.

The wind slid into the room, and the scent of sage melded with the scent of their heated bodies and the bloom of sex. Skin met skin, breath intermingled and their sighs became a symphony of want and desperate need.

Moving on him, sliding her body onto his, Gina found a magic she'd never expected. Her body quivered, her insides straining, reaching toward the release that built within. Her heart swelled, filling with the thrill of being a part of Adam at long last. And her mind raced with images she couldn't allow herself to indulge in. Images of Adam's eyes shining with love for her. Images of the two of them, together. Always.

But even though a part of her mourned, she relished the feelings coursing through her. She looked into Adam's eyes, lost herself in those dark, dark depths and watched as passion ignited, firing sparks she knew *she* had brought him.

Tension coiled tighter, tighter. Her body trembled. She held her breath and when she slid down his length one more time, the first explosion smashed into her.

"Adam!" She gripped his shoulders hard, trying to keep herself stable in a suddenly wildly *un*stable world.

"Let go," he ordered, his voice a low rush of sound, scraping from his throat. "Let yourself go, Gina."

She did. She couldn't help it. Didn't want to try.

Instead she gave herself up to the incredible sensations coursing through her. Riding wave after wave of tremors that continued to ripple through her long after that first tremendous burst had diminished.

And when Gina thought she couldn't take another moment, there was more. Adam dropped one hand to the spot where their bodies joined. Once again, he rubbed that tender piece of flesh that seemed to hold a store of electrical-like nerve endings. She jolted in his embrace and instinctively ground her hips against him.

"Adam…" She whispered his name now, a sigh of pleasure.

"Again," he said, pushing her even higher than she'd been before. Her mind splintered, her body shattered and when she felt herself falling, she heard Adam groan and knew he was taking the fall with her.

Adam's heart was racing and his body felt more lax than it had in years. He turned his head on the pillows to look at the woman lying beside him. Her eyes were closed, and she lay, one arm flung back behind her head, the other reaching toward him across the wide expanse of mattress.

Her skin was softer than the silk they lay on and her hair was a tumble of curls he couldn't seem to touch enough. Her sighs, her pleasures, tempted him to take her again and again. Even now, he felt himself stir, his body already hardening for her.

"You're watching me."

"Your eyes are closed," he pointed out. "How do you know?"

"I can feel it," she said and turned her head on the pillows to look at him. A smile curved her delectable mouth and Adam felt another jolt of desire slam into him. Maybe this bargain between them hadn't been such a good idea after all, he thought, at the realization that in the last hour with her, he'd *felt* more than he had in the last five years.

"Now you're frowning," Gina said, rolling to her side, unabashedly naked, her tanned, smooth skin nearly glowing in the moonlight. "No frowns allowed."

"Don't know if I can accommodate that request," he said.

She sighed, pushed one hand through her hair, throwing the thick mass over her shoulder. "Adam, you don't have to be worried."

"What makes you think I'm worried?"

She laughed and the sound of it sang through the otherwise quiet room. "Please. I know exactly what you're thinking."

"Is that right?" Turning to face her, he went up on one elbow. "Then what am I thinking?" he said with a slight smile.

She stroked the tips of her fingers across the sheet covered distance separating them and Adam wished she were touching him.

"That's easy. You're worrying that you made a mistake by agreeing to this little bargain."

He opened his mouth to argue, more because he hated knowing that she could read him so well than anything else, but she spoke up again.

"You're worried that I'm building up romantic notions. Hoping you'll fall in love with me."

He frowned harder, because damn it, she was right. He had been worrying about that, too. But he wouldn't admit it. "Wrong. I know you're not doing anything that foolish." At least, he hoped not. "After all, this was your idea."

"True." She smiled and rolled onto her stomach, coming closer to him. Close enough that he couldn't keep himself from reaching one hand out to stroke the line of her spine, the curve of her bottom. And he wondered how in the hell she'd managed to get a tan all over.

Shaking his head to get rid of the image of her stretched out naked in the sun, Adam asked, "Why?"

"Why what?" She looked at him, her golden eyes shining in the darkness.

"Why'd you offer me this bargain? I mean, I know you want a baby. I understand that. What I want to know is why me?"

She stretched lazily, moving that tanned, toned body on the white silk sheets until blood vessels started popping in Adam's brain.

"Easily enough explained, Adam," she said, glancing at him. "You wanted the land, so that gave me some leverage...."

"Yes..." He wanted the rest of her reason.

"And, I've known you forever, Adam. I like you. I think you like me—"

He nodded. He did like Gina. He'd just never paid much attention to that fact over the years. She was younger than he was, so they hadn't spent much time together when they were kids. Then, when they were grown, he'd had other priorities.

"—it seemed like the perfect answer to both of our problems." She lifted one hand to him and stroked her palm across his chest. Adam sucked in a gulp of air at the heat that instantly shot through him. "And...I think the two of us will make a beautiful baby."

A slice of something cold and dark cut through his mind at those words. He'd once made a vow to never have another child. To never open himself up to that kind of risk again. But this was different, he reasoned, so he pushed those thoughts into a corner of his mind. He'd made this bargain and he'd honor it. The child he and Gina made between them wouldn't be a part of his life. He wouldn't know it. Love it. Or lose it. In fact, best to not think about it at all.

"I'm sorry," she whispered and Adam cut her a look.

"About what?"

"Talking about the baby I want must make you remember your son."

Adam froze. He felt his features tighten and everything in him go hard and still as glass. Memories jumped into his mind, but he refused to acknowledge them. He turned them off as easily as punching the remote button aimed at a television. He'd had a lot of practice.

He wasn't open to talking about the son he'd lost five years before and they might as well get that straight right up front. "I don't talk about him. Ever."

Her eyes went soft in sympathy and Adam resented it. He didn't need her feeling sorry for him.

"I understand."

"You couldn't possibly," he told her.

A silent second or two passed before Gina said, "Fine, you're right. I don't understand. I hope I never learn the kind of pain you experienced and—"

He caught her hand in his and gave it a hard squeeze. Just enough to get her to stop talking. How the hell had they gotten onto the subject of his lost family anyway? Wasn't their bargain supposed to be about sex, plain and simple? "What part of 'I don't talk about it' didn't you get?"

She pulled her hand free of his, pushed herself up on the bed and leaned in close to him. Staring into his eyes, it looked as though she were searching for something, some sign that there was warmth hidden somewhere inside him. Adam could have told her to not bother looking.

After a long moment, Gina leaned in even further and kissed him, briefly, softly. "I get it, Adam. The subject's off-limits."

"Good."

"I don't want to talk anyway." Gina stroked his cheek with her palm and drew his head closer to hers.

"That's good, too." At her touch, his body heated and was instantly ready for her again. He'd been too long without a woman, that was all. He'd been a damn recluse for five years, with only the occasional, temporary woman to ease needs that couldn't be denied any longer.

That explained why his response to Gina was so overwhelming. It was just biological, that was all. It wasn't about her. It was about sex. Need.

And when she moved into him, he kept telling himself that, even as he inhaled her scent, drawing it deep inside him. Even as he twisted his hand into her hair, letting the silky feel of it slide over his skin. Even as he took her mouth and tasted the sweetness that was Gina alone.

He couldn't—wouldn't—allow anything else.

She tried to roll over in his arms, but he kept her on her stomach and shifted enough that he could trail kisses along the length of her spine. Such soft, honey-brown skin. Such long lines and rich curves. He heard her sigh and felt her tremble as his left hand swept down to stroke her bottom. He glanced at her, saw her eyes closed, her hands fisted in the bank of pillows.

"Adam…"

"We have all night, Gina," he said and suddenly knew that he wanted every moment of the night. He wanted her over him, under him. He wanted to taste and explore every glorious inch of her and then he wanted to start all over again.

Fire erupted in his blood as she moved on the sheets and he knew he had to have her. No more thinking. No more worrying about tomorrow or the day after that. For now, he would waste no more time with her.

Flipping her over with a quick twist, he grinned when she smiled up at him and lifted her arms in welcome. He slid into her embrace, covering her body with his and when he entered her, she arched her hips to take him completely. To hold him deep inside her heat. And Adam closed his mind to everything but her.

They moved together in a rhythm that left them both breathless. Bodies sang, minds emptied and when the first flash of release slammed into Gina, Adam held on to her, watching her eyes, dazzled with pleasure as he surrendered himself to the glory waiting for him.

Seven

Thanks to Esperanza Sanchez, Adam's longtime housekeeper, Gina was pretty sure she'd gained five pounds in four days. The older woman was so happy to see Adam married again, she hadn't stopped cooking all week. And every time Gina tried to help out in the kitchen, straighten up the living room or even to dust, she was shooed out of the room and told to go spend time with her new husband.

Not as easy as it sounded.

Esperanza was determined to see that Gina felt at home. Even if Adam was a little less than welcoming. Staring into a full-length mirror in the bedroom she now shared with Adam, Gina wasn't looking at her own reflection so much as at the gigantic bed behind her.

That was the only place she felt as though Adam was glad to have her in his home.

"Happy to have me in his bed anyway," she muttered and tried to find the bright spot in that statement. At least they shared passion. At least they connected occasionally. Even if it was only physically.

"Pitiful, Gina, just pitiful." She shook her head, met her own gaze in the mirror and gave her reflection one last glance. Not exactly a femme fatale, she admitted. In her pink T-shirt, worn jeans and boots, she looked more like a ranch hand than a newlywed. Her long dark hair hung down her back in a single braid and her eyes looked huge in her face.

She'd had a lot of hopes for this bargain. Had counted on Adam being a little easier to maneuver than he was proving. Instead he seemed determined to keep to himself. To keep their relationship as superficial as possible, despite the fact that they were married and living together.

Gina turned away, opened the French doors to their bedroom terrace and stepped out onto the glossy wood floor. The early morning sky was deep blue, but there were storm clouds banking out over the ocean. Now why, she wondered, did that sound like a perfect metaphor for her marriage?

They'd been back from Vegas for nearly a week, and it was as if that brief "honeymoon" had never happened. She leaned both hands on the second-story balcony railing and curled her fingers over the sun-warmed decorative iron. The minute they'd arrived back at the ranch,

Adam had closed himself off. She actually felt like they were a couple those days and nights together. It was as if a switch inside him had been flipped. He'd become the recluse he'd been for five long years. She hardly saw him during the day and when she did, he was distant, if polite. The only time he warmed to her was at night.

Then, he was the man she'd always dreamed he would be. Then, he gave himself and took from her. Every time they came together was better than the time before. Frankly the sex was incredible. Gina'd never known anything quite like it. But at the bottom of it, if all they shared was great sex, was there anything between them worth fighting for?

"Way to go, Gina," she muttered. "Depress yourself."

She squinted into the sun and watched Adam walk with long, determined steps into the barn. Once he'd been swallowed by the shadows, Gina sighed. She wondered what he was doing. What he was thinking. He didn't talk to her. Didn't share his plans for the day. Didn't let her into what was going on in his head. It was as if she were a boarder here at the ranch. Nothing more than a guest who would be moving on shortly.

Another sigh escaped before she could stop it. Bending slightly, she leaned her elbows on the railing and studied the shiny new gold band on her ring finger. She wasn't a guest. She was his wife. For now.

At least, for as long as it took her to get pregnant.

Which, she thought, explained why she was still using her diaphragm. A tiny thread of guilt whipped through her like summer lightning. She admitted at least to herself that what she was doing wasn't technically fair. But she was willing to risk everything for the chance at real love. Even if that meant Adam one day finding out what she'd done. If that day came, she'd confess all and hope that he understood.

Every night, he did everything he could to impregnate her, no doubt so that he could end the marriage quickly and send her on her way.

He just had no idea that she was sabotaging the bargain she had proposed in the first place.

"Gina, this might turn out to be a lot harder than you thought it would be." And maybe, she admitted silently, it would be impossible.

But even as that thought niggled away in her brain, she vowed she wouldn't give up so quickly.

She'd made the decision to keep using her diaphragm before the wedding. Yes, she wanted a baby. Adam's baby. But she also wanted a chance to make Adam want her for longer than the duration of their arrangement. She wanted time for them to get used to each other. Time for him to realize that they could have something special together.

Time to make him fall in love with her.

Risky?

Oh, yeah.

But if she could pull it off, so worth it.

While her mind wandered down the "what if" paths it was getting so used to lately, she noticed a bright red sports car turning into the driveway. Before she could even wonder who their visitor was, though, another vehicle turned onto the ranch road right behind the zippy little car. This one was a huge horse trailer. Instantly excitement shot through her.

"They're here!" She grinned, turned and ran back into the bedroom she shared with Adam. She raced through the big room, hardly looking at it, then down the hall and took the stairs two at a time. She was already standing in the driveway when the car and then the horse van pulled up in the yard and stopped.

A tall, gorgeous man stepped out of the car, took one look at Gina and said, "I'm guessing that eager welcome isn't for me?"

Gina gave Adam's brother a quick smile. Travis was so easygoing. So relaxed. So ready to smile and quick to laugh. How much easier would her life had been if she'd only fallen in love with him? Unfortunately, though, when she looked at him, she didn't get that "zing" of something hot and sweet inside her. It was just pure female admiration for a gorgeous man.

"Hi, Travis. Nice to see you." She waved a hand at the trailer. "My horses are here."

"Upstaged by a truck full of horses?" Travis walked around the front of his car, then leaned lazily against the front fender. "Must be losing my touch. Came by to see my new sister-in-law and say welcome to the family."

She knew that Travis and Jackson had a feeling of the true circumstances of her marriage, but he'd come anyway. Wanted to welcome her, however briefly, into the King family. For that, she wanted to kiss him. She walked to him and gave him a brief hug. "Thanks. I appreciate it, really."

He gave her a hard squeeze and held on to her when she would have backed away. Looking down into her eyes, Travis asked, "How's it going, Gina? Adam making you nuts yet?"

"Not completely." She smiled, grateful for the understanding.

"Give him time," Travis said with a wink. Then the smile faded from his face. "Gina, I just want you to be careful, okay? I don't want to see you get hurt and—"

"Why're you hugging my wife, Travis?" Adam's voice boomed as he walked out of the barn.

"Well, she's just so damn huggable, isn't she?" Travis sounded amused as he gave her another squeeze. He winked down at her before letting her go.

Adam's features were tight and his eyes were narrowed. Gina wished she could pretend he was actually a little jealous, but she had the feeling it was more about Travis showing up unannounced than about a hug.

Adam looked at her, then shifted his gaze back to his brother. "What're you doing here?"

"And hello to you, too, big brother," Travis answered.

Gina looked at her husband and tried to rein in her instant physical response. But it was way too late. No matter how she tried to control it, her body lit up the moment she saw Adam. Where she could look at Travis or Jackson, for that matter, and see a handsome man with a great body and lots of charm, that's as far as it went. When she looked at Adam, though, her stomach fluttered with the nervous clip of butterfly wings and her heartbeat quickened into a fast gallop.

Even with his crabby nature and tendency to shut out anyone who threatened to get close, she loved him. Somewhere inside that perpetual crab, there was still the guy who at sixteen had helped her home after she'd fallen off her horse. Inside Adam, there was still the young hero who'd come to her rescue at a school dance when her date had gotten too grabby.

She looked at him and saw not only the past, but their possible future and the love for him she'd carried around inside her for years was alive and well. God help her. She took a deep breath, waited for him to look at her and then said with a forced brightness, "My horses are here."

"I see that," he said, shooting a glare at the trailer as it parked close to the corral. "Why?"

That she hadn't expected. "What do you mean, why?"

"Simple question, Gina," he said, folding his arms over his chest, planting his booted feet wide apart as if readying for battle. "Why are they here? Why didn't you just keep them at your folks' place?"

Gina stared at him. He was mad about her horses being shuttled to the ranch? "Because I live here now."

"Temporarily," Adam said.

Direct hit, she thought and inwardly winced.

"For God's sake, Adam." Travis straightened up and walked to Gina's side, clearly aligning himself with her.

"This is none of your business, Travis."

Gina appreciated Adam's brother's attempts at help, but she needed to take care of this herself. "He's right, Travis. This is between Adam and me."

She walked over to her husband, whose scowl looked fierce enough to strip paint and tipped her head back to look up at him. "Adam, we're married. I live here. I work with the Gypsies every day. It's not exactly convenient to drive over to my parents ranch every morning to do that work."

Adam did a quiet seethe. She could see it in his narrowed eyes and the tense lock of his jaw. Then she watched him flick a glance at Travis before turning his gaze back to her. Clearly there was more he wanted to say, but Travis being a witness wasn't something he was interested in.

Taking her upper arm in a firm grip, he steered her farther away from his brother and didn't stop until they were standing in the shade of the open barn doors. "You don't have to put on a front, Gina. We both know that this marriage isn't *real*."

Another barb that hit home with deadly accuracy. But damned if she'd let him know it. If she was going to make Adam see her, really see her, then she had to stand up to him. Let him know right up front that she wasn't going to be ignored or placated or pushed around.

"You're wrong," she said shortly. "This marriage is *very* real." She held up her left hand and wiggled her ring finger at him. "Whatever you'd like to think, Adam, we're legally married, for however long it lasts."

He released his grip on her arm, but her skin kept buzzing as if his touch had branded her. "I know it's legal, but it's not your ordinary marriage, now is it?"

"What marriage is ordinary, Adam?"

He blew out a frustrated breath. "You're purposely misunderstanding me."

"Oh, I understand just fine," she said and tapped the tip of her index finger against his chest. "You want to pretend that I'm not really here. The only place you want to see me is our bedroom. Well, get over it. I am here. And I'm not going anywhere just yet."

"I know that." He shot a look at Travis, lowered his voice and said, "I'm just saying it doesn't make much sense to uproot your horses. Besides, there's no room for them here. Not to mention the fact that you could have talked to me about this before arranging for their arrival."

Okay. Love him or not, Gina wasn't going to be walked on. "There's plenty of room on this ranch for the horses, Adam. You don't even use the front corral and the barn's half empty."

"That's not the point—"

"You just made it the point. Plus," she said, rushing on before he could get started again, "you knew going in that I work with those horses."

"I didn't think—"

"What?" Her eyes widened and she waved both hands in the air. "You didn't think I'd work with them here? Where I live?" She lowered her voice a little and leaned in. "What did you think, Adam? That I'd just stay tucked up in the bedroom waiting for you to service me? I said I wanted a baby, but I also have a life. One I'm not interested in giving up."

"You could have told me—"

"Maybe I should have. But I didn't realize I would

have to discuss every one of my decisions with you to get your approval."

"I didn't say that—"

"What did you say then?" She was almost enjoying this, Gina thought. Adam looked confused and off balance. But it was better than disinterested. At least he was looking at her. Talking to her. Actually, she thought, keeping him off balance might be just the answer.

He scrubbed one hand across his face in an impatient gesture. "Fine. I'm not going to argue about this."

"Too late."

"You want the damn horses here, then fine."

"Oh," she said, laying one hand on her chest. "Thanks so much."

His mouth worked, he pulled in a long breath and then said, "You're really starting to irritate me, Gina."

"Good," she said and gave him a smile. Irritated meant she was getting to him. Keeping him confused could only help her. "I like knowing that I can make you feel *something*."

When she turned to leave, he grabbed her arm again, spun her around and before she could ask what else he wanted to complain about, he kissed her. He covered her mouth with his in a fast, hungry kiss that left her knees wobbly. He let her go then took a step back as if even he were surprised by what he'd done. "Be careful what you wish for, Gina. Not all feelings are pretty."

She lifted one hand to her mouth, rubbed her lips

with her fingertips and looked up at him. "Even that would be better than feeling nothing."

"Now you're the one who's wrong," he said. Then he jerked his head at the trailer, where the driver was jumping down from the truck cab. "Go get your horses settled in."

He turned his back on her and walked away, stepping into the darkness of the van without another look her way.

Adam stalked to the rear of the barn and turned into the small ranch office that had been built into what had once been just another stall. He took a seat behind the battered desk his ranch foreman usually used. Today, though, he was damn glad that Sam was somewhere out on the ranch.

Travis stopped in the open doorway, leaned one shoulder against the jamb and looked in at him. "You really enjoy being a jackass?"

"Butt out." Adam propped one boot up on the corner of the desk and folded his hands atop his middle. He could still taste Gina and that wasn't good. He hadn't meant to kiss her. But she'd prodded him until damned if he could control the urge to touch her.

Since coming back home from Vegas, he'd done his damnedest to avoid spending much time with her. If he kept himself busy enough, it was almost possible to pretend that she wasn't living there. That nothing had changed in his life. He went about his normal routine during the day.

But every afternoon, his mind started drifting to thoughts of her. His body started yearning. And every night, he went to her like a man on fire.

He hadn't counted on this. Hadn't planned on being affected by Gina's presence at all. This was just one more deal made. One more bargain struck.

But she was wriggling her way into his thoughts, his life, with a surety that bothered him more than a little.

"Gina deserves better than the way you're treating her."

Adam shot Travis a look through narrowed eyes that should have fried him on the spot. Naturally Travis was unaffected. "What's between Gina and me is just that," Adam said. "Between Gina and me."

Travis pushed away from the doorjamb, walked into the room and pushed Adam's foot off the edge of the desk before sitting down. One eyebrow lifted and a corner of his mouth tipped into a half smile. "She's getting to you."

"No," Adam lied. "She's not."

"She could if you let her."

"And why would I do that?" Adam's fingers, laced together atop his stomach, tightened until the knuckles went white.

"Let me answer that with another question. Do you really like living like a damn monk?" Travis demanded. "Do you enjoy locking yourself away on this ranch? Shutting out everybody but me and Jackson?"

Adam inhaled slowly, deeply, getting a rein on the flare of anger that had erupted inside him. "I'm not shut away. I'm working. The ranch demands a lot of time and—"

"Tell that to somebody else," Travis said, neatly interrupting him. "I grew up here, too. I know what it takes to run this place. Didn't I watch Dad do it year after year?"

"Dad didn't have the same plans for it I do."

"Yeah," Travis agreed amiably. "Dad wanted a *life,* too."

"I have a life."

Smiling, Travis nodded. "After seeing that kiss, I'm guessing you've got a shot at one, anyway. If you don't screw it up."

Adam fixed him with a frown. "Is there a reason you came by here today? Or are you just here to be another thorn in my figurative paw?"

"The thorn thing appeals, I'll admit. But I did have a reason." Standing up, Travis stuffed both hands into the pockets of his black slacks. "I'm taking one of the family jets to Napa for a couple of weeks."

"Bon voyage," Adam said, standing himself. "But what's that got to do with me?"

"Just wanted to let you know. There's a winery there doing some interesting stuff with cabernets. Want to see what I can find out about their operation."

"So why is it when you do something related to the vineyard it's okay, but when I'm concentrating on the ranch I'm a recluse?"

"Because—" Travis grinned "—I make time for the ladies, too. I don't live and die by the grape, Adam. And now that you've got yourself married again, maybe it's time for you to remember that there's more to life than this damn ranch."

"You know exactly why I'm married. Don't make it out to be more than it is."

"Doesn't mean it couldn't work out. For both of you."

"Not interested."

"Just because you and Monica—" He stopped short when Adam flushed a dark red. "Fine. We won't talk about it. Even though you should—"

"I don't need to be psychoanalyzed, either."

"Wouldn't be too sure of that," Travis said, then continued. "Go ahead, Adam. Bury your future because of your past. But—" he half turned to point toward the ranch yard beyond the barn "—that's a fine woman out there. Too good for you to use and toss away. She deserves better." When his brother didn't say anything else, Travis added, "Hell, Adam, *you* deserve better."

He didn't want to talk about any of this. "Don't you have a winemaker to seduce?"

"I do indeed." Travis headed for the door and stopped on the threshold. "But do me a favor while I'm gone?"

"Depends."

"Try not to be such a complete ass all the time. Give Gina a chance. Give *yourself* a damn break, will you?"

When Travis was gone, Adam couldn't settle. He paced the narrow confines of the office and listened to the sounds from the yard. The clatter of hooves on a metal gate, the nervous whinnies, Gina's delighted laughter.

He stopped dead, concentrating on the near magical music of it.

And he told himself that no matter what he felt or didn't feel for Gina, once she was pregnant, deal done. Marriage over. She'd move out and he'd move on.

Despite what Travis seemed to think, there was no hope for a future here. Adam had already proven to himself that he simply wasn't the marrying kind.

Eight

Gina left Adam sleeping in their big bed. She grabbed her robe from a nearby chair, tugged it on and belted it at the waist before slipping out of the bedroom. She couldn't seem to fall asleep no matter how long she lay there in the darkness. So why not get up, make some tea and have a few of Esperanza's cookies?

At the doorway, she looked back at her husband and her heart turned over as she studied him in the dim light. Even in sleep, Adam managed to look powerful, aloof. As if his emotions were closed up so tightly they couldn't even find the surface when he wasn't actively guarding them. Apparently she would have to do battle with his subconscious, as well.

She sighed a little, shut the door quietly behind her and

wandered down the hall toward the stairs. The house was quiet, tucked up for the night, resting after a long day. Gina only wished she could rest, too. But her mind was just too busy. She couldn't stop thinking about Adam, their argument earlier and the way he'd watched her from afar as she settled the Gypsies into their new home.

Why had she thought she'd be able to reach him easily when he'd spent the last five years sealing himself off from the entire world? What if he didn't want to be reached? Would she be able to outlast him? Would he guess there was something going on when she didn't get pregnant right away? A headache burst into life behind her eyes and she blew out a breath as she headed downstairs.

There were no lights on, but moonlight shone through the skylights, illuminating the dark staircase in a pale silver glow. Her bare feet made no sound on the carpet runner and as she walked downstairs, she looked at the framed photographs lining the wall.

Pictures of the King brothers from infancy to adulthood stared back at her. There was a smiling Jackson, boasting a black eye, standing between his older brothers, each of them with an arm draped over his shoulders. There was Travis, holding the trophy the high school football team had won when he was the quarterback. There was even a twenty-year-old photo taken at a Fourth of July picnic. The King brothers were there, but so were Gina and her brothers. Adam was the tallest and he was standing right behind a ten-year-old Gina. As if even then, she'd been arranging things so she could be close to him. Had he noticed? Smiling to herself, her gaze continued over the faces frozen in time and as she looked, she noticed that there weren't any pictures of Monica, Adam's late wife. Or even of his lost son, Jeremy.

That made her frown thoughtfully for a minute and think about the other photographs she'd noticed throughout the house. Now that she was considering it, she realized there weren't *any* pictures of the family Adam had lost five years ago. Strange. Why would he not want to see them? Remember them?

Then she pushed those thoughts aside and went back to studying the framed photographs on the wall. She blurred her vision to all but the shots of Adam.

Gina studied them, one at a time, remembering some, wondering about others. There was Adam as a kid, with torn blue jeans and a baseball cap shading his eyes. Adam as captain of the high school baseball team. Adam at his prom. Adam with a blue ribbon won at a local rodeo. Adam smiling. God, he should do that more often, she thought.

Reaching out, Gina touched her fingertips to that captured smile and wished she could reach the man as easily. He was so close to her now, yet he felt even further away from her than ever.

A chill swept along her spine and she hunched deeper into the soft folds of the green cashmere robe. But this chill came from her heart, not the temperature of the room, so nothing she did helped with it. She took the last of the stairs and stopped in the foyer.

In the silence, she looked down the long hall toward

the kitchen and Esperanza's cookies——then to the front door and the night beyond. She made up her mind quickly and opened the door to step outside.

The night air was cold and damp and still. Not a breath of wind moved. Overhead, the sky was clear and spatter-shot with bright stars. The moon was half-full and the light that shone down was bright enough to cast shadows across the ground.

Gina stepped onto the dirt driveway and walked quietly across the yard toward the corral where the Gypsies slept. Tomorrow, they'd be assigned stalls in the barn, but for tonight, they were here, getting used to their new home.

She leaned her forearms on the topmost rail and whispered, "I hope you guys catch on faster than I am."

One of the mares whickered softly and moved to her. Gina reached out, stroked the horse's nose with a gentle touch and smiled when the animal moved in closer for more. "Hi, Rosie. Did you miss me?" The horse shifted from foot to foot, the long, delicate feathers about its hooves waving lightly. Gina looked from Rosie to the other horses beyond and then back to the mare that had been her very first Gypsy.

"Feeling a little out of your element?" she asked, fingers stroking through the mare's silky mane. "Yeah, I know just how you feel. But we'll get used to it here. You know, Adam's not a bad guy at all. He just acts crabby."

"I *am* crabby."

His voice came directly behind her and Gina jolted so hard, the mare skipped away, dancing back from the fence to join the rest of the horses on the far side of the corral. Gina caught her breath and turned around to face him.

"You could have said something instead of sneaking up on me and giving me a heart attack!" Her hand slapped to her chest and she felt her heartbeat thundering hard and fast. "Jeez, Adam."

"What the hell are you doing out here in the middle of the night?"

Gina fought back the last of the adrenaline pumping through her and took her first good look at him. His naked chest gleamed gold in the soft light. His hair was rumpled from sleep and his jaw carried the shadow of a dark beard. Barefoot, he wore a pair of threadbare jeans that he'd apparently dragged on in a hurry. The top couple of buttons were undone and her gaze tracked the narrow line of dark hair that disappeared beneath the denim fabric.

He looked way too good.

Shaking her head, though, Gina asked, "Is this another rule, Adam? Do I have to ask permission to come outside, too?"

"That's not what I meant."

"Then what?"

He came closer and the scent of him, soap and male, drifted to her and seemed to coil in the pit of her stomach. She took a breath, hoping to steady herself, but all she succeeded in doing was dragging more of that scent deeper inside.

"I woke up and you were gone." He said it with a shrug.

A small note of hope lifted inside her. "You were worried about me?"

He glanced at her, then shifted his gaze to the animals wandering the corral enclosure. "I wouldn't go that far," he said. "I...wondered about you."

That was a start, Gina thought.

"You were sleeping and I couldn't," she said, turning to lean on the railing again and watch the horses moving through moonlight. "I was going to go for some of Esperanza's cookies, then I decided to come out and check on the Gypsies."

He shook his head and took up a spot beside her at the fence. Amusement colored his voice when he said, "What is it about these horses that's so damn special?"

She shot him a quick look, smiled and said, "Everything."

"Care to vague that up for me?"

"Wow. A joke?" She laid one hand on his forearm and when he didn't flinch and pull away, Gina considered it a win. "This is a real moment for me, Adam."

"Very funny." He turned to look down at her. "But that doesn't tell me why you're so nuts about these horses."

"They're gentle. And smart. And so good with kids, its nearly eerie." She blew out a breath and watched as one of the foals jolted into a one-horse race around the corral. Smiling as she watched the spindly legged baby run, she said, "They've been bred for centuries to become part of a family. They're strong and loyal. I admire that."

"Me, too," he said and when she looked at him, she noticed he hadn't been watching the horses, but her.

Nerves fizzed inside her, but in a good way. The night was quiet, but for the sounds of the horses. The wind was still, the sky brilliant with stars and it suddenly felt as though the world itself was holding its breath.

He was silent for so long, her nerves buzzed even harder, so she spoke to break the hush building between them. "I saw my first Gypsy about six years ago, at a horse show." Her gaze slid from his to the corral again. "They were so beautiful. Elegant somehow, yet their eyes were liquid and kind, as if there were very old souls looking back at me."

"If you love them so much, how do you bring yourself to sell them?"

She laughed. "It's not easy. And I'm very careful who they go to. I check out prospective buyers so thoroughly, the CIA would be impressed."

"I know I am."

"Really?" Gina turned her head to look up at him again and saw his dark eyes flash with something she couldn't quite read.

"Really," he said and leaned his bare forearms on the top railing of the corral fence, alongside hers. Jerking his chin at the horses milling around like wallflowers at a high school reunion, he continued, "I've seen my share of horse breeders who couldn't care less about the animals in their charge. They're only interested in the money they can make."

Gina's mouth tightened. "I've seen a few like that myself."

"Bet you have." Glancing down at her, he said, "Sorry about earlier today."

"Sorry?" Gina blinked at him, shook her head as if she hadn't heard him right and smiled. "Wow. A joke *and* an apology. This is a red-letter night for me!"

"You've got a smart mouth on you, that's for damn sure."

"True. My mom always said it would get me in trouble someday."

"Do you always listen to your mother?"

"If I did, we wouldn't be married right now," she pointed out, then wished she hadn't when he frowned.

"She was right, you know. About me. About warning you off."

"No, she wasn't. I love my mom, but sometimes she worries more than she should." Gina looked up at him and felt that maybe, just maybe, he was reaching out to her for the first time since their hurried wedding. Everything in her yearned for it to be true. She laid one hand on his forearm and tried not to notice that he nearly flinched from her gentle touch. "I know you, Adam…"

"No, you don't." He looked down at her hand on his arm and his stare was so steady, she finally pulled her hand away in response. When she had, he said, "You used to know me, Gina. I give you that. But I'm not that kid anymore. Time's gone by and things have changed. *I've* changed."

"You're still Adam," she insisted.

"Damn it." He pushed away from the railing, grabbed her shoulders and turned her around to face him. In the starlight, his features were hard and cold and his eyes were deep, dark, filled with shadows. Gina felt the strength in his hands and the heat of his skin, burning through the thick, cashmere robe right into hers.

"Don't mistake what's happening here, Gina."

She wouldn't be intimidated. And she wasn't afraid of him at all—even if that's what he was trying to do. "What's that supposed to mean?"

"You know exactly what I mean." His grip on her gentled slightly even as his eyes became darker, nearly black with the intensity of his gaze. "You're fooling yourself, Gina. You think I don't see it? Feel it?"

"Adam—"

"This bargain we made? That's *all* we share," he assured her. "We each want something from the other and when that bargain's fulfilled, it's over. Don't get comfortable here. Don't expect more from me than there is. And for God's sake, stop looking at me with those golden eyes of yours all soft and dewy."

"I don't—"

"Yeah, you do. And it's time to stop, Gina. For your own sake if nothing else. There is no *us*. There won't ever be."

Her heart *ached*.

Literally ached.

Her stomach churned and tears stung the backs of her eyes, but she fought them back, buried the swell of emotion that threatened to choke her. Everything he said, she knew he really meant, and yet, wasn't there more here than he would—or could—admit? Or was she just fooling herself as he thought? Was she setting herself up for a crashing fall at the end of their time together? Was she expecting to find the boy she'd once known inside a man too changed to remember him?

"We have now," she said, lifting both hands to lay her palms on his chest. The hard, sculpted muscles felt warm beneath her hands and the pound of his heart shattered something inside her. When he hissed in a breath, she took it as a sign to continue. "And for now Adam, there *is* an us."

"Gina…" He shook his head and blew out a breath riddled with frustration. "You're making this harder than it has to be."

"Maybe," she admitted. "And maybe you're making this far less fun than it could be."

She moved in toward him, closing the spare distance between them with a single step. Her hands moved over his chest, fingertips exploring, smoothing across his flat nipples until he took a breath and held it, trying not to surrender.

But she wanted his surrender and was willing to fight for it.

He caught her wrists and held them, staring down into her eyes like a man lost in unfamiliar territory. "You're playing with fire here, Gina."

"I'm not fragile, Adam," she said. "I don't mind a burn or two."

"This kind of fire consumes."

"And that's a bad thing?" she asked, smiling up at him despite the blackness of his eyes, the tight, grim slash of his mouth. Whether he wanted to admit it or not, the Adam she'd once known and fallen in love with was still there, hidden inside him, and she wanted to set him free again. To remind him that love and life and laughter were worth having. Worth cherishing. "We're married, Adam. This fire is what most people dream of finding."

"Fires usually burn out fast."

"Sometimes," she said with a short nod. "But while they burn, it's an amazing thing."

"You're not going to listen to anybody about this, are you?"

"No," she admitted.

"Thank God."

He released her wrists and without a word, reached for the cloth belt at her waist. Pulling it free, he silently swept the sides of the robe back, baring her naked body to his gaze.

Gina shivered a little as the cool, night air kissed her skin, but that minor chill dissipated under Adam's steady, heat-filled gaze. Her nipples peaked, tightening in the cold, aching for the touch of his lips, his mouth. His hands moved over her body, the hard calluses on his fingers scraping against her skin with an erotic friction that sent heat directly to her center.

Shifting from foot to foot in an unconscious attempt to ease the throbbing at her core, she let her head fall back against the fence post. Adam stroked her from breast to core and back again.

"Your skin glows in the moonlight," he said softly and leaned in to take one of her nipples into his mouth.

She gasped, arched into him and cradled the back of his head in the palm of her hand. He nibbled at her, scoring the tip of her nipple with the edges of his teeth. Ripples of something amazing rolled through her and Gina held her breath as she watched him suckle her. With each draw and tug of his mouth at her breast, Gina was swamped with more tenderness for this man who tried so hard to keep her at a distance for her own sake.

Holding him to her, she watched him as his mouth worked her body, teasing, tormenting, drawing out her pleasure as if he could taste her all night. She felt his connection to her, despite his warnings. His feelings were communicated in his touch. Tender strokes, gentle bites and licks. The brush of his breath across her skin and the sweep of his hands down her body, along her curves, down her hips and behind to cup her bottom.

In his touch, she felt everything she'd ever dreamed of.

Her hands fell to his shoulders and she reveled in the strength of him. The warm, solid feel of him beneath her hands. He lifted his head from her breast and she wanted to weep with the loss of him.

"I need to have you," he whispered and Gina quivered from head to foot.

"You *are* having me," she said on a choked-off laugh.

He smiled up at her and her heart stuttered in her chest. Those smiles of his, so rare, so breathtaking, tugged at her more than anything else.

"I want more," he said, sliding down the length of her body, trailing his lips and tongue along her skin as she leaned against the corral fence and hoped she didn't simply topple over.

"Yes, Adam." Two words, softly spoken, nearly lost in the quiet, moonlit darkness surrounding them, cradling them in the cool night air.

Then he was kneeling in front of her, pushing her thighs apart with his big hands and lowering his mouth to cover the very heart of her.

Gina groaned and gripped his shoulders tighter, her short nails digging into his skin to stabilize her hold on him. But even as she found her balance, the world tipped crazily around her. He stroked her damp heat with his tongue and had her gasping for air that never seemed enough to fill her straining lungs.

Wicked, she thought wildly. Here. Outside. In the ranch yard, she was naked and letting Adam have his way with her. More, *needing* him to have her. The thrill of being outside with him, beneath the stars, only added to the amazing feelings churning inside.

Again and again, he tasted her, torturing her with sweet, intimate caresses that sent waves of electrical-like surges moving through her. Then he lifted one of her legs, draped it across his shoulders and Gina was forced to reach back, grabbing hold of the fence behind her. She wanted this so badly she could hardly breathe anymore. Her world had shrunk to this one spot. Just she and Adam and what he could do to her.

The only sounds were her ragged groans, his steady breathing and the nervous stamping from the horses gathered at the other side of the corral. She stared blindly up at the stars, concentrating on what she was feeling, experiencing. The night was soft, and the magic of what Adam was doing to her was almost more than she could bear.

While his tongue and lips moved over her, he slid one hand around the curve of her hip and deftly slipped first one finger, and then two into her depths. He worked her with a steely determination that had Gina shaking unsteadily as a soul shattering climax coiled tightly within and prepared to spring.

His fingers explored her depths while his mouth continued its delicious torment. She wanted to keep him just like this. Forever. She wanted the orgasm that was just out of reach to stay poised where it was for eternity. She never wanted this moment to end.

Shifting her gaze from the sky to the man kneeling before her, Gina swallowed hard as she watched him take her. She looked at him and seeing what he was doing to her, watching as his mouth took her higher and higher, only seemed to intensify the very feelings he was stoking within. She couldn't look away now. Couldn't tear her gaze from Adam as he took her more intimately than anyone ever had before.

She felt him inside, outside. Her body shook. Her mind splintered. And when the first punch of release crashed through her, she called his name on a broken shout that trembled in the darkness.

Trembling, she rode that silky wave until it ended and when it was over, she swayed into him as he stood slowly, skimming his hands up her body as if memorizing the feel of her. "You taste sweet," he said, dipping his head to kiss her lips, her jaw, neck.

"Adam, that was—" Her forehead hit his chest as she struggled for air. Her body was humming and when he pulled her in close, she felt the hard length of him pressing into her abdomen. And fresh need erupted like a fireball.

Adam sensed her quickening desire as surely as he did his own. He hadn't come out here for this. Had only followed her into the yard to see if something was wrong. If she was all right.

He'd felt her leave their bed and told himself that he should let her go. But in moments, he'd been following her and when he'd seen her here in the moonlight, something inside him had fisted into a hard knot of pure lust.

Looking into her eyes now, he knew this was dangerous. He knew that she would be building on this encounter, turning it into something romantic. Something that might lead to a future for the two of them. But he'd warned her, hadn't he?

They'd gone into this with their eyes open, both of them. He was only doing what he could to keep his end of the bargain. Making love with her was just a part of the deal. That's all this was.

All it could be.

All he'd allow it to be.

He shook his head, letting thoughts and worries fly from his mind as he concentrated only on this moment with her. He wouldn't question this fire. Wouldn't try to define it.

As Gina had said, they had *now.*

Keeping his gaze locked on hers, Adam reached for the fly of his jeans, undid the last two buttons and freed himself. She sucked in a gulp of air and curled her fingers around him. Now it was Adam's turn to hiss in a breath through clenched teeth. Her touch was torment and pleasure rolled into one.

As she slid her hand up and down his thick length, he fought for control and knew he was losing.

Knew he didn't care.

Nine

She wrapped her legs around his waist and Adam turned, bracing his bare back against the fence post. The weathered, rough wood scraped at his skin but he couldn't care. All he felt, all he *wanted* to feel, was the woman in his arms.

He balanced her slender, curvy weight easily as he lowered her onto his body, inch by tantalizing inch. She slid over him in a slick heat that enveloped him in a rush of sensation like nothing he'd never known before.

Every time with Gina was like the first time.

And damn it, he didn't want to admit that. Not even to himself. But she was so much more than he'd expected. Her laughter filled him. Her temper challenged him. Her passion ignited his.

Adam held her, hands at her bottom, supporting her weight, easing her up and down on his thick erection. Every move dazzled. Every withdrawal was agony. Every thrust was victory. He filled her and her body opened and held him as if made to fit his.

Her head fell back as she rode him and arched into him. He could watch her all night. Listen to her sighs. Smell the sweet, slightly citrus scent of her skin. He watched every movement she made and saw the moonlight kiss her flesh with a silvery wash that made her seem lit up from within. And when she lifted her head to look at him, that same moon danced in her eyes.

He snaked one hand up her back, cradled her head in his hand and drew her mouth to his as his body tightened, fisting in anticipation. Again and again, she moved on him, rocking, swiveling her hips, driving him faster, harder than he'd ever gone before and still it wasn't enough.

He wanted.

He…needed…*her.*

Her tongue tangled with his and he took everything she offered. Her breath mingled with his. She trembled as her climax hit and when she groaned into his mouth, he swallowed it, taking that, as well. He wanted all of her. Needed all of her. And knew, bone-deep, that he would never get enough of her.

Then all thought ceased as he finally surrendered to a shattering release. And as he filled her with everything he had, he wondered if *this* was the night they would make the child that would end what was between them.

* * *

She still wasn't pregnant.

Gina'd worried a little after that night in the ranch yard two months ago. But the fates were apparently on her side, because her period had arrived right on time.

So she was still married and still trying to find a way to convince the man she loved that he loved her, too.

"You're thinking about Adam," her mother said. "I see it on your face."

Gina looked up from her place at the Torino kitchen table. She'd been assigned that chair when she was a little girl and she still headed straight for it whenever she came home again.

Sunlight speared through the wide windows her mother kept at a high gloss at all times. A clock on the wall chimed twelve times and in the backyard, Papa's golden retriever barked at a squirrel. Soup simmered on the stove, filling the air with the scents of beef and oregano.

Nothing in this room ever changed, Gina thought. Oh, there was fresh paint—same shade of bright yellow— every couple of years, new rugs or curtains and the occasional new set of pans, but otherwise, it was the same as it had always been. The heart of the Torino house.

The kitchen was where the family had breakfast and dinner. Where she and her brothers had complained and laughed and sometimes cried about whatever was happening in their lives. Her parents, the foundation of the family, had listened, advised and punished when necessary. And each of their children came home whenever they could, just to touch base with their beginnings.

Of course, if there was something they didn't want their parents to know, it was best to stay away. Especially from Mama. She didn't miss much.

Her mother was standing at the kitchen counter, putting finishing touches on the lunch she'd insisted Gina eat, while waiting for her daughter's answer.

"I must look happy then, huh?" Gina quipped and smiled too brightly.

"No, you do not." Her mother picked up the plate holding a sandwich and some homemade pasta salad. Carrying it to the table, she plunked it down, poured two tall glasses of iced tea and took a seat opposite her daughter. "I worry about you, Gina. Two months you're with Adam. You do not look happy. You think I don't see it in your eyes?"

"Mama…"

"Fine," her mother said, grabbing her glass to chug some of her tea. "You want a baby. I understand. How could I not? I, too, wanted babies. But you want them with the man you love. With a father who will also love the child you make."

"I do love him," Gina said and took a bite of the roast beef sandwich, because knowing her mother, she'd never be allowed to leave until she did. She chewed, swallowed and said, "Adam loved his son. He would love our child, too. He wouldn't be able to help himself."

Teresa crossed herself quickly at the mention of Adam's dead son and conceded, "He did love that boy. Such a tragedy. But you know as well as everyone else he changed when he lost his family."

Gina shifted uneasily on her chair and used her fork to move bow tie pasta around on her plate. "That's natural enough, isn't it?"

"Yes. It is. But he does not want to move on, Gina. The darkness in him is thick and heavy and he doesn't want it lifted."

"You don't know that."

Her mother snorted. "You do not want to see it."

Gina sighed, dropped her fork and said, "We've been over this."

Teresa Torino set her glass down, reached across the table and patted her daughter's hand. "And we will again. Until I make you see that you are making a mistake that will only cause you pain."

"Mama…"

The older woman sat back, folded her arms beneath her copious breasts and frowned. "So. You get pregnant. Then what? You leave? Then you walk away from your baby's father? You believe you can do this? With no pain?"

Just thinking about it was painful, but admitting that would probably be the wrong move. Besides, she was still hoping she wouldn't have to walk away. That Adam wouldn't want to let her go. "Adam and I made a deal."

"*Sì.*" Her mother sniffed in disgust. "So your papa tells me all the time. A deal. What kind of a way is that to start a marriage?"

"Um," Gina said, picking her fork up again to take a bite of her mom's pasta salad—only the best in the known universe, "excuse me, but didn't Papa go to Italy to meet you because his parents knew your parents and they thought you two would make a good couple?"

Teresa's big brown eyes narrowed on her daughter. "You think you're so smart, eh?"

"Pretty smart," Gina acknowledged with a smile. "I know my family history anyway."

"Yes, but you also know this," her mother said, sitting forward suddenly and leaning her forearms on the yellow-and-white-vinyl-cloth-covered table. "My papa told me I should marry Sal Torino and move to America. I argued with him. Told him I wouldn't marry a man I didn't love. Then I took one look at *your* papa and loved him in that instant." She lifted one hand and wagged her index finger at Gina. "One look. I *knew*. I knew it was right. That this marriage would last and be a good one. Can you say the same?"

Spearing another piece of pasta, Gina met her mother's worried gaze and said softly, "I've loved Adam since I was a kid, Mama. One look. I *knew*."

Teresa blew out an exasperated sigh. "Is not the same."

"No, it's not," Gina said wearily. "Papa wanted to get married. Adam didn't. But," she added, "we *are* married. And I know he cares for me."

"Care is not love," her mother warned softly.

"No, but it could be. Mama, Adam needs me. I love him and I'm going to try to make this work. For both of us. Can't you be on my side? Please?"

Astonishment crossed her mother's features as her brown eyes widened and her mouth dropped open. Standing up, Teresa moved around the kitchen table to stand beside Gina. She cupped her daughter's face between her palms, then drew her in close, wrapped her arms around her girl and held on tightly. "Of course I am on your side, Gina. I'm your mother. I want for you all that you want. Always. I only wish to spare you pain."

Gina held on and let herself be rocked for a while, taking comfort from the one source she'd always been able to count on. She thought of Adam, saw his face in her mind, felt his touch in her memory and her heart lifted, despite the odds being stacked against her. For two months, she'd lived with him, loved with him. She'd wormed her way into his house and could only hope she was worming her way into his heart, as well.

The chance she was taking was worth it. She had to believe that. She had to try. Otherwise, she'd always wonder if she'd given up on Adam too soon.

"I know that, Mama, I do," she said, her voice getting more determined with every word. "But sometimes, you can only get to happy by going through the pain."

"That wife of yours is a real hand with horses," Sam Ottowell said as he thumbed through a sheaf of receipts for ranch supplies.

"Yes." Adam smiled. "She is." Then he leaned over his foreman's desk and pulled a notebook toward him. Making a few quick notations, he dropped it again. "I want you to call Flanagan's. Get an extra order of oats out here. With Gina's horses here, too, we're going through twice as much."

"Right," Sam said, leaning back in his chair, propping his hands on his abundant belly. "She's really something, you know? Got those damn animals following her around like trained puppies or something. Girl's got a gift with horses."

She had a lot of gifts, Adam thought. Most particularly, she had a gift for throwing his perfectly organized life into turmoil. He'd hardly had a moment to himself since entering into this little wedding bargain. And the moments he *did* manage to find, his thoughts usually turned to her anyway.

"You hear those kids?" Sam asked, cocking his head as if to better hear the laughter drifting to them from the corral.

"Hard not to," Adam snapped. Though God knew he was trying.

Sam's features went stiff and blank in a heartbeat. He sat up, reached for the Rolodex and asked, "You going to call Simpson about the hundred-acre lot he wants to lease?"

"Yeah," Adam said, grabbing on to the change of subject with both hands. He checked his watch, then said, "I'll call his office tomorrow. We can work out—"

Whatever else he might have said was cut off at the sound of a scream shredding the air.

With Sam right behind him, Adam raced out of the barn, heart in his throat and skidded to a stop when that scream turned into peals of laughter. His gaze shot to the corral and everything in him fisted into a tight knot.

A boy, no more than four or five, was seated on the back of one of the Gypsy horses. The child's parents were standing outside the corral, watching the scene with indulgent smiles as a daughter, no more than ten, hopped up and down impatiently awaiting her turn on the horse.

Gina walked alongside the tiny would-be cowboy, her hand on the boy's thigh, holding him in place while she grinned up at him. The boy's delighted laughter spilled into the air like soap bubbles and Adam wrestled with the pain lodged in the center of his chest.

He couldn't move. Couldn't tear his gaze from Gina and the boy as they moved slowly around the inside of the corral. He noticed everything. The sunlight on the boy's blond hair, the steady gait of the horse, the patient smile on Gina's face. Again and again, the boy laughed as he petted and stroked the mare's neck, his tiny fingers getting lost in the thick, black mane.

"Uh, I'll just head on back to the office," Sam said, and slipped away unnoticed.

While his vision narrowed to that solitary child, Adam's mind filled with images of another boy. On another sunny day. Another lifetime ago.

"I want to stay with you, Daddy." Jeremy's big brown eyes were filled with tears and his lower lip trembled.

"I know you do," Adam said, checking his wristwatch and inwardly wincing. He was already late for a meeting. There were offers to be made, documents to be signed, dreams to be crushed. Instead of that wince, he smiled to himself. Since taking over the family ranch, he'd already made a difference.

He'd found new buyers for their grain and cattle.

New tenants for the farmland and he had plans to rebuild the King stables.

If that meant spending less time with his wife and son than he would have liked, that's the price he would pay. He was doing this for their future.

"Please let me stay," Jeremy said and a single tear rolled down his cheek. "I'll be good."

"Jeremy," he said, going down on one knee long enough to look his son in the eye. "I know you'd be good. But I've got work. I can't play now anyway. You'll have more fun with Mommy."

Adam lifted his gaze to the woman standing behind his son. Monica didn't look any happier than Jeremy, but rather than tears in her eyes, there was fire. Anger. An expression Adam had become more and more used to seeing.

Jeremy's chin hit his chest and his narrow shoulders slumped in dejection. He rubbed the toe of his bright red tennis shoe in the dirt, sniffed loudly and ran one hand under his nose. "'Kay."

As the boy turned and walked with slow, miserable steps toward the silver sedan parked in the driveway, Adam stood up to face his wife.

"That's so typical of you, Adam," she muttered, shooting a look over her shoulder at their son to make sure he was out of earshot.

"Let's not do this right now, all right?" He checked his wristwatch again and Monica hissed in a breath.

"You never want to 'do' this, Adam. That's the problem."

"I don't have time for it, all right?"

"Why don't you schedule me in for a week from Tuesday, Adam? Will I get one minute? Or two?"

He blew out a breath, reached out one hand to her, but she skipped back to avoid his touch. Adam sighed. "You know as well as I do, I've got responsibilities."

"Yes, you do."

He was irritated, angry and just a little weary of this whole situation. Monica had less and less patience with what she saw as Adam's "preoccupation" with the King ranch. And as she pulled further away from him, he did the same. The ranch was his family's legacy. It took time. Dedication.

The car door closed behind Jeremy and he looked to see his son pull the seat belt across his chest and hook it securely.

Glancing back at his wife, Adam said, "Can we not do this now? I've got a meeting."

"Right." She shook her head, blond hair flying in a tight, short arc around her jawline. "Wouldn't want you to miss a meeting just because of your family."

"Damn it, Monica."

"Damn you, Adam." She turned and stalked to the car without another look at him. Just before she opened the car door, though, she allowed her gaze to lock with his. "Not that you'll notice or anything, but I thought you should know—we're not coming back. Jeremy and I are driving to my mother's in San Francisco. I'll let you know where to send our things once we're settled."

"Just a damn minute," Adam said, starting for her.

But she hopped into the car, fired the engine and raced

*down the driveway before he could get to her. He watched
dust and gravel fantail up behind the wheels of her car.
The sun beat down on his head and shoulders and despite
the heat, he felt cold. Right down to his bones.*

*The dust settled and still he stood there, watching after
the car carrying his wife and son away from him. Then
the alarm on his watch beeped and he idly reached to turn
it off. He had to leave for the meeting. He'd give Monica
a chance to cool off. Then they'd talk. Work this out.*

He headed for his SUV.

*First things first. He had just enough time to make
that meeting.*

Twenty minutes later, Jeremy and Monica were dead.

Adam came up out of the past with a jolt.

It had been years since he'd allowed himself to remember that day. But now, it had all rushed back at him
because of the child, still laughing, in the corral.

Adam felt as though a steel clamp was on his chest
and it was tightening with every strangled breath he
took. His eyes narrowed until he was looking at Gina and
the boy as if down a long, dark tunnel. He might as well
have been miles away. Sunlight splashed down on the
two of them, as if defining the difference between Adam
in the shadows, and his wife, in the golden rush of light.

Then Gina caught sight of him, smiled and waved.
He stiffened at the warmth in her gaze, the welcome in
her smile. He hadn't wanted this. Still didn't want it.

He could admit that over the last couple of months,
he'd become too accustomed to her presence. The scent
of her in the house. The feel of her in his arms. He

turned to her in the night and listened for her during the day. This was a temporary arrangement that was beginning to seem far too permanent.

When he didn't answer her wave, only stared at her out of cold, empty eyes, Gina frowned slightly, then shifted her gaze back to the boy on the horse.

"She's good with kids, isn't she?"

Adam slowly turned his head to nod at Gina's brother Tony, walking toward him. He hadn't even known the man was on the ranch.

Tony pulled the brim of his hat down lower over his eyes to combat the glare of the sun. He stopped beside Adam and shot a look at his sister. "Mama sent me over with some of her homemade bread. Thought I'd watch Gina for a while before going back to the ranch." He turned an interested look on Adam. "Looks like I'm not the only one watching her."

Adam frowned at him. "Did you have a point?"

Tony grinned. "Only one. That look you were giving Gina just then makes me think that maybe this temporary arrangement might be coming to mean a little more to you."

"You're wrong." Couldn't have been more wrong. If anything, watching Gina with that child had just brought home to Adam the fact that he had to get her out of his life. The sooner the better. He wanted his old insular life back.

"See, I don't think so." Tony wandered to the barn, leaned back into a patch of shade and folded his arms over his chest. "I admit, I sided with Mom about this marriage. Seemed like a bad idea all the way around to me. But," he said, pausing to briefly look at his sister again, "Gina's happy here. And I think you're happier with her here, too."

Adam's features closed. He stared at Tony, deliberately keeping his gaze from the temptation of Gina. "You're wrong about that, too. Haven't you heard, Tony? I don't do happy."

"You used to."

"Used to do a lot of things," he said shortly, turning his back on his uninvited guest, as well as his wife, and heading back into the barn.

Tony, of course, followed him. "You just determined to be a miserable bastard, Adam?"

"Go with your strengths," he said, never stopping, never turning for a look back at the other man. He didn't want to make nice with Gina's family. He didn't want to watch Gina and feel a yearning. He wanted his world back the way it had been before Gina had become a part of it.

He walked straight to the rear of the barn and into the tiny office. Jerking his head at his foreman, an unspoken message was passed between them. The other man jumped out of the chair, nodded to Adam and Tony, then hurried out of the office, muttering something about seeing if Gina needed any help at the corral.

Adam didn't watch him go. If there'd been a door on the office, he'd have slammed it. But he had a feeling, that wouldn't have slowed Tony down anyway. Like his sister, the man refused to be ignored.

"So what's the deal, Adam? You too scared to admit you care for my sister?"

Adam's head snapped up and he shot Tony a glare with so much ice in it, the man should have been sliced to ribbons. Naturally Tony looked unmoved. "My brothers don't get away with talking to me like that. What makes you think you can?"

Tony shrugged indolently, then took off his wide-brimmed hat and ran one hand through his hair. Lifting his gaze to Adam's, he said, "Because I'm worried about my sister and I figure you can understand that."

Damn, he was right. Adam did understand all too well. Family loyalty. The instinct to defend and protect. These were things the Kings were raised with as well as the Torinos. So he was willing to cut Tony some slack in that department. But that didn't mean that he was willing to discuss his private life. Or his marriage to Tony's sister.

"I get it," Adam said. "But I'm still telling you to butt out. Gina and I will handle what's between us without your help or anyone else's."

"That may be the way you want it," Tony mused, stepping into the room. He put his hat back on, bent down and planted both palms on the edge of the cluttered desk. "But that's not how it works. Gina's family. My baby sister. I look after my own."

"So do I," Adam countered.

"That right?" Tony's eyebrows lifted. "Not how I remember it."

Adam flushed and felt the rising tide of anger rush up from the soles of his feet to fill his head and his vision until the very edges of it were a cloudy red. "You got something else to say, say it and get out."

Tony pushed up from the desk and scrubbed a hand over his mouth as if he could physically call back the words he'd just said. "That was out of line. I'm sorry."

Adam nodded, but he wasn't willing to give more than that.

"All I'm saying is, you're an idiot if you don't give what you've got with Gina a real chance, Adam. And I don't figure you for an idiot."

"Tony, *what* are you doing?"

Both men turned to face Gina, standing in the doorway of the small office. She looked from one man to the other, fury flashing in her eyes and Adam felt a solid punch of something that was much more than desire.

That's when he knew for sure he was in trouble.

"I thought you were with the horses."

She brushed that aside with a wave of her hand and narrowed her eyes on her older brother. "Not that it's any of your business, but Sam's taking Danny around and talking to his parents. I want to know what you're doing here."

"I'm having a talk with my brother-in-law," Tony told her easily, but being a wise man, he took a short step back.

"And you?" She shifted her look to Adam.

"Let it go, Gina," he said.

"Why?"

"Because it's over," Adam said with a glance at Tony as if to make sure of that fact. "Isn't it?"

"Yeah." Tony nodded and edged toward the door, clearly trying to slip past his sister before she could turn her fury directly on him. "It's over. Adam? Good to see you."

Adam nodded again and waited until Tony was gone before looking at the woman who was his wife. And only then did Tony's words reverberate through his mind.

It's over.

If only, Adam thought, staring into Gina's amber-colored eyes, it were that easy.

Ten

When Tony left, it was as if Gina were alone in the small, cramped office. Adam, though physically present, had shut himself down so completely, it was as if he'd forgotten she was even there.

"Adam," she said, moving in closer, despite the unwelcoming chill in the room, "what's going on? What were you and Tony talking about? And why do you look so angry?"

"Angry?" He glanced at her and his eyes were cool, dispassionate. "I'm not angry, Gina. I'm simply busy." To make his point, he picked up a sheaf of papers, straightened them and tucked them into a manila file folder.

"Uh-huh. Too busy to talk to me but not too busy to talk to Tony, is that it?"

He swiveled in the desk chair, propped his elbows on the narrow, cushioned arms and folded his fingers together. Tipping his head to one side, he said, "Your brother showed up, I had no choice but to talk to him. Just as I had no choice but to put my own work aside when I heard that boy screaming."

Gina shrugged and tried a smile. It didn't get a reaction out of him. "Danny was excited, that's all. His parents are buying the young mare for him and his sister and it was his first ride."

"I didn't ask why the child screamed," Adam said, then reached for a pen laying on the desk. Absently clicking the top of it, he continued. "I only said the noise is distracting. I'm not used to having all of these people coming and going from the ranch. And I don't like it."

Now Gina flushed a little with the small whip of anger that jolted her. The way he sounded, she might as well have been holding parades every day. One or two people a week was nothing. It was normal. And hey, if he'd come out of the barn or his office and talk to them, maybe he might not hate it so much. Instead he kept himself in solitude. He was always working. On the phone, riding the ranch on one of his horses, closeted in the office with buyers.

Fine for him to lose himself in his own business, but he didn't want to allow her the same privilege. Her business was as important to her as the ranch itself was to Adam. You would have thought he could appreciate that, at least.

Still, no point in arguing with a man whose expression clearly stated he was looking for a battle. She didn't really want to fight with him anyway. Instead she wanted to reach him. Reach the Adam she'd known as a girl. The one who'd always stood up for her. The one she knew was still locked away deep inside him.

So when Gina spoke, she kept her tone reasonable, despite the flare of what her mother liked to call the Torino Temper.

"I've only had a few people a week over, Adam. They have to come to see the Gypsies in person. I have to see the way they are around the horses. There's simply no way to avoid it even if I wanted to. Which, by the way, I don't."

"I don't want these people around."

"I'm sorry to hear that." She wouldn't give in. She loved him, but she wasn't going to stand still for having *Welcome* tattooed on her forehead, either.

His mouth flattened into a slash of disapproval. "This isn't working out, Gina."

"This?" she repeated, with a wave of her hand. "This what? The horses? The people?"

"The marriage," he said shortly.

She rocked back on her heels a little from the force of that smack down. Her stomach tightened and an ache settled around her heart. But through the pain, her mind started racing. What had brought this on? She thought back over the day and all she could find was little Danny's scream. Then something hit her and she felt badly that it hadn't occurred to her before.

"It was Danny, wasn't it?" Her voice was a whisper of concern. "Little Danny's scream started all this."

His face froze, so Gina knew she'd touched on the truth. She should have realized. He'd lost a son. Of course that child's scream would tear at him. Bring back memories of another child, that one lost to him forever.

"The boy has nothing to do with this."

"I think you're wrong."

"Of course you do," he said. "But that doesn't really matter."

"Adam, it does matter." She took a step closer to him, her momentary rush of anger dying in a swell of sympathy. "Hearing Danny made you think of Jeremy."

If possible, the scowl on his face deepened. His dark eyes shuttered and before she could say anything else, Adam stood up and faced her.

"This isn't about my son. Don't bring the past into this."

"The past colors everything we have now," she argued.

"Maybe in your world, but the past does not influence me." He glared at her and Gina knew he actually believed that lie. But she also knew the truth. She knew that when he'd heard Danny's joyful scream, it had touched something inside him. Something he kept locked away from everyone.

"This isn't about that boy. This is about the deal we struck. I realize we made a bargain," he said, his eyes as cold as ever, his words as unaffected by emotion as the robotic voice of a computer. "One which, I'm sure you'll admit, I've done my very best to honor."

"Yes," she said tightly, trying to ignore the rush of heat that swam through her at the mere thought of the nights she spent in his arms. If she hadn't been using her diaphragm religiously, she had no doubt that she'd be pregnant. Her mom had always said they were a fertile bunch and heaven knew Adam had certainly put everything he had into making the child they'd agreed on. "You have. As have I," she pointed out quickly.

"True."

Did his eyes warm up there for a second? Was he, too, thinking about their nights together? Or was it only wishful imagining on Gina's part?

"But," he said, capturing her attention again, "since we've been married more than two months and you're not pregnant yet, it might be time to reconsider the bargain."

"What?" She hadn't expected this. Hadn't thought that Adam would want to walk away from a deal that promised him the deed to the land he wanted so badly. But if he did want out, what could she do about it? Clearly she hadn't been able to get him to open up yet. So was she supposed to pick up her toys and go home? Forget about her time here? With him? Try to move on?

Oh, good God.

As if needing more room for this conversation, Adam stepped past her and walked into the shadow-filled barn. The mingled scents of horses, fresh hay and old wood made an almost comforting aroma. She walked to join him and kept her gaze on his even when he turned his head to stare out at the sun-washed yard beyond the open doors.

"You want to end the bargain?" she asked, and winced when her voice came out so small, so reluctant. "Because if you do, I won't agree."

She should, of course. What kind of woman would stay with a man who didn't want her? Where the hell was her dignity? Her sense of Torino pride? But the moment those questions rose up in her mind, she mentally provided the answers.

Her pride had been swallowed by her love. It wasn't as though she had a choice in this, Gina thought in her own defense. It wasn't as if you got to *choose* who to love. She had loved Adam for most of her life. Sometimes, she felt as if she'd been born loving him. And the time spent with him these last few months only confirmed her feelings.

She wasn't an idiot, though. She knew he wasn't perfect. Far from it, in fact. He could be cold and calculating. He wasn't an easy man to get along with, but he was never cruel or deliberately unkind, either. There were shadows of pain in his eyes that she only rarely caught glimpses of and his even rarer smiles were enough to melt her heart even when she was doing her best to stand strong.

Not perfect, no. But he'd always been perfect for *her.*

And wasn't that what loving was all about?

He shifted his gaze, stared at her for a long time and she really wished she could read whatever he was thinking in his eyes. But he was too good at masking his emotions. Too good a negotiator in business to let his opponent get a good read on him.

Finally, though, he spoke. "No, I don't want to end our bargain."

Gina pulled in a slow, deep breath, relief swamping

her even while anxiety hovered nearby, ready to pounce. "All right," she said. "Then what are you talking about?"

"I think it would be in both our best interests to redefine the bargain, that's all," he said quietly. "You're not pregnant yet…"

"It's only been a little over two months," she argued.

"True. But what if it takes a year? Two?"

She didn't say anything, even though on the inside, she knew she wouldn't have had a problem with it. The more time she had with Adam, the better her chances of getting through to him, making him see just how good they could be together.

"My point is," Adam said, pushing his hair back from his forehead with one hand, "I think we should set a time limit on this endeavor."

"Endeavor?"

He paid no attention to the sarcasm coloring that single word. "If you're not pregnant by the end of six months, then we end this. We each go our separate ways and—"

She shook her head and blurted, "You get your land and I get what?"

"I wasn't finished." He frowned a little, but continued. "If you're not pregnant by the end of six months, then we end the marriage and the bargain. We both lose."

"You'd give up on the land you want so badly?" Was he really so anxious to get her out of his life? Was marriage to her really so hideous? God. Hadn't she reached any part of him yet?

Yes, she had. She knew she had. She could feel it in his touch every night. See it in the flash of need and desire in his eyes when he came to her bed. Why was he fighting this so valiantly? Why was he so determined to keep her at bay? To stave off any chance they might have had at happiness together?

And *why* was she still here? How could she continue to love a man who so obviously wanted her gone?

"I'll find another way to get the land. Surely your father would change his mind eventually." He shoved both hands into the back pockets of his jeans and shook his head. "It's the only way, Gina. What would be the point in drawing this out? Making it harder on ourselves?"

"Thanks very much," she said.

At last, he gave her a very brief smile. More of a twist of the lips even than a smile, really. And it was a sad statement of fact that Gina's insides jumped when she saw it.

"I like you, Gina. Always have. And frankly, I'd prefer to end this between us while we still like each other. If you're not pregnant at the end of six months, neither one of us is going to be satisfied with this arrangement."

"You like me."

"I do."

She choked back a laugh. She loved. He liked. *Big* difference.

But he was still talking, so she focused on Adam. "I think the only fair thing to do is cut our losses at the end of six months. That way, we both have a deadline. We know there's an end in sight and we can plan around it."

"Right." She nodded, swallowed hard and tried to keep the bubble of frustration she felt rising within from spewing out her mouth. "The master negotiator at work.

Gotta have a plan. Good idea, Adam. Wouldn't want to relax into this."

"Gina…"

"No, no!" She held up both hands and started walking. She couldn't stand still another minute anyway. Honestly she didn't know who she'd rather kick more… Adam or herself. He was so damn stubborn and what was she? A glutton for punishment?

She took a few steps away from him, thought better of it and spun around to walk right back. "Do you even see how crazy that is? No, of course you don't. I'm not pregnant yet, so by putting a deadline on me, that'll be sure to take the pressure off." Gina threw her hands high then let them slap back down against her thighs. "Hey, maybe you should send a memo to my eggs? You know, something short and sweet like, *Get in line to be fertilized. What's the holdup?*"

He scowled at her. It had no effect of course, because if there was one thing Gina was used to, it was that scowl.

"Sarcasm doesn't really accomplish anything, does it?"

"Didn't know it was supposed to," she countered. "It's sort of an end all in itself." Tipping her head back, she glared up at him. "Adam, don't you get it? A deadline isn't going to help anything. What we need is to be closer, not more focused on a damn ticking clock."

One dark eyebrow lifted. "As I recall, we've been *damned* close almost every night for the last couple of months."

"That is so male," she said with a shake of her head. "Naturally you assume that having *sex* is being close."

"It's not?"

"No, it's not!" She reached up and yanked her hair in pure frustration. "What is it with your gender?"

"Just a minute…"

"No. You wait a minute." Blowing out a breath, she tried for calm and just barely managed it. "Adam, don't you get it? We're together, but not. We sleep together and then you ignore me during the day. You make love with me all night and then the next morning, you shut me out. How the hell are either one of us supposed to loosen up enough to make a *baby?*"

His features went cold and stiff again. Typical.

"In case you've forgotten, this isn't a standard marriage."

She staggered back dramatically, slapped one hand to her chest and let her jaw drop. "Really? It's not? Wow. That explains so much!"

His eyes narrowed. "If you're not willing to discuss this like a rational human being…"

"You'll what?" Gina asked, tapping the toe of her boot against the dust-covered concrete floor. "Hire someone to do my talking for me? Or no, wait. Better yet, you could hire someone to do *your* talking. Then you wouldn't even have to look at me until it was time to come to bed and do your duty for the King ranch and dynasty."

He gritted his teeth and the muscle in his jaw twitched. "You think I treat lovemaking as a chore?"

"Isn't it for you?" she countered and immediately wished she hadn't. Never ask a question if you don't think you'll like the answer. But too late now. Yes, he seemed to enjoy making love with her. But what if she was wrong about that? What if he really was doing only what he considered keeping up his end of the bargain? What if she hadn't even reached him in bed? Didn't she *have* to know? And wasn't pushing him the only way to know for sure?

"We made a deal," she accused, hoping with everything she was that he would deny what she was thinking, "and you come to me every night to check sex off your to-do list."

"Now you're not making any sense at all." He snorted a dismissive laugh.

"No? Then tell me you want me, Adam. Tell me that making love to me is more than a chore. More than just holding up your end of the bargain." She stepped in close to him, felt the heat pouring off his body and reaching for hers. "Prove me wrong, Adam," she taunted. "If I'm more than that to you, prove it to me."

Seconds ticked past as she stared into his eyes. Heat flared in those dark chocolate depths and Gina almost wondered if she'd pushed him too far.

Then he grabbed her, yanked her flush against him and took her mouth with a fierce aggression that melted every bone in her body.

Looked like she'd pushed him just far enough.

Adam couldn't breathe.

The anger that had been choking him was drowning now in a molten sea of desire. He pulled her in close, wrapped both arms around her and gave himself up to the raging need within. She opened her mouth for him and his tongue delved into her heat. He tasted and took, grabbing as much of her as he could, as if his life depended on it.

She was a contradiction in so many ways. Sweet, and yet not afraid to stand up for herself. Even to him. Sexy and warm and hot tempered, as well. She shook up his life. Brought chaos to order. Dragged strangers onto his property. Made him feel too much. Want too much.

His hands fisted in her hair and he pulled her head back, bending her back as he took all she offered. All she promised. He felt her like a drug in his system. She filled every cell. Awoke every nerve.

She was dangerous.

At that thought, he pulled himself up from the spell he was under and broke the kiss like a man surfacing for one last gasp of air before he drowned. He released her and she lurched unsteadily until she found her footing. Then she lifted one hand to her mouth and raised her glassy eyes to his.

Adam fought to bring air into straining lungs. Fought to ignore the throbbing in his groin, the near-frantic demand for release clamoring at him. When he finally felt as though he could speak again, he said only, "You're not a chore, Gina. But you're not permanent, either. You can't be."

Pain flickered in her eyes and he steeled himself against it. He wouldn't be moved by concern for her. Would hold himself to the course he'd set when he embarked on the bargain that had shattered the peaceful solitude of his world.

"Why, Adam?" Her voice was soft and sounded as bruised as her eyes. "Why are you so determined to feel nothing? You were married before. You loved Monica."

Ice flowed through his veins just as quickly as the fire had only moments before. "You don't know anything about my marriage."

He hoped she would drop it, but of course, being Gina, she didn't.

"I know that she's gone. I know that the pain you felt at losing your wife and son will never really go away."

"You know *nothing*."

"Then talk to me!" Her shout was loud enough to rattle the window glass in the old barn. "How can I know what you're thinking if you won't talk to me? Let me in, Adam."

Shaking his head, he fought for words, and couldn't find any. He didn't want her *in*. Didn't want this to be anything more than the impersonal bargain they'd first begun. His past was just that. *His*. He didn't make decisions based on guilt or pain or any other emotion that could cloud judgment, impair thought.

Adam ran his life as he ran his portion of the King business. With calm, cool reason. Something Gina clearly was unaccustomed to.

"The pictures of your family in the hall?" She looked up at him, a silent pleading in her golden eyes. "The photos all over the house? They're of you and your brothers. Your parents. Cousins. But—"

He knew what she was going to say and still swayed with the slap of her words.

"There are no pictures of Monica and Jeremy any-where. Why is that, Adam?"

Steeling himself, he kept his voice steady, emotions hidden. "You'd prefer that I filled the house with photos? You think I want to look at pictures of my son and remember him dying? Does that sound like a good time to you, Gina? Because it sure as hell doesn't to me."

"Of course not." She grabbed his forearm with both hands and he felt the strength of her grip, the heat of her touch right down to his bones. "But how can you just shut it all out? How can you refuse to remember your own son?"

He remembered, Adam thought as an instant image of Jeremy leaped up into his mind. Small, with blond hair like his mother and his father's brown eyes. Smiling, always smiling, that's how Adam remembered him. But that was private. Something he didn't share.

Slowly he peeled her hands off his arm and took a step back from her for good measure. "Just because I don't surround myself with physical mementos doesn't mean I could or *would* forget him. But I don't run my life on memories, Gina. My past doesn't infringe on my present. Or my future." He forced himself to look at her and distance himself from the regret, the disappointment shining in her eyes. She'd known going into this that he wasn't looking for love. If she'd allowed herself to hope for more, that wasn't his fault, was it?

When she didn't speak, Adam continued. "We have a business arrangement, Gina. Nothing more. Don't expect what I can't give and we'll both come out of this with what we want."

Eleven

For days, Gina wrestled with that last conversation she'd had with Adam in the barn. She kept forcing herself to remember not only the fierce fire of his kiss, but the icy shards in his eyes.

Had she been fooling herself for months? Had she really been holding on to a childish dream that had no basis in reality? Was it time to admit defeat and bundle her heart up before it could be shattered completely?

She tugged on Shadow's reins and urged the gentle Gypsy mare down a well-worn path to the King family cemetery. As she approached, storm clouds that had been crouched at the horizon all day suddenly moved forward, sweeping across the sky like an invading army.

The temperature dropped in an instant and the sun's

light was obliterated. Grayness surrounded her and a cold wind kicked up, lifting her long braid off her shoulder, tossing it behind her back. Shadow danced uneasily beneath her as if the horse sensed the coming storm and wanted nothing more than to return to the warm comfort of the stable.

But Gina was on a mission, and wasn't going back to the house until she'd completed it. How had Adam cut his dead family so neatly out of his life? With surgical precision, he'd sliced off that part of his past and shuttered it away completely. What kind of man could do that?

The last of summer was slipping away into fall. Soon, the trees guarding the old cemetery would be awash in brilliant golds and reds, their leaves shuddering in the wind and falling to the ground in a patchwork of color. Already, the wind was colder, the days were shorter.

Shadow blew out a breath, shook her head and again tried to stray off the worn path. But Gina was determined to face the past Adam had locked away.

The scrollwork in the iron trellis fence surrounding the cemetery looked time worn yet still elegant and strong. As if it had been built with love to last generations. Like the King family itself.

Bougainvillea vines twisted through the metal work, their deep scarlet and pale lavender flowers fluttering in the wind. Headstones crowded the small cemetery that had stood in this place since the early eighteen hundreds. Some tipped drunkenly, the letters carved into their stone rubbed away by time and weather. The newer additions stood soldier straight, their stones still bright, the engraving deep and clear, hardly touched by wind and rain.

Gina swung off of Shadow, tied the reins loosely to the iron fence and cautiously as a thief, opened the intricately worked gate. A squeal of metal on metal scraped at her nerves and the wind pushed at her, as if someone or something were warning her to turn back. To stay away from the home of the dead and to return to the living.

She squinted into the wind as the first raindrops pelted her. Icy drops soaked into her shirt, snaked along her neck and down her back. The leaves on the trees rustled, sounding almost like a crowd of people whispering, wondering what she would do next.

Walking carefully across the wet and getting-wetter grass, Gina eased around the older graves and made her way back to the last row, where brilliantly white granite tablets awaited her. Adam's parents were buried side by side more than ten years ago, after the private plane they were piloting went down outside San Francisco. There were fresh flowers on their graves. Roses from the ranch garden.

But Gina hadn't come to see Adam's parents. It was two other graves, silent and chill beneath the splattering raindrops that called to her.

Monica Cullen King and Jeremy Adam King.

There were flowers here, too. Roses for Monica, daisies for Jeremy. The now-steady rain made streaks across the surface of the granite and the brass nameplates affixed there. And the silence that reached for Gina nearly choked her. Here lay the family that Adam couldn't forget and wouldn't allow himself to remember. Here was the reason he was living only a half life. Here was the past that somehow offered him more than a future with her ever could.

"How do I make him love me?" she asked, her gaze sliding from one of the stone tablets to the other. "How do I make him see that having a future doesn't take away from the past?"

There were no answers of course and if there had been, Gina would probably have run screaming from the cemetery. But somehow, she felt as though her questions were being heard. And understood.

Going down on one knee in front of the twin graves, she felt the cold wet soak into the denim fabric as she smoothed the flat of her hand across the neatly tended grass and absently picked up fallen twigs to toss them aside. "I know he loved you. But I think he could love me, too." She glanced at the stone bearing Jeremy's name and the too-brief span of years that marked the life he'd led. Her eyes filled, remembering that sunshiny boy and the devastation she'd felt for Adam when Jeremy had died.

"It's not that I want him to forget you. Either of you. I only want…" Her words trailed off as she lifted her gaze to the horizon where black clouds roiled.

"I have been fooling myself, haven't I?" she whispered finally, the wind throwing her words back in her face. "He won't risk it again. Won't risk loving when he's already paid too high a price for it."

The rain thundered out of a sky gone black and dangerous, coming down in a torrent that soaked her to the skin. A fierce wind wrapped itself around her and cold settled in Gina's bones. She knew the storm wasn't the only reason though. It was the chill realization that what she'd longed for would never happen. It was time to surrender. She wouldn't put herself through staying with a man in the hopes that he would one day love her.

Time to throw away the diaphragm.

Standing up slowly, she looked down at the graves of Adam's family and whispered, "Look after him when I'm gone, okay?"

Adam was in the barn saddling his own horse by the time Gina rode into the ranch yard, soaking wet and looking as miserable as a woman possibly could. He'd been getting ready to go out looking for her—which even he'd had to silently admit was practically useless. On a ranch the size of the King spread, it could have taken him days to find her. And still, he would have searched because not knowing where she was, if she was safe or maybe hurt or lost or God knew what else, was making him insane.

Looking at her now, though, he was torn between relief and fury. Mindless of the pouring rain, he left the barn, stalked across the ranch yard and didn't stop until he reached her side. He snatched her off the back of her mare and held her shoulders in a death grip while he looked down into her eyes and shouted, "Where the hell have you been? You've been gone for hours."

"Riding," she said and pulled out of his grasp. She

stumbled a little, caught her balance and looked around herself as if trying to remember where she was and how she'd gotten there. "I was riding. Storm came…"

Her voice drifted off and whatever else she said was lost in the pummeling thunder of the falling rain and the slam of the wind. She looked down at herself as if surprised to find she was completely drenched. The heavens were still torn open, with rain coming down in thick sheets that made it almost impossible to see clearly more than a few feet.

Adam's insides were still rattled even as he fought for the legendary calm that was normally such a huge part of his life. Damn it, he'd been going nuts wondering where she was. If she was safe. He'd spent the last two hours alternately watching the storm roll in and searching the horizon for a sign of her returning. He felt as if he'd been running all day. Exhausted and pushed to the edge of his limits.

He reached out, swiped her wet hair off her forehead and said, "Damn it, Gina, you don't go riding without telling someone where you're going. This is a big ranch. Anything could happen, even to an experienced rider."

"I'm fine," she mumbled and rubbed water off her face with her hands. Hunching her shoulders, she added sternly, "Stop yelling."

"I haven't even started," he warned, still riding the rush of emotion that had damn near choked him when she rode into the yard. Didn't she know what could have happened?

Rattlesnakes could have spooked her horse. Wildcats

down from the foothills looking for food could have attacked her. Hell, her mare could have stepped into a hole and broken a leg, leaving Gina stranded miles from help. His heart was pounding, his brain was screaming and the temper he'd kept a close rein on ever since he'd discovered she was gone finally cut loose.

Grabbing her upper arms, he shook her until her head fell back and her wide, golden eyes fixed on his face. "What the hell was so important that you felt you had to ride out with a storm coming in?"

She blinked up at him and the rain fell like tears down her face. "Never mind. You wouldn't understand."

She might as well have slapped him. Fine. She didn't want to tell him what was going on? Worked for him. But damned if he'd stand in the yard and drown. "Come on." He turned and dragged her toward the house.

She struggled in his grasp but no way was she going to get loose. "I've got to see to Shadow."

"*Now* you're worried about the mare?" He shook his head. "One of the men will take care of her."

"Will you just let go, Adam?" she argued, dragging her heels trough the mud. "I can walk on my own. I take care of myself. And I can take care of my own horse."

"Yeah?" He looked her up and down. "Looks like you're doing a hell of a job there, Gina. Nice one." Then he glanced over his shoulder, pointed and said, "There. Sam's got Shadow. He'll rub her down and feed her. Satisfied?"

She looked, too, and watched her mare being led into the warm, dry stable and it was as if the last of her strength just drained away. She swayed in place and something inside Adam turned over. She'd thrown his life into turmoil and now she was making him yell like a maniac and he *never* yelled.

"Come on," he muttered and took hold of her again, leading her behind him and he didn't stop until he'd reached the front door. He threw it open, stomped off as much mud as he could from his boots, then stepped into the house. "Esperanza!"

The older woman scuttled into the hall from the kitchen and immediately raced toward Gina. "*Dios mio,* what's happened here? Miss Gina, are you all right?"

"I'm fine," Gina said, still trying to get out of Adam's tight-fisted grip. "I'm sorry about the mess," she added, waving one hand at the rainwater and mud sliding across the once-gleaming entryway floor.

"No matter, no matter." Esperanza threw a hard look at Adam. "What did you do to her?"

"*Me?*"

"No," Gina interrupted quickly, briefly. "It wasn't Adam. I got caught in the storm."

Still, Esperanza shot Adam a death glare that clearly said, *you could have stopped this if you'd tried.* Whatever. He wasn't going to stand there and defend himself while Gina froze to death.

"I'm taking her upstairs," Adam said, already heading for the wide staircase. "We'll want something hot in, say, an hour? Maybe some of your tortilla soup, if there is any."

"*Sí, sí,*" Esperanza said. "One hour." Then she

clucked her tongue as Adam swung Gina into his arms and started up the stairs, taking them two at a time.

"I can walk," she complained.

"Swear to God, don't you say another word," he snapped. At the head of the stairs, he glanced back to see Esperanza making short work of the mess he and Gina had left behind. Time for another raise for his housekeeper.

Gina, apparently unaffected by the fury pumping through him, slapped one hand to his chest and said, "Damn it, Adam, I'm not an invalid."

"No, you're not. Just crazy," he said, sparing her only a quick look before continuing down the hall to the master bedroom. He walked inside and never paused until he reached the connected bath. A huge room, with miles of white and green tiles, it boasted a double sink, a shower big enough for an orgy and a hot tub with a wide bay window that overlooked the spectacular back gardens. Now though, rain sluiced down the glass, making the view blurry and the distant horizon nothing more than a smudge of gray and black.

"Strip," he said when he set her down.

She glared at him. "I will not."

"Fine. I'll do it for you then. Not like I don't know my way around your body." Adam reached for the buttons on her shirt, but Gina slapped at his hands. Didn't hit him very hard, since she was shaking and so cold her teeth were chattering.

"You might want to wait until you're stronger to make a fight of it," he said tightly and reached down to turn the faucets on the hot tub. He flipped up the latch to set the plug and turned back to her while hot water rushed into the tub.

He began tearing the buttons from her shirt and peeling the sodden garment off of her. "You're half-frozen." Then he undid her bra, leaving Gina to clasp one arm across her breasts in a useless bid for modesty.

"A little late for maidenly concerns, don't you think?" he asked as he shook his head at the defiant glare shooting out of her eyes.

"I don't want you here," she said, and her words might have carried more weight if her voice hadn't trembled.

"Tough," he said, kneeling down in front of her to tug off one of her boots. "What the hell were you thinking? Why did you go out today? You saw the storm. Heard the forecast."

"I thought I had time," she said, reaching out to slap one hand on the counter to keep her balance while he lifted first one of her feet, then the next. "I needed to—"

"What?" He looked up at her from where he knelt in front of her. Still furious, still relieved, still battling both sensations, he grumbled, "Needed to *what?*"

She shook her head. "Doesn't matter now."

It irritated him that she wouldn't tell him what she was thinking. Where she'd been. What had put the look of utter devastation on her face and in her eyes. He wanted to…damn it, he wanted to make her feel better. When the hell had this happened? When had he begun to care what she thought, how she felt? And how could he stop it?

Shaking his head, he tugged off her boots, then her socks and went to work on her jeans. The denim fabric was so soaked, it was hard to maneuver and he had to put some real effort into dragging them down her thighs and calves. Cold water ran in rivulets down her pale, blue-tinged skin. She shivered again and Adam fisted his hands to fight the urge to caress her, to warm her with his touch.

Instead he hissed in a breath. "You're cold to the bone."

"Pretty much."

Behind them, hot water rushed into the gigantic tub and steam rose to fog the bay window, shutting out the night, sealing them into that one room together.

"Get in," Adam said flatly.

She looked at him. "First you get out."

"Not likely," he told her and picked her up as if she weighed nothing, then plopped her down into the tub. Gina sucked in a gulp of air as warm water met her cold legs, but an instant later, she sat down and let that heat reach down inside her and somewhat ease the cold that seemed locked deep.

Gina closed her eyes and leaned her head back, focusing only on the delicious feel of the hot water surrounding her tired, aching, freezing body. She heard Adam hit the switch to turn on the hot-tub jets, and an instant later, she felt hot, steady pulses hitting her poor, abused body like tiny, miraculous blessings.

Okay, he was bossy and irritating and right now, the last human being on the face of the planet she wanted to be alone with, but he'd been right about the hot tub. And she wanted to thank him for turning on the jets.

When she opened her eyes to do that, though, she saw Adam peeling out of his own wet clothing. "What are you doing?"

He glared at her and tugged his jeans down to join the wet shirt he'd already tossed to the floor to lay atop both pairs of boots. His broad chest ran with water and droplets of the stuff fell from the tips of his wet hair. "What the hell does it look like?"

"I know just what it looks like," she said and scooted back in the tub as far from him as she could get. Yes, her body was starting to fire into life, but it wasn't as if she wanted it to happen. It was simply a biological imperative. See Adam naked, go all hot and tingly.

God, would it be that way forever?

No. Eventually if she could go without seeing him for ten or fifteen years, she'd probably be able to control her reaction to an occasional sighting. At the moment, though, she was having a hard time fighting down her body's urges. Despite the warnings and dire predictions her brain kept screaming.

He stepped into the tub, settled against the side opposite her and as the frothy water splashed at his bare chest, he looked at her and said, "I was worried."

A ping of something warm and sweet echoed inside her for a moment or two. A few weeks ago…heck, even a few days ago, she would have loved to hear Adam say that to her. It would have given her hope, made her think that there was still a chance for them.

Now she knew better.

Gina looked into his eyes and could only think that

now, it wasn't enough. The worry for her, the fear that she'd been hurt was no more than he would have felt for a neighbor. An acquaintance.

She wanted more.

And she wasn't going to get it.

"You're still cold," he said.

"I am." So very cold. Colder than she'd ever been and Gina had the distinct feeling she'd better get used to the sensation.

"I can fix that." Adam lunged forward, grabbed her arms and then swept back, pulling her up against him, stretching his long legs out in the hot tub.

He wrapped his arms around her and pulled her head down to his chest. She nestled in, listening to the steady beat of his heart beneath her ear.

"Don't do that to me again," he said, his voice rumbling through his chest.

Hot water sprayed up onto her face and the pummeling jets pounded at her back as Adam stroked her skin. She thought he might have kissed the top of her head, but Gina dismissed that notion immediately, sure she was only fooling herself.

"I won't." Not that she'd have the chance to worry him for much longer. Her time at the King ranch was definitely coming to a close. And when she left here, Adam wouldn't give her another thought. He wouldn't have to be concerned about her whereabouts. He'd have what he wanted. A twenty-acre parcel of land to make the King holdings whole again.

In a few months time, she'd be nothing more than an

inconvenient memory. Maybe he'd walk that acreage he'd worked so hard to earn and think about her. Maybe he'd wonder then what she was doing, or where she was. But then, he'd put it out of his mind. He'd lock the memory of her away as completely as he had that of Monica and Jeremy.

"At least take your damn cell phone with you next time," Adam said, stroking his big, rough hands up and down her back in long, steady caresses, a silky counterpoint to the hot tub jets. "About made me insane when I called you and heard the phone ringing up here."

"I will." She hadn't been thinking when she left the ranch or she would have told someone where she was going. She'd been raised to know better. Accidents could happen anywhere, anytime and finding someone on a ranch the size of Adam's could have taken weeks. As to the cell phone, she hadn't wanted it with her. Hadn't wanted anyone to be able to intrude on her ride into Adam's past.

"Damn it, Gina…" This time his voice was more of a growl. She heard the need in it, felt the hard, insistent throb of his erection beneath her. His body was tight, his heartbeat quickened and in seconds, his hands were moving over her with more hunger than care.

"You could have been hurt," he muttered thickly and turned her face up to his. He bent his head and kissed her, hard and long and deep. His tongue swept into her mouth, his breath dusted her cheek and the low moan that issued from his throat slipped inside her, becoming one with her own.

The rhythm of the jets pounded at her, pushing her closer to Adam, hammering home her need as if in punctuation to the raw desire rising up in her.

He was hard and thick and ready. His breath came in strangled gasps as she slid one leg over his middle. His big hands came down on her waist and settled her atop him. Their eyes met and held as Gina felt the slow slide of his body into hers. He filled her and she savored it. Relished it. Imprinted the feeling on her memory so that she'd always be able to recall with perfect clarity the feel of his hands on her slick skin. The scent of him. The taste of his kiss.

Because without her diaphragm standing in the way, she knew she'd be pregnant soon. Knew that even as he touched her, even as his body and hers became one, they were already pulling apart.

And she knew that every touch from this night on, would be a silent goodbye.

Two months later, Adam was in his study, going over reports from his brokers and projections from several of the smaller companies the King ranch held an interest in. At least once a week he was holed up in this room, going over the insane amount of paperwork a huge corporation like his generated.

The study hadn't changed much since his grandfather's time. The walls were a dark hunter-green. There were floor-to-ceiling bookshelves on two of the walls and a bank of windows displaying the wide lawn at the front of the house. A mahogany wetbar took up one corner of the room and a fifty-inch plasma television was hidden behind a copy of one of his mother's favorite Manet paintings. There were two sofas, facing each other, waiting for someone to sit down and have a conversation, along with two oversize club chairs in maroon leather. And for winter, there was a stone fireplace with a hearth big enough for a child to stand up straight in.

It was his sanctuary. No one came in here, except Esperanza, and that was only to clean. Completely caught up in the columns of figures and the suggestions on further diversifying, he didn't even notice when the study door opened quietly.

He heard it shut, though, and said without looking up, "I'm not hungry, Esperanza. But I could use more coffee if you've got some."

"Sorry," Gina said, "fresh out."

Surprised, Adam lifted his gaze and saw her look quickly around the one room in the house she'd never been. She was wearing worn blue jeans, a long-sleeved red T-shirt and boots that looked as old as the ranch itself. Her hair was pulled back into a ponytail at the base of her neck and she wasn't wearing a speck of makeup. Yet her golden eyes seemed alive with fire and emotion and he knew he'd never seen a more beautiful woman.

He felt the now all-too-familiar rush of a near electrical charge jolt through him as he watched her. Instantly his groin went hard as granite and an ache settled deep inside him. They'd been married for months and still he hadn't become immune to her presence.

Irritated by that thought, he deliberately lowered his

gaze to the stacks of papers in front of him. "Didn't know it was you, Gina. I'm kind of busy right now. Is there something you need?"

"No," she said softly, walking across the thick red Oriental carpet toward the massive oak desk that had once been his father's. "You've already given me everything I need."

"What?" Her solemn tone, more than the words, caught his attention. He lifted his gaze to her again and for the first time, noticed the sad smile curving her mouth and the gleam of unshed tears making her eyes shine brilliantly. "What're you talking about?" he asked, standing to face her. "Is something wrong?"

She shook her head, brushed away a single tear that escaped her eye to roll down her cheek and pulled a folded piece of paper from her back pocket. "No, Adam. Nothing's wrong. In fact, everything's just right."

"Then…?"

In answer, she handed him the piece of paper and watched him as he unfolded it carefully. The first thing Adam saw was one word, in chunky black lettering.

Deed.

His fingers tightened on the paper, making it crackle in the stillness. This could only mean…looking at her finally, he said, "You're pregnant?"

She gave him a smile that didn't quite reach her eyes. "I am. I did a pregnancy test on my own, then went to the doctor yesterday to confirm." She took a deep breath and said, "I'm about six weeks along. Everything looks fine."

Gina. Pregnant with his child. Emotion he didn't

want and refused to acknowledge ran crazily through his mind. His gaze dropped to her flat belly as if he could see through her body to the tiny child already growing within. Child. *His* child. He waited for the pain to cut at him, but it didn't happen and he didn't know what to make of that.

"Congratulations, Adam," Gina said, shattering his thoughts with her quiet, somehow broken, voice. "You did a great job. Held up your end of our deal. Now, you've got the land you wanted, and our bargain's complete."

"Yeah." Congratulations to him. His fingers smoothed over the paper he held and knew he should be feeling a sense of satisfaction. Completion. For five years, he'd dedicated himself to acquiring the last pieces to his ranch. And here it was. The final parcel in his hands and he felt...nothing.

"I'm all packed," Gina was saying and Adam frowned, narrowed his gaze and looked at her.

"You're leaving? Already?"

"No point in staying longer, is there?" Her voice got brighter, sharper.

"No." He glanced at the paper in his hand again. Gina was leaving. The marriage was over. "No point."

"Look, Adam, there's one more thing." She took a deep breath, then blew the air out in a rush. "It's something you should know before I go. I love you, Adam."

He swayed a little as those four words punched at him. She loved him and she was leaving. Why wasn't he saying something? Why the hell couldn't he *think?*

"Always have," she admitted and wiped away another

tear with an impatient gesture. "You don't have to say anything or do anything, so don't try, okay? I don't think either one of us could take it." She gave him a brief smile, but he saw her bottom lip tremble.

He started around the edge of his desk, not sure what he was going to do or say, only knowing that he had to do *something*. But she stopped him by holding up one hand and backing up a little. "Don't, okay?" She shook her head. "Don't touch me and don't be nice." She laughed shortly and it sounded like glass breaking. "God, don't be nice. I uh, wanted you to know, I won't be staying in Birkfield. I'm leaving. Tomorrow."

"Leaving? For where? For how long? What? Why?"

"I'm moving to Colorado." She gave him a smile that didn't fool either of them. "Going to stay with my brother Nick and his family until I find a place of my own." She was backing up toward the door, keeping her gaze fixed on him as if worried he'd try to keep her from leaving. "I can't stay here, Adam. I can't raise my child so close to a father who doesn't want it. I can't be near you knowing that I'll never have you. I need somewhere fresh, Adam. My baby deserves to be happy. So do I."

"Gina, you're throwing this at me too fast. What the hell am I supposed to do about this?"

"Nothing, Adam." Her hand fisted around the doorknob behind her. "This isn't about *you*. So anyway…goodbye."

She was changing her whole life because of him. He felt like a jerk, but couldn't quite bring himself to say it. She shouldn't have to leave. Move away from the home she loved all because of him. "Gina, damn it—"

She shook her head. "It's just how it has to be, Adam. So, have a good life, okay? Be well."

Then she was gone and Adam was alone.

Just the way he wanted it.

Twelve

"You are a fool."

Adam didn't even look up when Esperanza served his breakfast along with her opinion. Morning sunlight splashed across him as he sat at the head of the long, cherrywood table in the dining room. One man at a table for twelve.

Quite the statement on his life.

His coffee was cold, but he had the distinct impression asking for a refill wouldn't get him far. Glancing down at his breakfast plate, he noticed the scrambled eggs were runny—he loathed wet eggs and Esperanza knew it. The bacon was charred on one side and raw on the other and his toast was black.

Pretty much the same breakfast he'd been served every morning since Gina left.

Complaining about it wouldn't change anything, he knew. Esperanza had been with the family for way too long. Once a woman's paddled your backside for you when you were a kid, you no longer had any authority over her, no matter what you'd prefer to think.

"Thanks," he said, picking up his fork and wondering if he could just eat the *tops* of the eggs. Damn it, he hadn't *told* Gina to leave. That had been her idea. She'd walked away under her own power, but facts didn't seem to matter to his housekeeper.

Did they matter to him, either? Not for the first time since she'd been gone, Adam wondered what she was doing at that moment. Sitting around her brother's breakfast table? Laughing, talking, enjoying herself? Or was she missing him? Did she think about him at all?

"You are going to simply sit here and do nothing while the *mother of your child* is off somewhere in the wilderness?" Esperanza stood alongside the table, arms folded over her chest, the toe of her shoe tapping briskly against the wood floor. Her dark eyes snapped with fury and her mouth was so thin a slash, it had almost disappeared.

Adam pushed thoughts of Gina away, though they didn't go far. He blew out a breath and nibbled at a bite of egg before grimacing and giving it up. He and his housekeeper had had this same conversation for three weeks now. At every opportunity, Esperanza alternately cajoled, harangued and berated him for allowing Gina to leave him. "Colorado is hardly the wilderness," he pointed out.

"It is not *here*."

"True." Adam dropped his fork onto the plate and resigned himself to another hungry day. Maybe he'd drive into town for a decent breakfast. But as soon as he considered it, he changed his mind. In town, there would be people. People wanting to talk to him. To tell him how sorry they were to hear his marriage had ended. People fishing for more information than he was willing to share.

"You should go after her."

He finally shot his housekeeper a dirty look. She remained unmoved. "Esperanza, Gina left. She *wanted* to go. We had a deal, remember? The deal's finished."

"Deal." That single word carried so much disgust, it practically vibrated in the air. "What you had was a marriage. What you are going to have is a child. A child you will never see. This is what you want, Adam? This is the life you wish to lead?"

No, he thought grimly, looking at the chair where Gina used to sit. Imagining her smile. Her laughter, the gentle touch of her hand when she reached out to pat his arm. He hadn't even realized how much he'd come to depend on seeing her every day. Hearing her. Talking with her. Arguing with her.

In the last few weeks, life on the King ranch had returned to "normal." The Gypsy horses were gone, back at the Torino ranch until Gina sent for them to join her in Colorado. The constant stream of visitors who'd come to buy those horses had ended. There were no more vases of fresh flowers in his bedroom, because Gina wasn't there to pick them. There were no more late night movies played or bowls of popcorn eaten, because Gina had left him.

There was no more *life* at the ranch.

His world had become the stark black and white he'd once known and cherished. Only now…he hated it. He hated the sameness. The quiet. The everlasting ordinariness of his existence. It was like the breakfasts Esperanza had been serving him. Tasteless.

But he couldn't change it. Gina had gone. She'd moved on to build a life without him and that was for the best. For her. For their baby. For him. He was almost sure of it.

"She has been gone three weeks already," Esperanza reminded him.

Three weeks, five days and eleven hours. But who was counting?

"You must go to her. Bring her back where she belongs."

"It's not that simple."

"Only to a man," she pointed out, grabbing up his untouched breakfast and heading for the kitchen.

He half turned in his chair to shout after her, "I *am* a man!"

"A foolish one!" she shouted right back.

"You're fired!"

"Hah!"

Adam slumped in his chair and shook his head. Firing her would do no good. Esperanza would never leave. She'd be right here for the next twenty years, probably making him miserable at every opportunity.

But then, he wondered as he shoved himself up from the table, did he really deserve any better? He'd let Gina go without a word because he hadn't been able to risk caring for her. For their child.

Which made him, he knew, a coward.

And everybody knew that cowards died a thousand deaths.

By afternoon, Adam had irritated, angered and annoyed all of his employees and was even starting to get on his own nerves. So he closed himself up in his study, made some phone calls and started looking for new projects. After all, he had the precious land he'd wanted so badly. Now he needed something new to concentrate on.

The knock on the study door aggravated him. "What is it?"

Sal Torino opened the door and gave him such a long, level stare that everything in Adam went cold and hard as ice. He jumped up from his chair. There was only one reason for Sal to be there. "Is it Gina? Is she all right?"

Gina's father stepped into the room, closed the door behind him and studied Adam for a moment or two before speaking. "I've come because it's only right you know."

The ice moved through his veins, sluggishly headed for his heart. Adam clenched his fists, gritted his teeth and fought for control. "Just tell me. Gina. Is she all right?"

"Gina is fine," Sal said, walking slowly around the big room, as if seeing it for the first time.

Relief swept through Adam so fast, it left his knees shaking. He felt as though he'd been running in place for an hour. His heart was pounding, his breath was laboring in his lungs and his legs were rubbery. What the hell kind of stunt was Sal up to?

"Damn it, Sal. What was the point of that?" He shouted the question, as adrenaline drained slowly away. "Want to see if you could get a rise out of me? Is that it?"

"It was a test of sorts," Sal admitted, stopping on the opposite side of the wide desk. "I wanted to know," the older man said, his dark eyes narrowed, his mouth grim, "if you loved my Gina. Now I know."

Adam shoved one hand through his hair, then wiped his face. Love. There was a word he'd avoided thinking about over the last few weeks. Even when he lay awake at night, alternately planning on either flying to Colorado to kidnap Gina or burying himself in work, he'd trained himself to never think that word.

It wasn't part of his plan.

He'd tried love before and he was no good at it. Love messed people up. Ruined lives. Ended some. He wasn't going there again. Even if the heart he'd thought long dead was now very alive and aching.

Not something he was going to admit to anyone else.

"Sorry to disappoint. Naturally I was concerned for her. But if she's fine, then I don't see a reason for this visit." Sitting down in his desk chair again, he picked up a pen, lowered his gaze to the papers in front of him and said, "Thanks for stopping by."

Sal didn't leave, though. He leaned forward, bracing

his work-worn hands on the edge of the desk and waited until Adam lifted his gaze before saying, "I have something to tell you, Adam. Something I think you have the right to know."

"Say it then and get it done," Adam muttered, bracing himself for whatever news the older man had come to deliver. How bad could it be? Was Gina already in love with someone else? That thought sliced through him, even as he discounted it. It might feel like years since she'd been gone, but it had only been a few weeks. So what could possibly have happened?

"Gina lost the baby."

"What?" He whispered the word and the pen he held dropped from suddenly nerveless fingers. "When?"

"Yesterday," Sal said, his features full of pity and sorrow.

Yesterday. How had that happened and he hadn't sensed it? Felt it somehow? Gina had been alone and he'd been here. Tucked away in an insulated world of his own design. She'd needed him and he hadn't been there.

"Gina? How's Gina?" Stupid question, Adam thought instantly. He knew how she would be. She'd wanted that child so much. She would be devastated. Crushed. Heartsick.

And a moment later, he realized to his own astonishment that he felt those things, too. A profound sense of loss shook him to the bone and he was so unprepared for it, he didn't know what to think.

"She will be fine in time," Sal told him softly. "She didn't want you to know, but I felt it was only right."

"Of course." Of course he should know. Their child was dead. Though it hadn't taken a breath, Adam felt the loss as surely as he had the loss of Jeremy years ago. It wasn't just the death of the child. It was the death of dreams. Hopes. The future.

"Also," Sal added, waiting now for Adam to look at him, "you should know that Gina will be staying in Colorado."

"She. Staying. What?" Adam shook his head, trying to focus past the pain that was threading its way through his bloodstream.

"She's not coming home," Sal said, then added softly, "unless something happens to change her mind."

Adam hardly noticed when Sal left. His mind kept flashing with images of Gina until the pain in his heart was almost too much to bear. For weeks now, he'd thought of nothing but her, despite trying to shut himself off from the world. Return to the solitary existence he'd become so accustomed to.

But no matter how hard he tried, thoughts of her had remained. Taunting him. Torturing him. Wondering how she was. Where she was living. What she would tell their child about him.

Now there was no baby. Gina was in pain, so much more pain than he was feeling and she was alone in this, despite her family, she was as alone as he was. And suddenly, Adam knew what he wanted more than anything. He wanted to hold her. Dry her tears. Comfort her and wrap himself up in the warmth of her.

He wanted to fall asleep holding her and wake up to look into her eyes. Standing up again, he turned, looked out the wide window behind him at the sweep of lawn leading to the main road. The ancient trees lining the driveway danced in the wind, leaves already turning gold breaking free to twist and fly through the air. Fall was coming fast and soon, the days would be cold and the nights far too long.

Just as his *life* would be long and cold and empty without Gina.

"Esperanza was right," he muttered, turning to reach for the phone on his desk. "Half-right, anyway. I *was* a fool. But no more."

Gina laughed at the little boy bouncing around in the saddle. He was so excited at being a "cowboy," he hadn't stopped grinning since Gina had put him on the horse.

Thankfully, even though her brother Nick was technically a high school football coach, he had a small ranch outside of town. You really could take the boy off the home ranch but couldn't take the ranch out of the boy, she thought. And being here, working on Nick and his wife's small spread had been good for her. She'd spent time with her nephews and niece and had kept herself so busy that she'd only had time to think about Adam every *other* minute.

Surely that was progress.

"You're thinking about him again."

She turned to smile and shrug at her older brother. "Only a little."

"I talked to Tony last night," Nick said, leaning his forearms on the top rail of the corral fence. "If it helps any, he says Adam looks miserable."

Small consolation, Gina thought, but she'd take it. She leaned back against the fence and said, "Is it wrong to say 'glad to hear it'?"

"No. Not wrong at all." Nick tugged at her ponytail. "Tony's willing to go beat him up for you. You just say the word."

"You guys are the best."

He grinned and his golden eyes twinkled. "So we keep telling you."

She smiled again and turned to look when a car pulled into the yard behind them. She didn't recognize the bright yellow van, so her heartbeat didn't stutter until the driver opened the door and stepped out.

"What d'ya know?" Nick mumbled.

"Adam," Gina said on a sigh, straightening up and wishing she were dressed a little better. Silly, she knew. But the purely female part of her couldn't help being irritated that she was wearing worn jeans and dirty boots for Adam's surprise arrival.

He started toward her and Gina took a step before turning back to her brother. "Nick, would you keep an eye on Mikey?"

"Sure thing," her brother said with a brief nod. "But if you need me to get rid of Adam, just call out."

Get rid of him? No. She didn't want to get rid of him. She wanted to luxuriate in just looking at him. How pitiful was that? God, he was gorgeous. Even better than the dream images she saw of him whenever she closed her eyes. Her blood was humming, her heartbeat pounding and her mouth was so dry, she could hardly swallow.

Gina forced herself to take slow, even steps toward him when her instincts were telling her to run, throw herself into his arms and never let go. How long did it take, she wondered, before love faded? Months? Years?

"Gina," he said and his voice was a deep rumble that seemed to reverberate inside her chest.

"Adam. What are you doing here?"

He scrubbed one hand across the back of his neck. "I had to see you. Took one of the family jets. Rented a car at the airport—" He paused to give the van a dirty look.

"Yeah, nice color."

"All they had," he said.

She smiled. "I didn't ask how you got here. Just why you *are* here."

"To see you. To tell you—"

His eyes were flashing with emotion—more than she'd ever seen in those dark depths before and Gina wondered frantically what was going on. Hope reared up inside her and she quickly squashed it. No point in pumping up a balloon that Adam would undoubtedly pop.

Then he frowned, looked her up and down and said, "Are you all right? Should you be up and around?"

"What?" She laughed at him. "I'm fine, Adam. What's going on?"

"I brought you something." He dug a folded paper out of his back pocket and held it out to her. "This is yours."

It only took a glance to tell her it was the deed to the

land he'd wanted so badly. "What?" She shook her head. "I don't understand."

"Simple to understand. I'm breaking our bargain. The land's yours again."

She looked from him to the paper and back again. "You're not making any sense."

"Your father told me."

A niggling doubt began tugging at the edges of her mind. What had her interfering father been up to now? "Told you what exactly?"

Adam stepped close, dropped both hands onto her shoulders and looked into her eyes. "He told me about you losing the baby."

She swayed, but he kept talking.

"I'm so sorry, Gina. I know that's not enough. I know 'sorry' doesn't mean a damn at a time like this, but it's all I've got to give you." His hands moved to her face, his thumbs stroking her skin. "I'm so sorry I didn't appreciate the miracle we made together."

Her father had lied to him. And thinking she was in pain, Adam had raced to her side. That bubble of hope lifted inside her again. She sucked in a breath and despite the cold Colorado wind buffeting her, Gina felt warm for the first time since leaving California. "Adam…"

"Wait. Let me finish." He pulled her in close, held her tightly to him and stroked his hands up and down her back as if trying to convince himself that she was really there. With him. And Gina did nothing to stop him. She gave herself up to the wonder of being held by him again. To the scent of him filling her. To the feel of his strength wrapped around her.

When he spoke, his voice was quiet, torn. "You asked why I don't have pictures of Monica and Jeremy in the house."

She stiffened a little, but he felt it and held her tighter.

"I haven't forgotten them. But there's something you don't know, Gina." He pulled back to look at her. "Monica was leaving me. I was a terrible husband and not much better at fatherhood."

That explained so much. "Oh, Adam. You blame yourself for—"

"No." He shook his head now, sadly. "I don't feel guilt for the accident—though if I'd been a better husband, maybe it wouldn't have happened. No, Gina. What I feel is regret. That I couldn't or wouldn't be what they needed."

Her heart hurt for him, but there was more than grief in his eyes, there was determination, as well. And hope. Something that lifted her heart even as she wanted to soothe him.

Adam tipped her chin up with his fingertips and said, "I want to be a husband to you, Gina. I want a real marriage. That's why I'm giving you back the stupid land. I don't want it. You hold it. Give it to the next child we make together. Just give me a chance to make it up to you."

"Oh, Adam..." It was everything. Everything she'd hoped and dreamed and prayed for. All of it was here, within arm's reach. She saw what she'd always wanted to see in his eyes and knew that they would now have the life together that she so craved.

"I miss you," he said, gaze moving over her face like a dying man taking his last look at the world. "Like an arm or a leg. I miss you. A part of me is gone without you. Nothing means anything anymore because you're not with me. Gina, I want you to come home. Be my wife again. Let me be the husband I should have been to you. I do love you, Gina. I'm not too stubborn to say it anymore. Will you take me back? Will you help me try again for another baby?"

Gina was staggered by his presence, his words, by the love shining in his eyes. She could even forgive her father for interfering this time.

"I love you, too, Adam," she said, reaching up to cup his cheek in the palm of her hand.

"Thank God," he whispered and pulled her in close again. When he kissed her there was desperation and adoration and the hunger Gina knew so well. Finally, though, when they broke apart to smile at each other, Gina had to tell him.

"I'll come home with you, Adam, and we'll make that wonderful life together. But—"

He scowled at her. "But?"

"There's no need to work on another baby just yet," she said, taking his hand and laying it flat against her belly. Meeting his gaze, she smiled wider, brighter and saw realization dawn in his eyes. "Our first child is just fine."

He looked confused. "You're still—"

"Yes."

"So your father—"

"Yes," Gina said, grinning now as she went up on her toes to link her arms around his neck.

"The old fraud," Adam muttered, grinning back at her as he lifted her off her feet and swung her in a wide circle. "Remind me to buy your father a drink when we get home."

"That's a deal," Gina said.

"Let's seal this bargain right, shall we?" Then Adam kissed her and felt his world shift back into balance.

* * * * *

Maureen Child's **KINGS OF CALIFORNIA**
continues next month with
Marrying for King's Millions
only in Mills & Boon® Desire™.

THE WEALTHY FRENCHMAN'S PROPOSITION

by
Katherine Garbera

Dear Reader,

Since I was a little girl I've been in love with all things French. I think it's because my great-grandmother, though Italian, spent a few years in a girls' school in Marseilles before coming to America. She spoke French as fluently as Italian. And my grandmother, her youngest child, would sometimes speak to me in French.

During school I took French as my required language, and I sent letters to my grandmother in French. It was our little thing that only the two of us did. My youngest sister took French, as well, and we used to speak in French when we didn't want our other sister to know what we were saying!

My obsession with French men began when I was working at Walt Disney World in Florida. Before Disneyland Paris opened, they sent three young Frenchmen to our office to learn how Disney worked in order to set up the Paris finance office. These men were dreamy. Tall, dark-haired and *very* flirtatious. One in particular used to sit on the edge of my desk and talk to me. I can still hear the rhythm of his words, that accent he had whenever he spoke. So Tristan is an amalgam of these men.

Sheri is a lot like me in some ways. She is used to blending into the background. When she finds herself in the spotlight, she struggles to find her footing. But knowing that she has Tristan helps her find her way.

Happy reading!

Katherine

KATHERINE GARBERA

is a strong believer in happily-ever-after. She's written more than thirty-five books and has been nominated for *Romantic Times BOOKreviews* career achievement awards in Series Fantasy and Series Adventure. Her books have appeared on the Borders bestseller list for series romance and on the *USA TODAY* extended bestseller list. Visit Katherine on the web at www.katherinegarbera. com.

This book is dedicated to Rob Elser
who is my knight in shining armour.

Acknowledgements

I have to acknowledge my children Courtney
and Lucas who were wonderful while I was
writing this book during their summer break.
They were extremely understanding in letting
me plan events for them around my writing
schedule. I know that every mother says she has
the best kids in the world – but I really do!

One

"*Bonjour*, Sheri. Did the interoffice pouch arrive yet? I have sent something special in it for you!"

Sheri Donnelly smiled into the phone at Lucille Dumont's greeting. She loved her job at the Sabina Group. She'd been unsure what the future would hold six months earlier, when the small magazine company she worked for had been purchased by the large French conglomerate. But the change was working out beautifully.

Lucille was Sheri's counterpart at the publishing company's Paris office. Though they'd never met, Sheri always pictured Lucille as a chic Parisian. Partly because of the way she sounded over the phone and partly because their boss, publisher Tristan Sabina, had said that Lucille was nothing like her when she'd asked what his other assistant looked like.

"No, why?"

"I sent you the latest copy of *Le Figaro*." Lucille was a devoted reader of all tabloid magazines. She often sent Sheri the French tabloids and loved to receive the gossip rags from the U.S.

"Tristan hates it when you do that."

"He doesn't have to know. And he's on the cover with a gorgeous woman."

"I might be interested in it," Sheri said. Tristan had become kind of an obsession with her. Not anything unhealthy that bordered on stalking, but more of an unquenchable curiosity. She wanted to know all about him. So far, she'd learned that he was demanding but gave praise easily. Plus he was extremely cute. And a widower.

"I thought you would be."

Sheri grimaced. Was she that transparent, even over the phone? "Was there anything else?"

"Yes. I want to know about the woman. She's a

blond American actress, Kate or Jennifer or something. Do you know if he is seeing her?"

An actress? She'd been jealous of the coffee girl from downstairs whom Tristan flirted with every morning. No way could she compete with a beautiful blond actress. Sheri personified plain and dowdy, two things she knew about herself but had never been able to change.

"I don't have any details," Sheri said, smiling at the office mail guy as he dropped off the pouch. Now she was curious to see exactly what was in there.

"See what you can find out when he gets in to the office. You have the inside scoop on this one."

"I'm pretty sure that Tristan will fire me if I start gossiping about his personal life."

"You are right about that." The deep, velvety cadence of Tristan Sabina's voice made her start guiltily.

She gulped and looked up into his steel-gray eyes. "I've got to go, Lucille." She hurriedly said goodbye and hung up the phone, still holding Tristan's gaze.

His thick brown hair was longer in the front than in the back and his face had the healthy glow that came from spending time outdoors and not on a tanning bed. This morning he wore a blue pin-striped shirt, open at the collar, and a tailored navy suit. The sight of him made her want to stare dreamily, which was *so* not like her.

"Talking about me again?"

"Lucille and I have to talk about you," she said, trying for the cheeky tone she usually pulled off easily. "We're your assistants."

"True, but that did not sound like work."

She shrugged, unable to stop her speculative thoughts. Was he dating a Hollywood starlet? And when had it happened?

"What was Lucille calling you about?" he asked as he reached for his messages, and began thumbing through them.

"Oh, you know how she is, always thinking there's something exciting going on here in New York," Sheri said, looking down at her computer screen and hoping he'd just go into his office. She couldn't look at him and not tell him the truth.

"Ms. Donnelly?"

"Hmm…?" she said, still not looking up. Her computer screen was infinitely fascinating at this moment. *Please let him go away.*

"Look at me." She finally did. "What did Lucille ask you about?"

"I told you," she said, dropping her gaze to his open collar.

"Why will you not look me in the eye?" he asked, his accent very pronounced.

"Because I don't want to lie to you."

"Then do not lie to me."

She shrugged again. The last thing she wanted to talk about was his personal life. *Liar.* "It was something she saw in *Le Figaro.*"

"About me and a woman?" he asked.

She nodded.

He didn't say anything else, just stared down at her, and she started to feel really self-conscious. What if, somehow, he could read on her face that she was attracted to him? What if he picked up on that and it made working for him awkward? What if…?

"You have a conference call with Rene in fifteen minutes, and he just sent a lengthy e-mail that you should at least glance at before you talk to him," she said, holding out a copy of the e-mail, which she'd printed out for him.

For a moment she didn't think he was going to let her steer the conversation back to business.

"You are right, of course," he said, taking the papers.

"I highlighted the topics for you and jotted down the information I had on each one."

"Thank you, Ms. Donnelly. I don't know what I would do without you."

She flushed at the compliment. "You're welcome."

She watched until he walked into his office. She was going to kill Lucille. Not that the other woman could have known that Tristan would arrive while they were talking about him, but still....

She reached for the interoffice pouch and opened it. The magazine spilled out. The cover featured Tristan's publicity shot but inset was another picture. The paparazzi hadn't gotten a very good photo, but he looked very amorous, as did the woman wrapped around him. Sheri traced her finger over the line of his eyebrows, ignoring the headline and just concentrating on Tristan.

She was careful never to stare at him at work, that wouldn't be appropriate, but—

"Ms. Donnelly?"

"Yes."

"Put that magazine away."

She blanched and opened her bottom desk drawer, tossing the tabloid in there. "Was there something you wanted?"

"I need the book for the *Global Traveler*."

"Yes, sir. I think that Maurice has it down the

hall," she said, standing and leaving the office before he could say anything else to her.

Oh, man, this was so not good. Twice in less than ten minutes, he'd caught her slacking on the clock. One of his big no-nos. To be honest, she didn't do a lot of it. But she had a feeling that wasn't going to matter. If she wanted to move up the managerial ladder, perhaps someday become an associate publisher, she'd better not get fired.

She grabbed the book, the big mock-up binder of the issue they were currently working on for their *Global Traveler* magazine, and hurried back to Tristan's office. He was on the speakerphone with his brother, Rene. The conversation was in French and she understood only about every third word they said. Tristan gestured for the book and she handed it to him before leaving the room.

She got back to her desk and saw an instant message from Lucille.

[L.Dumont] Did T walk in while we were talking?
[S.Donnelly] Yes.
[L.Dumont] Did you tell him what we were talking about?

She thought about filling Lucille in but then decided better of it.

[S.Donnelly] I really can't IM right now.
[L.Dumont] OK. Ping me when you can.
[S.Donnelly] Later.

Later, she thought. If she still had a job. She doubted that Tristan would fire her for talking on the phone, especially to Lucille, but she knew he wouldn't hesitate if she gave him enough reason to believe she was more interested in his personal life than in her job.

"Do you need anything else before I go, Mr. Sabina?" Sheri asked right at five o'clock. Not that she had anything really interesting to go home to. But she'd made it a point not to stay late since Tristan had become her boss. She found she liked the office a little too much when only the two of them were still there.

Tristan glanced up from his phone, which he'd been staring at in...amazement? His bangs fell over his forehead, making him look devilishly handsome.

He looked at her assessingly, making her

more nervous. "Actually I do have one more thing to discuss with you, something that has just come to my attention. Please come in and shut the door."

Sheri tried to school her features as she entered the office but guessed she'd failed when he gave her another odd look. Was the tabloid conversation going to come up again?

She walked across the Italian marble floor to the thick Arabian carpet that lined the area in front of his desk. The Sabina Group was a first-class outfit all the way. No cheaply made faux-wood desks or cubicles for their offices. And Tristan's office was a lush as they came. She took a seat on one of the leather wingback chairs that he had for guests.

"Before you say anything, let me apologize for looking at that magazine earlier. Sorry about that. I couldn't resist seeing what Lucille was talking about."

He shook his head. "No need to apologize. I think I let my temper slip a bit when I saw what you were reading."

"Why?"

"The paparazzi are always following me around. They can be a real nuisance," he said.

He sounded almost bored, an air she knew he

used to hide his anger. "You've been making the headlines a lot, lately," she said.

"Our family always has. My grandmother was a famous actress in France, and my grandfather was a director. My family always generates a lot of interest."

"I'm sorry. I wish there was something I could do."

"Well, actually, there is."

"What?" She hoped he wasn't going to ask her to be some kind of paparazzi lookout. "I'm not sure the celebrity photographers who follow you are going to disappear if I ask them to."

"No?" He arched one eyebrow at her in a totally arrogant way, giving her a half smile that melted her brain.

"Maybe you should stop partying," she said before she thought better of it.

His lips twitched and he shrugged one of his shoulders in a very Gallic way. "Unfortunately it is too late for that." He rubbed the back of his neck. "I have a proposition for you, Ms. Donnelly."

"And that is?"

"A personal one."

"How personal?"

"Pretty personal."

"I thought it was important to you to keep things strictly business among everyone at the office," she said.

"Well, this is personal business. What would you say to an all-expenses-paid trip to the island of Mykonos in Greece?"

Her breath caught. "Tell me more," she said.

"One of my best friends is getting married there next week."

She stared at him, confused. "Do you want me to go in your stead?"

"No. I'm asking you to come with me and be part of the bridal party."

Come. With. Him. Oh, God, she wanted to jump up, say yes and leave before he changed his mind. Maybe he had noticed the real Sheri beneath the plain clothing. But she wasn't that naive. There had to be more to this than any kind of latent attraction.

"Why me?"

"The bride, Ava Monroe, is American."

"You know other Americans," she said, thinking of the actress.

"It's short notice and I want to bring someone I am comfortable with. Someone who won't be nosing around in Christos's business."

This wasn't the most flattering invitation she'd ever had. It reinforced something she knew but hated to face. That she wasn't a forever kind of girl. That men moved on, always leaving her behind. Starting with her father, the pattern had repeated again and again over the course of her life. She tried not to dwell on it or mope around, but sometimes she forgot and hoped…hoped that those little-girl dreams of a white knight would become reality.

She still wanted to say yes.

"Christos Theakis?"

"Yes. Do you know him?"

"Only what I've read about Christos and the Theakis heir in the papers." The Greek shipping tycoon had recently come to America and been photographed with a lovely woman and a young boy. The tabloids had speculated that the child was his secret son.

"What did the scandal rags say?"

"Not too much," she said, taken aback by the vehemence in his tone. She should change the subject. "What exactly does this proposition entail?"

He pushed to his feet and walked around his desk. He leaned back against the polished walnut surface, crossing his legs at the ankle.

"I want you to be my date for the week during

the wedding activities. They need a few women to round out the bridal party. The bride has one close friend she has asked, and she and Christos would like the groomsmen to invite the other attendants."

She stared at him for a minute, unsure she'd heard him right. She shook her head and opened her mouth, but no words came out. Then she closed her eyes. "Okay, did you say *date?*"

"That is correct."

Her eyes popped open. "Are you crazy?"

"Maybe. But I am serious about this."

"Serious about taking me to Greece for a week." She crossed her arms over her chest and settled back into the chair.

"Actually, ten days. And I already told Christos that you will be there."

"Shouldn't you have asked me before you started announcing that?" she asked, not even trying to keep the surprise from her voice.

He lifted one eyebrow at her. "I apologize. There wasn't time to discuss it with you. Christos just called to ask me and wanted a name to include in the wedding program. As my assistant, you were the first suitable woman to come to mind."

"Mr. Sabina—"

"Call me Tristan."

She stared at him. "Are you asking me because one of your lovers might get to thinking that marriage to you might be in the cards?"

He shrugged.

"Don't you care for any of them?"

"I care for all of them, but that isn't the point. I've had my once-in-a-lifetime love. Marriage is something I won't share with anyone else."

She'd heard through Lucille that he'd deeply loved his first wife, and that she'd died, but knew few other details. "Why not?"

"That's irrelevant. The only fact that concerns you is that I'd like you to accompany me to Greece for this wedding. It is a proposition, Sheri," he said in that low-toned voice of his. It was the first time he'd said her first name. He always addressed her as Ms. Donnelly.

"Like a business deal?" she asked.

"Yes, exactly. You do this for me and then I do something for you in return."

"What kind of favor?" she asked.

"Any. Your choice."

He seemed to have given this some thought. "I don't know. I'm not really that good at social stuff."

"I'll show you. That will be part of my favor to you."

"I'm still not sure… I can't make a decision like this so quickly."

"There is not much time. I'm leaving at 8:00 a.m. tomorrow on my jet.

"Sheri, I need you," he said, walking over to her and putting his hands on the arms of the chair. He leaned in close, and she shut her eyes as she breathed in the delicious scent of his aftershave.

He needed her. Oh, man, there was no way she was going to say no. Ten days of just her and Tristan… She couldn't resist the opportunity to get him to see her as more than just his assistant.

Two

The marriage of his best friend was a good reason to celebrate but, since Cecile's death, weddings had become painful for Tristan. Still…on this day, with the sun shining brightly in the Greek sky and the champagne flowing freely, he wasn't focused on the past.

In fact, as the reception progressed, he was becoming more and more obsessed with *Sheri*. He'd invited his assistant because he knew that bringing a real date to a wedding always made the woman start looking at him like he had the potential to be a husband.

He wasn't going down the aisle again.

Yet…there was something about Sheri that he found comforting. She was fun to work with, she was pleasing to look at it. Not a world-class beauty, but so unassuming about her looks that it was refreshing to be around her.

But today she looked exquisite. The pale bridesmaid's dress made her skin glow and the subtle makeup that someone had applied to her face gave her an understated beauty that he couldn't keep his eyes from. Seeing her move lithely through the stately, beautiful Theakis home and grounds where the wedding was being held had put her into a new light.

"You're staring at your secretary," Gui said as he came up behind Tristan.

"Am I?"

Gui arched one eyebrow at Tristan but said nothing more. Count Guillermo de Cuaron y Bautista de la Cruz was one of his two best friends, Christos Theakis, the groom, being the other member of their triad. They'd met at boarding school in Switzerland when they'd all been ten, three young hell-raisers who had nothing in common except being second sons, boys who'd grown up with no pressure or expectations.

In their twenties, they'd started a business called Seconds, a string of nightclubs in posh hot spots all over the world. The exclusive clubs were *the* place to see and be seen the world over, and every night the bouncers turned away more celebrities, wannabes and hangers on than they let in.

He heard the husky sound of Sheri's laughter and Lucille's familiar snort and smiled to himself. Lucille, who knew Christos well from working with Tristan for so long, had also flown up for the wedding, and the two women had hit it off in person. He wasn't really surprised, because Sheri was one of those women that everyone got along with, and she and Lucille had already been friendly via the phone.

He didn't examine too closely why he'd asked Sheri, and not Lucille, to be his companion for the wedding.

"You're staring again...are you falling for her?"

"Falling for who?"

"Your secretary."

"You know how I am. She's pretty and available."

"And that's enough for tonight," Gui said.

Tristan shrugged. He didn't like to talk about his attitude toward women. He had two sisters and had been married to the love of his life. If he'd been a different man with a different sex drive, he would have lived the rest of his life as a celibate. A part of him had died with Cecile.

But he had never been able to turn off his attraction to the opposite sex. Six months after her death, he'd found himself starting a string of one-week affairs. Sex was the only thing he'd ever take from the women he became involved with.

He suspected that would not be enough for Sheri. She also worked for him, and that complicated things. He shook his head and signaled the waiter for another glass of wine. The vintage was a very nice one from his family's vineyards.

"Tris?"

"Hmm?"

"She's not like your other women—"

"I know that, Gui."

Gui nodded. "I can't believe that Christos is married."

"It's not the death sentence you think it is." Though he'd never admit it, Tristan envied Gui his attitude. Gui had never been serious about one woman, and he moved through life with a kind of light charm that Tristan admired.

The music changed and a sweet, slow song came on. Couples filled the dance floor with Ava and Christos in the center. They seemed so… He shook his head, not willing to go there.

"I have to go," Gui suddenly said.

"Why?"

"Those men are too old for Augustina," Gui said, acting the protective older brother to his sister, who had been Gui's companion in the wedding party. Tristan bit back a smile as he watched his friend wedge his way between Augustina and her suitors.

He felt a small hand on his arm and glanced down at Sheri. "Having fun?" he asked.

"Yes. I can't believe I was reluctant to come," she said. Her breath smelled faintly of champagne. She held a half-empty glass in her right hand. She tucked her left hand between his arm and body.

She closed her eyes and swayed to the music. Just a little movement and humming under her breath.

"Are you enjoying the reception?" he asked.

"Yes, I am. Ava's so sweet. Thank you for inviting me to join you this week."

"You're welcome. I believe I owe you something."

"What do you owe me, Tristan?"

There was a dreamy quality to her voice. From the first it had been obvious to him that she was attracted to him. But she was careful to keep that attraction to herself and had put a barrier between them. Put him into a box, so it seemed. But tonight…tonight, with the trio playing romantic music and the wine flowing freely, none of that mattered.

"Dance with me, *ma douce?*"

She smiled up at him. "I'd love to."

He had never seen that exact look in her eyes before. "You seem different."

"Maybe that's because we're not in the office."

"No, we are not. What difference does that make to you, Sheri?"

"It makes all the difference in the world, Tristan."

She wrapped her arms around his shoulders and leaned up on tiptoe, brushing her lips against his neck. "This is so nice."

Tristan knew he should pull away and let her go but instead he leaned down, put his hand under her chin and tipped her head up toward his. His lips found hers easily and she sighed into his mouth as their lips met.

The wedding that she'd been nervous about participating in had taken on a certain dreamlike state. The champagne was good. Very good. There really was a difference between that stuff she bought in the grocery store and fine French champagne.

The music was chic and sexy and, as Sheri

leaned closer to Tristan, she realized that he was, too. His cologne was one of a kind and smelled delicious. She'd never get enough of it. Even at work the scent lingered in his office when he was away.

She knew it was partly the alcohol she'd drunk that gave the evening the magical quality that it was taking on as she danced with Tristan, but just this once she felt as if she was woman enough for him.

The right kind of woman for Tristan Sabina, international playboy, her boss and the sexiest man she'd ever danced with.

"What are you thinking?" he asked, his French accent nearly as appealing as the strong line of his jaw.

"About you."

"Really?"

"Um…yes. What are you thinking?"

"That maybe I should pull you closer," he said, suiting action to words.

She rubbed her cheek against his shoulder and closed her eyes. She knew this was another part of the wonderful dreamland she'd been in for the last week. Being on Mykonos was like being in a fantasy world.

Tristan and his friends were wealthy in every sense of the word and, when she was with them, she was living a life that was far removed from everything she'd ever known.

"Okay?"

"Yes," she said, her words a sigh. "Though I thought we'd decided that…um, we'd just have a professional relationship."

"Did we? I think we can both be forgiven for making the most of this moment, on a night like tonight."

She looked up at him, trying to judge if he was sincere, and she saw something in his eyes. Something she'd never seen in them before.

Lust.

Everything feminine in her clenched at that expression. Here was what she'd dreamed of. And how sad was it that she wanted to accept whatever he had to offer?

"For just this night?" she asked, to make sure she understood what he was offering.

"That's all I have in me," he said, but in his eyes she saw the hint of something more.

Some kind of emotion that intimated that he did feel more, but why did she care? Being in Tristan's arms was enough for her. This moment dancing together was better than she'd ever imagined it could be. She kept breathing deeply, trying to imprint the scent of him in her soul. She ran her hands down his shoulders and back, feeling the strength of his body under her touch.

If she were braver she'd press her body closer to his so she'd have the imprint of him against her to recall when she was back in the office and they were simply employer and employee again.

His finger under her chin startled her into opening her eyes and when he tipped her head back and their eyes met, she realized that there was more happening here than just a dance. She saw something else in Tristan's gaze. There was such sadness there, she thought. A kind of pain that she recognized all the way to her lonely soul.

Tristan Sabina, lonely?

The thought was ludicrous.

She shook her head. What the hell was she doing? This was her boss. She pulled back, put a respectable few inches between them, and he let her.

She got the message loud and clear. There *wasn't* more to this than Tristan feeling lonely at the reception and wanting…what exactly?

She tipped her head to the side as he brushed his finger along the line of her jaw. "Why are you looking at me like that?"

"I never realized how beautiful your eyes are."

She caught her breath. She wasn't beautiful and

she knew it. Her eyes were brown. Not the kind of luscious chocolaty color that poets wrote about, just plain brown. She shook her head.

"Yes, gorgeous. I could get lost in them."

"Tristan—"

He rubbed his thumb over her lower lip and her thoughts dissolved. She felt a tingling from that contact that spread down her neck and shoulders. And she realized that the safe little way in which she'd been obsessed with Tristan had turned into a dangerous and exciting attraction.

She knew that he wasn't himself tonight. That Monday morning, when they were back at work, they would return to the relationship they'd always had.

A sane person would turn around, walk off the dance floor and go back to her room.

But she'd been alone in her room for much of her life. In a box of her own making where she was safely insulated from pain. From the men who always left her.

She looked up at Tristan. He stared at her lips. His own parted as he stroked hers. And she wondered if knowing he was leaving, figuratively speaking, after one night would somehow lessen the pain of being left once again.

And she didn't kid herself that it wasn't going to be painful when he left. It was always painful, but being with Tristan…being in his arms and experiencing the things she'd dreamed of since the first time he'd walked into her office…well, that might be worth it.

Wouldn't it?

She didn't know and didn't want to analyze it. For once she wanted to forget that she was a plain-Jane kind of woman. That she was the kind of girl who usually went back to her room alone. For tonight, she was the woman that Tristan Sabina was looking at with lust in his eyes.

He and Sheri danced together for the rest of the evening and once Christos and his bride left, Tristan thought of leaving, too. But he glanced over at Sheri and was unable to walk away.

He drew her back out onto the dance floor, moving their bodies together. Feeling the rightness of the way she fit in his arms and against his body.

If she pulled back, of course he'd let her walk away. He had never had to coax a woman into his bed. But with Sheri, he was tempted. He was tempted to ply her with champagne and kisses.

Kisses.

He'd tasted her lips once, and now that was all he wanted to do. Stroke his tongue over the seam between her lips until she sighed and opened her mouth. Let his tongue sweep into the softness of her mouth. She would taste sweet…of champagne and something else that was uniquely Sheri.

He could not resist. He lowered his head, and she rose to meet him. She moaned into his mouth, wrapping her arms around his neck and leaning up on her tiptoes to keep their mouths together. He held her waist, lifting her against him. He felt the impact of her breasts against his chest and wanted to groan out loud. How could he ever have missed the fact that Sheri was a damned attractive woman?

He pulled back and looked down into those deep chocolate eyes of hers. They were wide and dreamy-looking. She brought one hand from his shoulder to her mouth and traced her lips with her forefinger.

"Sheri?"

"Hmm?"

"Would you like me to kiss you again?" he asked.

"Oh, yes," she said, licking her lower lip and leaning her weight on him as she stretched up toward him.

He bent lower and as soon as his lips brushed hers she opened her mouth and her tongue met his.

Just a soft, tentative touch, and then she made that little moaning sound and he felt the gentle edge of her teeth against his lower lip as she sucked him into her mouth.

He opened his eyes and saw that hers were closed and she was absorbed totally in the moment. He realized things were going too far for a public dance floor. Sheri's burgeoning passion was for him, and him alone.

Damn, he'd never felt this possessive about a woman before.

He lifted his mouth from hers, tucked her head into the curve of his neck and shoulder. Rubbed his hands down her back until he thought he could walk without each step being painful.

The crowd at the reception had thinned. The photographer from the Sabina Group was still there, but otherwise the event was paparazzi free. The guards that Christos had hired had provided an environment where his bride and his guests could relax and not have to worry about being pursued.

"Sheri?"

"Yes, Tristan?"

He couldn't ask her to stay with him tonight, he thought. This was his assistant. The woman he counted on to be cheeky and funny and to keep his

New York office running efficiently. Yet he wanted her, and he wasn't in the habit of denying himself anything he wanted.

"Did you like that?"

"Kissing you?"

"Mmm, hmm."

"Oh, yes. Very much. And dancing with you," she said, her eyes sparkling as she shimmied against him in time to the slow jazz number playing. "Did you enjoy it?"

"Kissing you or dancing with you?" he asked, just to tease her.

"Both."

"Yes."

She arched both eyebrows at him. "Really? I know you're used to more sophisticated women."

"How do you know that?" he asked. He never discussed his private life at the office.

"I searched you on Google. I read the *Post*. And Lucille sends me the French tabloids with pictures of you."

"Why?" he asked, realizing that Sheri was a lot more talkative when she drank. Normally, she'd try to play off her interest in him, but not tonight.

"You're my obsession," she said, her tone airy and breathless.

"Obsession?" he asked.

She flushed and pushed out of his arms. Her hands came up to cover her face. "Oh, my God. I can't believe I said that."

Tristan cupped her elbow and led her from the dance floor. Sheri grabbed a glass of champagne from a passing waiter. Taking a delicate sip, she drew to a stop.

"Will you please forget I said that?"

Not in a million years, he thought. She was totally unique in a world of women who fawned over him. There was a freshness to her. An innocence that he'd never experienced. Not even with Cecile, who'd been ten years his senior.

"Tristan? Did you hear me?"

"Yes, I did."

"And?"

"No, Sheri, I will not forget you said that."

"Why not?"

"Because I like being your obsession. What have you obsessed about doing with me?"

She shook her head and he wondered if she'd back down now. Instead she took a sip of her champagne and smiled up at him. "I'm not sure you're ready to know about that."

"When do you think I will be?"

She shrugged. Her delicate shoulders moved underneath the pretty silk straps of the bridesmaid's dress. "I'm not sure you'll ever be ready."

"Why not?"

"Because of what I said earlier."

"And that was?"

"You're not used to a woman like me."

"*Ma petite,* that I may not be, but I'm definitely ready for a woman like you."

Three

Sheri kept her hand in Tristan's as they walked toward the front of the mansion, where the valet was stationed, to get his car. Suddenly she hesitated, realizing that this was going to change her life. She forced herself to look around and acknowledge that, if she kept walking, her life *would* change.

"Sheri?"

She bit her lower lip, wondering if she was going to pass up the chance of a lifetime. And the answer was…she had no idea. She was torn between what she wanted—the man she'd wanted for so long—and self-preservation.

"Yes?"

"Would you like to stay here?"

No, she thought. But now she couldn't say that she was swept away by the moment. He was putting the onus on her, which was exactly where it should be. Clearly, he was leaving…and the thought of watching another man walk away was too much for her. The decision was made that easily.

She had no idea what the future would hold, but on this night she was going to be with Tristan. And it could only be this night, because she was flying back to the States in the morning.

"Where are you taking me?" she asked.

"My villa."

"You have a villa on Mykonos?"

"Yes. I own property all over the world," he said.

"Why? There's no real reason for you to be here for the magazine."

"One of my best friends lives here. Plus, in the summer, it's a nice place to holiday."

She nodded. "I don't own any property." She was very lucky that her brownstone in Brooklyn was a fixed-price rental. She'd taken over the lease upon her aunt's death.

He arched one eyebrow at her. "Is that important?"

She shrugged and realized that, to him, it wouldn't be. And unless she wanted to ruin the wonderful attraction that was flowing between the two of them, she needed to stop being so mired in who she was.

"It's not. So where is this villa?"

"Not far. Ready to go?"

She nodded.

She started forward but he stopped her with a hand on her arm, drawing her back against his chest. He leaned down and whispered something in French that she couldn't understand and kissed her neck.

Tingles of arousal spread down her body, tightening her nipples and making her breasts feel fuller. He wrapped his arms around her from behind, one hand at her waist, one hand right under her breasts.

She tipped her head to the side to give him better access to her throat. He whispered her name and kept her close to him before biting her softly and lifting his head.

He took her hand in his and led the way out of the building. They waited for the car. Tristan kept his gaze on the night sky. But Sheri couldn't help looking at him and marveling that, for tonight, he was hers.

Tristan Sabina is going to be mine. The future didn't matter at this moment, because she wanted him with the kind of keen longing she'd never experienced before with a man.

He turned to her and lifted one eyebrow as if he were asking her what she was thinking. She flushed and shook her head.

He smiled then lowered his head and kissed her, his lips feathering over hers and his hands skimming down the sides of her body. His fingers brushed against the curves of her breasts and came to rest at her waist, pressing her up into his body.

She liked the way he felt against her. His height made her feel delicate and very womanly. His hands were large enough to span her waist and she felt them wrap around her. Everything else dropped away.

There was just her and Tristan. His lips on hers, his hands on her body and the very essence of him seeping into her cold and lonely soul.

She suckled his lower lip, drawing it into her mouth. His hands tightened on her and his erection brushed against her lower belly. She swallowed hard and pulled back, looking up at him.

She had a little sexual experience, but nothing that had made her feel like Tristan was.

"What is it?" he asked, bringing one hand up to cup her cheek. His thumb stroked her skin and she looked up into his warm gray eyes and felt something shift inside her.

"Why me?"

"Why not you?"

She shook her head and realized that, if she asked questions, she should be prepared to hear an answer that might not be what she was searching for.

But she'd never been a coward, and this night with Tristan…well, she wanted to make the most of it. Be someone she'd never been before.

"Seriously, why are you making a move now?"

"That sounds so crass, *ma petite*. I have no ulterior motive. I have a beautiful woman in my arms and I don't want to let her go."

"I'm not beautiful," she said, because she knew it was true. There were truly beautiful people in the world and she wasn't one of them. She was more apt to be described based on her sterling personality. It wasn't that she was unattractive, it was just that there was nothing that really made her stand out.

"Tonight you sparkle," he said.

She felt her cheeks heat up with a blush. He lowered his head once again, kissing her, and in his arms she realized she did feel beautiful. She felt worthy to be on his arm as they got in his black Lamborghini and drove through the narrow streets of Mykonos.

He kept her hand on his thigh and his hand on top of hers, moving only to shift gears, and occasionally to lift her hand to his mouth to kiss the back of it.

She leaned her head back against the leather seat and turned to watch him. Tristan Sabina…she couldn't believe she was alone with him at last.

Tristan parked the Lamborghini behind his villa and got out. Sheri had her door opened before he got there. He offered his hand to help her out of the car. He saw the surprise in her eyes as she took it.

He realized that no one had ever been good to her in the way that men should be toward women. He wanted to change that, at least for tonight.

When she was standing next to him, he tucked a loose curl behind her ear. He couldn't get enough of touching her. He led the way into his house, tossing his keys on the kitchen countertop and hitting the light switch. She stood awkwardly just inside the doorway. Was this the moment when she'd change her mind?

He wouldn't pressure her into staying, he thought.

Then she nibbled on her lower lip and his entire body went on point. God, he wanted her. Why now?

He'd had a few inconvenient fantasies since they'd arrived here on Mykonos. Away from the office, Sheri had dropped her barriers and started to relax. He'd always liked her cheeky attitude, but seeing her in shorts on Christos's yacht during the week and tonight in this dress that actually fit her…well, it got to him.

He tried to remind himself that she was his assistant and that this was the kind of situation that Rene always warned him against. Fraternization was firmly frowned upon at the Sabina Group, especially by the CEO, Tristan's older brother, Rene.

And frankly, now that she was here in the villa, she seemed nervous. Not at all like the sexy woman he'd held in his arms on the dance floor.

"Would you like a drink?"

"No thank you," she said. "I… Show me your place."

He shrugged out of his tuxedo jacket and tossed it on the bar stool at the kitchen counter. He led her out of the kitchen into a formal reception room and up the stairs to the living room. He'd put on some music and dance with her again. That would relax her like nothing else would.

And he'd have her back in his arms.

"Look at the view," she said as they stepped into his living room. One wall was all windows, showcasing the view of the city of Mykonos and the Aegean Sea.

"It's even more spectacular from the balcony. Would you like to see that?"

She nodded.

He put his hand on the small of her back and lowered his mouth to hers and kissed her slowly. She shifted in his arms, turning to wrap her arms around his shoulders.

Blood rushed through his veins, pooling in his groin. He lifted his head. Her lips were wet and a little swollen from his kisses. "Come, let me show you the view."

He led her outside and the cool evening air surrounded them. She rubbed her hands over her arms. He brushed her hands aside, caressing her and pulling her back against his body.

He kissed her neck and shoulders as she stood still under his touches. Then she turned around and rose up on her tiptoes, taking his mouth with hers. Her tongue teased his and he realized that, though she was a little nervous, she was with him right now.

Wanting him the way he wanted her.

He felt her fingers at his neck, loosening his bow tie and then tossing it away. "Can I unbutton your shirt?"

"Yes."

She did with slow touches. "You have a great body, Tristan."

"How do you know?"

"I saw it in *People* magazine's spread on you last summer. A photo of you at the beach."

He growled deep in his throat when she leaned forward to brush kisses against his neck. Her lips were sweetly shy as she slowly unbuttoned his shirt. Then she nibbled her way lower, and he felt the edge of her teeth graze his skin.

He watched her, his eyes narrowing and his pants feeling damned uncomfortable. Her tongue darted out and brushed his nipple. He arched against her and put his hand on the back of her head, urging her to stay where she was.

She put her hands on his shoulders and eased her way down his chest. She traced the muscles that ribbed his abdomen and then slowly made her way lower. He could feel his heartbeat in his erection and he knew he was going to lose it if he didn't take control.

But another part of him wanted to let her have

her way with him. When she reached the edge of his pants, she stopped and glanced up his body to his face.

Her hand brushed over his straining length. "I guess you like that."

He muttered the French equivalent to the American "Hell, yeah," and pulled her to him. He lifted her slightly so that her breasts brushed his chest. "Now it is my turn," he said.

Blood roared in his ears. He was so hard, so full that he needed to be inside of her body *right now.*

Impatient with the fabric of her dress, he drew it up over her head and tossed it out of his way. No bra. He caressed her creamy thighs. God, she was soft. She moaned as he neared her center and then sighed when he brushed his fingertips across the *V* of her panties.

The cotton was warm and wet. He slipped one finger under the material and hesitated for a second, looking down into her eyes.

They were heavy-lidded. She bit down on her lower lip and he felt the minute movements of her hips as she tried to move his touch where she needed it.

He was beyond teasing her or prolonging anything. He pressed her panties aside, slipping two fingers into her humid body. She squirmed against him.

He pulled her head to his so he could taste her mouth. Her lips parted and he told himself to take it slow, that Sheri wasn't used to him. But one touch and he was out of control.

He held her at his mercy. Her nails dug into his shoulders and she pressed upward. He pulled away from her mouth, glancing down to see her nipples pushing against his chest. She closed her eyes and held her breath as he ran his finger over one nipple. It was velvety compared to the satin smoothness of her breast. He brushed his finger back and forth until she shifted on his lap.

He caressed her back, scraping a nail down the length of her spine to the indentation above her buttocks.

He wanted to give her so much pleasure, because he suspected she hadn't experienced true passion before.

Women were vulnerable when it came to sex. Not just in a physical way, but in an emotional one, as well, and Tristan made it a point to make sure that his lovers knew how sexy and beautiful he found them.

She moaned, a sweet sound that he captured in

her mouth. She tilted her head to the side immediately to allow him better access. She held his
shoulders and moved on him, rubbing her center
over his erection.

Gently he scraped his fingernail over her nipple
again and she shivered in his arms. He pushed her
back a little bit so he could see her. Her breasts
were bare, nipples distended and begging for his
mouth. He lowered his head and suckled.

He held her still with a hand on the small of her
back. He buried his other hand in her hair and
arched her over his arm. Both of her breasts were
thrust up at him. He had been with many women,
but he knew that he wanted Sheri more than he'd
wanted any other woman in a long time. What the
hell? This was sex, not about wanting her.

He wouldn't let this be about anything other
than the physical. One night together.

"Tristan?"

"Hmm?"

"Okay?"

Damn. He didn't want her out of the moment.
"I'm fine. Just enjoying you, *ma petite*."

Her eyes were closed, her hips moving subtly
against him, and when he blew on her nipple he
saw gooseflesh spread down her body.

He loved the way she reacted to his mouth on her breasts. Her nipples were so sensitive, he was pretty sure he could bring her to orgasm just from touching her there.

The globes of her breasts were full and fleshy, more than a handful. He licked the lily-white valley between them, suckling at her to leave his mark. He wanted her to remember this moment, what they had done, when she was alone later.

Soon her hands clenched in his hair and she rocked her hips harder against his length. He lifted his hips, thrusting up against her. He bit down carefully on one tender, aroused nipple. She cried his name and he hurriedly covered her mouth with his, wanting to feel every bit of her passion. He was so hard he thought he'd die if he didn't get inside her.

He glanced down at her and saw that she was watching him. The fire in her eyes made his entire body tighten with anticipation.

Since he'd always prided himself on being a conscientious lover, he knew he should ask about birth control, but that could be a mood killer with some women. So instead he reached for the condom he'd put in his pocket earlier before leaving for the reception. He'd planned to get laid so he could assuage the memories of his own wedding but he'd never anticipated he'd be here now with Shèri.

"Tristan." She said his name with the hint of shyness he'd noticed in her earlier.

"Yes," he said.

"I'm not…really good at this."

"You will be in my arms."

She shook her head. "Don't wait for me to… well, you know. It's hard for me."

"It won't be with me."

"Tristan—"

"Shh," he said, pulling her back into his arms and setting about arousing her again to the point where she would forget that she supposedly couldn't orgasm. Because of her cheeky attitude, he hadn't realized how innocent Sheri was. She seemed like a confident woman, comfortable with who she was, and only here on the balcony with her in his arms did he realize that she was as big a fraud as he was.

"Come to me now."

She reached between his legs and fondled him, cupping him in her hands, and he shuddered. He needed to be inside her now. He eased her panties off then shifted and lifted her thighs, wrapping her legs around his waist as he leaned back against the wall of the balcony. The sky was full of stars and the lights of Mykonos spread out below them. Her hands fluttered between them and their eyes met.

He held her hips steady and entered her slowly, deeply, pulling her down on him until he was fully seated. Her eyes widened with each inch he gave her. She clutched at his hips as he started thrusting. He leaned down and caught one of her nipples in his teeth, scraping very gently. She started to tighten around him. Her hips moved faster, demanding more, but he kept the pace slow, steady, wanting her to come before he did.

He suckled her nipple and rotated his hips to catch her pleasure point with each thrust, and he felt her hands in his hair clenching as she threw her head back and her climax ripped through her.

He varied his thrusts, finding a rhythm that would draw out the tension at the base of his spine. Something that would make his time in her body, wrapped in her silky limbs, last forever.

He turned them around so that she was pressed against the wall, then he tilted her hips, giving himself deeper access to her body. She scraped her nails down his back, clutched his buttocks and drew him in. He tightened, and his blood roared in his ears as he felt everything in his world center on this one woman.

He called her name as he came. She tightened around him and he looked down into her eyes as he kept thrusting. He saw her eyes widen and felt the minute contractions of her body around his as she was consumed by another orgasm.

He rocked his hips against her until she stopped moving. She wrapped her arms around his shoulders and kissed the underside of his chin.

"Thank you."

"For what, *ma petite?*"

"For giving me this night. It's like something out of one of my dreams."

With those words she brought him completely out of himself and into a place he'd been only once before. A place of vulnerability that he'd hoped never to find again.

Four

Tristan carried her back into the villa. Sheri didn't get a chance to look at the place though, as he carried her straight to the bedroom.

He put her on her feet next to the bed.

As she stood naked in front of him, he traced the strawberry birthmark on her right hip. She felt so vulnerable, standing with him looking at her. He'd refastened his pants and his shirt hung open, but he was still essentially dressed and she was naked.

She crossed her arms over herself, one across her breasts, the other over her lower body.

"What are you doing?" he asked, his voice deeper than normal, his French accent more pronounced.

"I'm not…"

"Not what?"

"I look better with clothes on," she said at last.

He shook his head. "Not those baggy frocks you wear in the office."

"You don't like the way I look at work?"

He traced his finger over the edge where her right arm covered her breasts. His finger dipped beneath her arm to caress the upper curves of her breast. "I like the way you look. It is those frumpy clothes you wear that I don't like."

"Frumpy?"

"Yes."

"I'm not good with fashion," she said, not sure why she was telling him this. In the darkened bedroom, with her body still tingling from the incredible orgasms he'd helped her achieve, she felt oddly relaxed. If only she was wearing something. "Why don't you take your shirt off?"

"Would you like me to?"

"Yes, definitely."

He shrugged out of it, and she reached for it before he could toss it aside. She put her arms in the sleeves, but he held the two sides open. "I like you naked."

"I feel too exposed."

"Why?"

She felt more vulnerable now than she had just a second before. She just shrugged.

He didn't say anything else, just bent to trace her birthmark with his tongue. Could he want her again so soon?

She couldn't think as he stood back up and lifted her onto the bed. He slipped off his pants and underwear, then bent down to capture the tip of her breast in his mouth. He sucked her deep, his teeth lightly scraping against her sensitive flesh. His other hand played at her other breast arousing her, making her arch against him in need. Yes, he could.

She reached between them and took his erection in her hand, bringing him closer to her, spreading her legs so that she was totally open to him. "I need you now."

He lifted his head. The tips of her breasts were damp from his mouth and very tight. He rubbed his chest over them as he slid deep into her body.

She moved her hands down his back, cupping his butt as he thrust deeper into her. Their eyes met. Staring deep into his eyes made her feel as if their souls were meeting. She felt her body start to tighten around him, catching her by surprise. She climaxed before him. He gripped her hips, holding her down and thrusting into her two more times before he came with a loud groan of her name.

He held her afterward, disposing of the condom but then pulling her into his arms and tucking her up against his side.

She wrapped her arm around him and listened to the solid beating of his heart. She fought to remember that this was just for one night. Men leave, she reminded herself firmly. But, lying in his arms, she felt as if this could last forever. She burrowed closer to him, holding him tightly to her.

She wished she could say that she understood him better now than she ever had before. But she had the feeling that she'd simply revealed her own weaknesses. Showed how little she felt she was worth.

"Are you sleeping?" he asked.

She felt the vibration of his words in his chest and under her ear. She shifted in his embrace, tipping her head so she could see the underside of his jaw.

"No. Too much to think about." This had been the most exciting day of her life. She felt as though, if she went to sleep, she might wake up and find none of it had happened. He traced his fingertips over her body, starting at her forehead and moving slowly down. She felt him linger on the birthmark, tracing over it again and again.

He tipped her head up so that their gazes met. "Thank you for coming to Mykonos this week."

"You're welcome. I enjoyed it."

"Was the vacation what you thought it would be?"

She pushed herself up on one elbow, looking down at his dark features and tracing her finger over his brows. "I can safely say it wasn't at all what I expected it to be."

"Better?"

"Yes." She paused. "Thank you for wearing a condom," she said. "I'm not on the pill."

"No problem."

It bothered her that he'd had condoms on him. That spoke volumes about the differences in their attitudes toward sex and sex partners.

"I don't think either of us wanted to deal with an unexpected pregnancy."

"You're right." His words were a stark reminder to her that this was a one-night stand. No matter that he hadn't said anything; she could read between the lines. Though his attitude toward pregnancy was one she shared. When she was eighteen, she'd vowed she'd never have children. She'd been too young to make that kind of decision, but the emotions behind it had been real.

Sheri still slept in his arms. Tristan glanced at his watch. They were flying back to the States later this afternoon. Because he wanted to linger, he pushed himself out of bed. He wanted to pull her into his arms and hold her tightly to him so that he knew she'd stay right by his side. And he'd only ever wanted to stay in bed with Cecile.

"Tristan?"

"Right here," he said. He sat on the side of the bed with his back to her, because if he saw her in his bed one more time he'd make love to her again. And he needed to start building a distance between them again. Last night was fine, but this morning he needed to get her dressed and out of his villa.

"Is it morning already?" she asked, leaning up to kiss his shoulder blade.

He shifted away from her on the bed, putting some distance between them.

"Yes."

In the silence that followed, he sensed her confusion.

Her stomach growled, breaking the tension, and he laughed. "Hungry?" He dared a glance at her.

She buried her red face under the sheet. "Yes. I was too nervous to eat last night."

"Why nervous?"

"Ava wanted her wedding to be perfect and I didn't want to screw it up. And Augustina is gorgeous, as is Ava's maid of honor, Laurette. I was the only weak link in the wedding party."

"You were gorgeous, too," he said glancing over his shoulder at her again.

She was this morning, too, with her thick hair hanging around her shoulders. She didn't have a speck of makeup on, but the beauty that he'd somehow never noticed because of her ugly clothes now shone through.

She shook her head. "I'm not, but thank you for saying that."

She wrapped the sheet around her torso and leaned up, embracing him from behind. She kissed the junction where his neck and shoulder met. "Thank you for last night."

To hell with restraint. He pulled her around on his lap. Felt her hips brush his morning erection. He kissed her forehead. "Thank *you,* Sheri."

She hugged him. Just put her arms around him and held him close. And he knew that no matter what happened he didn't want to hurt her. He wanted to believe that he could find a way to make sure she didn't regret being with him.

"Have you thought about doing anything else at the magazine?"

She pushed away from him, sitting on the bed next to him. "I can't work for you anymore?"

He got to his feet and found his pants, pulling them on quickly. "Of course you can continue to work for me. But I wondered if you'd ever considered an editorial job, or sales?"

"Tristan?"

"Hmm," he said without turning to face her.

"Look at me please."

He turned, hands on his hips. "Yes?"

"I don't expect anything from you after this. This was just two people who hooked up at a wedding reception."

He doubted she was aware of how transparent her face was, or how she'd flinched when she said *hooked up*. He scrubbed his hands over his face. The morning sunlight seeped in under the wooden blinds that covered the windows, painting the room in cheery colors. But instead of seeing the promise of a new day, all he felt were last night's regrets.

He knew better than to take Sheri to his bed. She

wasn't like the women he usually dated. "We were friends before this."

"We were acquaintances," she amended. "And we'll go back to being them again. Don't worry about me. I might not be as used to this situation as you, but I can handle it."

He had no doubt that Sheri could handle anything that came her way. She was strong like that. "Very well. Would you like to take a shower while I see about breakfast?"

"You can cook?" she said, with the cheeky grin he'd come to know so well.

He flushed at the way she said it. "No, but my housekeeper can."

"What's on the menu?"

"Whatever you like," he said. Mrs. Thonnopulus was very skilled in the kitchen and he had no doubt she'd be able to fix anything that Sheri asked for.

"Raisin Bran and some coffee would be great."

He nodded. "We'll have breakfast on the balcony. I'll use the guest bathroom down the hall."

She shook her head. "Don't be silly. I can use that one." Then she turned bright red and looked around his room. "I'm going to need something to wear."

"I'll bring in some clothes for you. You wear a size six in the States?"

"Yes, I do. But…whose clothes are they?"

"My sister's." Thanks to Blanche, he had grown up in a household where discussions had routinely centered on fashion. He knew equivalent sizes. "Go and shower. I'll leave the clothes on the bed."

She nodded and tugged the top sheet completely free from the bed, wrapping it around her. She looked small standing there, and vulnerable.

He turned away before he did something else he'd regret, or said something he knew he couldn't possibly mean, because he never dated a woman for more than a week. He usually only took them to his bed for a night or two and then moved on.

Sheri was no different.

He wondered exactly how many times he was going to have to say that before he started believing it.

Sheri stood on the threshold between the living room and the balcony. Looking out, she saw the place where she'd made love with Tristan for the very first time. Her body was sensitive this morning, remembering the feel of him against her—inside her.

She shook her head, trying to force the images

of Tristan making love to her from her head. She wished she could forget him easily. Get the distance she knew she'd need before they were both back in the office on Monday morning.

Yet, at the same time, she didn't want the feeling of having his body inside hers to fade.

Tristan stood by the railing. He was on his cell phone, and he gestured for her to sit at the wrought iron table that was set for breakfast for both of them. He wore a pair of black dress pants and a short-sleeved, casual shirt. He looked suave, debonair, and she felt… Well, even in the sophisticated clothing he'd provided for her, she still felt a bit frumpy.

There was a plate of croissants with jam and butter, the cereal she'd requested but in European packaging with a different name than she was used to in the States, and a small French press coffeepot.

She fiddled with her hair, tucking it behind her ear, waiting for him to look back at her. And when he did, she wished he hadn't. There was too much knowledge in his eyes. It was clear that he knew she wasn't herself this morning.

Tristan put his hand over the phone. "I have to finish this call and I'll join you in a moment."

"No problem. I can take care of myself."

He gave her that steely-eyed look of his, but she ignored him as she seated herself.

"I'll be right back. Wait for me to eat?"

"If you'd like me to," she said, but inside a panic was starting. She wanted to forget about breakfast and get away as fast as she could. She also wanted to linger. Wanted him to be sitting here waiting for her. Maybe kiss her when she'd come out instead of being on the phone.

But that was just more of the fantasy she'd always wanted, and this was reality. One-night stands weren't the beginning of a romance. They were temporary.

Temporary.

Maybe if she said the word enough times she'd start to realize that her reality wasn't with Tristan.

Too bad she remembered the way he'd held her last night even when they were sleeping. There was some kind of closeness between them that she didn't want to let go.

"I would."

She nodded as he walked away. Watch him, she told herself. Watch him walk away and know that he's not the kind of man who'll stay. Temporary, she reminded herself again.

But dammit, she wanted him to be. Last night she realized that she'd been trapped in a box of her own making, that she'd let the men in her life dictate how she moved through life.

Last night she'd stepped outside of that box.

Instead of feeling unworthy of a man's attention, she'd felt as if she deserved to be with Tristan. She wasn't kidding herself that he might be the man for her. Their lives were too different. But he had changed her, and as she poured a cup of black coffee she realized she didn't want to go back to being the woman she'd been before.

It was time she started living.

She took another sip of her coffee and felt that nervous anticipation that came from waiting. It reminded her so clearly of the times she'd sat in front of Aunt Millie's house, waiting for her dad to show up. And he never did.

God, she was pitiful. She pushed to her feet and walked away from the table, taking her coffee mug with her. She went to the railing and looked down at the street. It was crowded this morning with cars and people. Strange for a Sunday.

A man glanced up at the balcony and took a photo. She shook her head, knowing he was capturing the architecture of Mykonos and not her.

She stepped back from the railing so that he could get a better picture.

"Come inside," Tristan said, and something in his tone put her on edge.

"What? Why?"

"We have to talk."

Man, she hoped he wasn't going to fire her. If he did, she could find another job as an executive assistant somewhere else in the city, but starting over was always hard.

"Let's talk here," she said.

"No. Come inside now."

"Why are you—"

"Sheri, inside now."

"Tristan, you can't speak to me like that. I'm not your pet or slave."

"I don't think of you that way. Things have happened. Come inside and I will explain."

"Is it Christos and Ava? Are they okay?"

"Yes, they are fine," he said, reaching for her elbow and drawing her into the living room. He closed the door behind her and then clicked a button on the remote in his hand. The blinds slid slowly down, covering the windows.

"If this is how you always behave the morning

after, I finally understand why women only stay with you for a short while."

"Sheri, this is serious."

"I was being serious," she said, knowing that she had to find a way back to being his humorous assistant.

"You are being cheeky and another time I'd appreciate that, but not right now."

He was starting to scare her. "Tristan, I can… Listen, it won't be weird at work. I'm not going to be all clingy or anything."

"I know you won't be."

"You're going to fire me?"

He crossed his arms over his chest and gave her a narrow look.

"I can handle it, honestly. I just need to know what I'm facing."

"You're not facing anything," he said, tossing her a newspaper. A Greek tabloid. "We'll face this together."

She saw the photo of herself naked in Tristan's arms as they were kissing on the balcony.

Five

Sheri had never wanted to be famous. Unlike other kids who dreamed of celebrity, she'd preferred her natural anonymity, so as she stared down at the newspaper in front of her, skimming the headline written in a language she couldn't read, she saw only her picture.

Her face got hot as she blushed harder than she ever had before. She was going to die. That was it. There was no way she was going to live through this.

It was bad enough that she'd made the highly questionable decision to sleep with her boss. But now the entire world would know… Hell, *Lucille* would know, and she wasn't going to let Sheri forget about this.

"Oh, my God."

"I don't think praying will help," Tristan said in a quiet voice.

"What do you recommend?" she asked, desperately wishing she could go back in time.

He put a hand on her shoulder. It was big and warm and as he squeezed so slightly, she felt a little better. Not much, mind you, with her face and the ecstasy she'd felt in his arms clearly on display for the world to see.

Tristan's expression wasn't visible, as his face was buried in her hair. Her hands shook as she looked at the picture.

"I don't look like myself," she said, tracing a finger over her face. Her eyes were half-closed and she was clutching at Tristan as he kissed her. Thank goodness his broad shoulders covered her naked chest fairly well.

He reached around her to take the paper. "You look like a woman in the arms of her lover."

"Yeah, ya think?" Sheri said, unable to help herself. She wished she could get good and mad. But this wasn't Tristan's fault. It was only that fact that was helping her keep it together. That and the strong belief that if she let go of her control she was going to crumple to the floor and never get up.

"Cheeky is cute, Sheri. Sarcastic is not," he said, his accent very strong and pronounced.

She hated when he did that arrogant thing. Actually it was attractive at times, but right now, while she was grappling with the shock of seeing her scandalous picture in a major newspaper, it wasn't.

"Sleeping with you was fun while it was our little secret," she said, mirroring his tone. "Having the entire tabloid-reading world know about it is not."

"Sheri—"

She cut him off and turned away, walking farther into the elegantly appointed living room. She stood underneath a painting, a large oil by someone famous, she was sure, but she didn't know art. Her aunt Millie's taste had run more to prints of the Brooklyn Bridge than real art.

"Sorry, was that too sarcastic? I'm not used to dealing with the paparazzi the way you are."

"You're right," he said. "This is my mess. I will take care of this."

"How, exactly?" she asked.

"Leave it to me."

"Do they know my name?" She pivoted to

face him. The morning sunlight streamed through the glass doors behind him, keeping his face in shadow.

Tristan lifted the paper and read the article.

"You haven't read it yet?" she asked.

"Not all of it."

"What does the headline say?"

"'Snagged. Elusive bachelor found in love nest.'"

"Oh, my *God*."

"If you're going to pray, you should at least ask for something."

"Tristan, I'm going to ask for lightning to strike you."

"Not a wise course of action," he said.

"You don't think so?" she asked, trying to keep the panic she felt rising inside her from her voice.

He wrapped his arm around her waist and drew her into his body. "I don't. You need me, Sheri Donnelly, and I'm going to get you out of this mess."

This close to him, it was hard to keep the distance she'd been struggling to maintain since she came down for breakfast.

"I can't believe this," she said.

"What?"

"I took a chance last night... Man, I knew that leaving the reception with you was a bad idea, but

I was only thinking about what you might think when you saw me naked."

Tristan drew back and tipped her head up toward his. "What I might think when you were naked?"

"Yeah, you know, stuff like, 'she's a lot flabbier than the women I'm used to....'"

"*Ma petite,* you were perfection in my arms last night."

"You don't have to lay it on that thick, Tristan. I look in the mirror every day and what I see staring back at me isn't perfection."

"Your mirror is not the best. Otherwise you'd never leave your flat in the clothes you wear."

"Um...are you trying to make me feel better?" she asked.

He gave her a quick pat on the backside and stepped away. "I was, smart-ass."

"So how are we going to deal with this?"

"*We* are not. I am."

She shook her head. No way was she going to leave everything to Tristan. Thus far he hadn't exactly been successful in getting the paparazzi off his own tail. And she wasn't like him. She couldn't afford a security detail, or a chauffeur. She took the subway to work and walked seven blocks from the station to her office.

"Tristan—"

"Enough. I said I will deal with it. Trust me."

Tristan wasn't surprised by the flash of temper in Sheri's eyes. But he was surprised that she backed down. She crossed her arms over her chest, and he saw tears gleaming in her pretty brown eyes.

He was angry. At himself for not anticipating that photographers would be bold enough to take advantage of an intimate moment. At Sheri for looking up at him with wounded doe eyes that made him realize he *had* to fix this. She simply wasn't as sophisticated as the heiresses and actresses he usually brought to his bed, and laughing off this kind of scandal was beyond her.

And mostly he was mad at the tabloid that had decided to print this picture. He suspected it was because the publisher, Gabrielle Damienne, was an ex-lover of his and they hadn't parted on the best of terms.

"Sheri?"

"Yes."

"Will you trust me?" he asked.

Distantly he heard the doorbell ring, but knew the housekeeper would answer it. He had the feeling that anyone who came to the door today he wasn't going to want to see.

"I'm not sure."

Was her trust really important to him? She was more than a one-night stand, she was a woman he cared for, but he wasn't going to love her. So was trust really that important?

Yes, he thought. He wanted her to say she trusted him to handle this for her. He wanted to demand it. To make her admit that she would rely on him to handle this media mess.

"You seemed sure last night."

She narrowed her eyes and then tipped her head to the side. "Last night was lust. Surely you knew that."

He felt the burn of her words and that sickly sweet tone she used. He knew he'd been rushing her out the door until he'd seen the paper. He hadn't really cared if she'd picked up on that fact earlier. But now, hearing those words come from her lips…he realized he already cared more for Sheri than was prudent.

She was dangerous because she made him feel way more than lust for her sexy little body, which she kept hidden under the ugliest clothing he'd ever seen on a woman.

Today, dressed in his sister Blanche's blouse

and trousers, she looked...almost beautiful. Actually, the only thing detracting from her beauty were those wounded eyes of hers. She was hurting, and a different man, a man who still had a romantic heart, would soothe her.

There was a rap on the door. "Mr. Sabina?"

"Please come in."

Mrs. Thonnopulus opened the door. "I'm sorry to interrupt, sir, but Count de Cuaron y Buatista de la Cruz is here to see you."

Gui. He must have seen the paper this morning. And Tristan was glad to have his friend interrupt this situation with Sheri, which was going from bad to worse.

"Send him in."

Less than a minute later Gui strode through the door. Wearing jeans and a designer one-of-a-kind shirt, Gui looked relaxed and casual. Not like the aristocrat he was, but more like the second son he also was.

"Ms. Donnelly, Tristan, please pardon my unscheduled visit. But I need a word with you, Tris."

"About?"

"A sensitive matter," Gui said.

"Does it involve the photos of us in the newspaper?" Sheri asked, all blunt American.

Tristan wanted to order her from the room so he could have a discussion with Gui without her sarcasm.

"Indeed. So you've already seen the papers."

"Paper*s?*"

"Reuters picked up the photo. It's in every tabloid I've been able to put my hands on this morning," Gui said.

Sheri started trembling. She turned her back on both men and dropped her head down to her chest. Tristan watched her, knowing she was dealing with the pain and unable to make himself walk across the room and comfort her.

He'd done enough of that this morning. He needed to keep a distance between them.

Gui arched one eyebrow at him and nodded toward Sheri. Tristan shrugged his shoulders and shook his head. Gui rolled his eyes and went to Sheri's side. He wrapped one arm around her shoulder and handed her a snowy-white handkerchief.

And Tristan saw red. It was that simple. He knew he'd just dismissed her, but he couldn't stand to see Gui touching Sheri. She was his. *His.*

He was across the room before he realized he was moving. He nudged Gui aside and pulled

Sheri into his arms. She put her head on his shoulder and he felt the warmth of her tears sinking through the cotton fabric of his shirt.

A wave of total helplessness swamped him. How was he going to fix this? He'd spent the last eight years since Cecile's death moving forward, never stopping to answer questions or challenge the paparazzi that followed him and the scandals he wove effortlessly.

He wrapped his arms around her and held her the way he hadn't held a woman in eight long years. He held her to give comfort. He felt the shackles he'd tried to wrap around his heart shift.

He lifted her face to his, aware that Gui had stepped out to the balcony to afford them some privacy at this moment.

"*Ma petite,* stop your tears."

"I… Yes, I will. It's just, I have no idea how to handle this," she said, sniffling delicately.

Damn those big doe eyes of hers, he thought. He wiped her cheek with his thumbs, brushed them down her face until the tracks from her tears were completely gone.

Step away, he told himself. Comfort was one thing, but kissing her now would be the kind of mistake he was too smart to make.

He'd started to lower his head, wanting to taste her one last time, and she rose on her tiptoes, eyes closing, and leaning into his body. And he knew that for her sake, so that he didn't hurt her any more than he already had, he couldn't kiss her.

So instead he brushed his lips against her forehead and stepped back. He turned away, but not quickly enough to miss the disappointment and hurt on her face.

Sheri had to get out. When Tristan turned his back and walked to the balcony, where she saw Gui waiting, she grabbed her handbag and made a beeline for the door. Enough of staying here. She was clearly not wanted.

And she had experienced more than enough of that in her life. She needed to move. She checked for her hotel-room key and her passport. Both were in her handbag. She also had enough money to pay for a cab.

She wondered if she should take the time to ask the housekeeper to call one for her or just take a chance at flagging one down on the street.

She heard the rumble of Tristan's and Gui's voices and knew that hanging around wasn't going to work for her. She was probably going to cry again, which was a stupid "girl" reaction to the situation, but she was tired. And she'd made love—no she'd *had sex*—with a man she'd been fantasizing about for too long. And now the entire world would know.

The only silver lining she saw was that Aunt Millie was dead and wouldn't see the picture.

She walked down the stairs to the ground floor and paused in the kitchen, looking around and remembering how excited she'd been when she'd followed Tristan through this room.

How very much she'd wanted that man.

And he'd wanted her, she thought. At least for one night.

She opened the kitchen door and stepped outside into a perfect February morning. Or at least, perfect on the island of Mykonos. It was a resort town. A place the trendy visited.

She should have felt out of place all week but there had been something very welcoming in Tristan's group of friends. Ava had made her feel so at ease, but then again the other woman was an American and had somehow recognized the attraction that Sheri felt for Tristan.

"Mademoiselle?"

"Miss?"

"Hey, lady?"

The cries came at her from every corner as a group of photographers moved closer to her. She scrambled backward, reaching for the handle on the kitchen door. She tried to open it but her hands were sweating and she couldn't get a good grip.

She covered her face with her hands, took a deep breath and then opened her mouth and screamed the way she'd been taught to in self-defense class. A deep-throated loud sound that actually stopped the questions that the photographers were throwing at her in every language imaginable.

Asking her name. What kind of lover Tristan was. Did she think she'd finally snagged the elusive bachelor?

The door opened behind her and she felt Tristan's arm come around her waist as he drew her back into the kitchen and slammed the door closed.

She glanced up, thinking to thank him, but he looked so angry. So…not in the mood to be teased. She'd had no idea he could ever look that mad.

"What were you thinking? Why would you leave the house without my permission?" he asked.

She backed away from him but he put his hands on her shoulders and held her in place.

"I want answers, Sheri. This isn't a game. The paparazzi are going to be all over you until this blows over."

"I needed to get away," she said.

"From me?"

She nodded. "I…I like you way too much to be your plaything."

Tristan cursed under his breath, using the few French words she'd become very familiar with since he used them regularly in the office.

"*Merde* is right. I'm trying to be cool about this whole thing but…I'm not ready to this morning. I'm tired and my body still tingles from the last time we made love, and you were pushing me out the door this morning."

She tucked a strand of her curly hair behind her ear and looked up at him from under her eyelashes. His expression was unreadable.

"So I was trying to leave," she said, concluding as quickly as she could.

Tristan turned away from her, leaning back against the wall and crossing his arms over his chest. "First of all, I'm not expecting you to be blasé about sleeping with me."

"Well, that's good. Because I'm not."

He started to speak, but she held up her hand. She couldn't bear to hear him say that she was one of many to him. "I don't expect you to feel the same."

He shook his head.

"I can still feel you on my body, *ma petite.* The remembered feel of your sheath clasping me is making it damned hard for me to let you go."

"Oh."

"Yes, oh. Maybe you don't know quite everything."

She looked down. "I never meant to imply that I did."

He nodded. "Good. Then stop trying to manage this on your own. We need to deal with this together, or else you're going to get hurt."

She wrapped her arms around her waist before realizing what she was doing. The move was a dead giveaway that she felt vulnerable, and Tristan already had seen her with tears in her eyes. She knew him well enough to know that weakness wasn't something he understood.

He was immune to that flaw. And if he wanted her by his side, wanted them to be a team, she wanted to be worthy of staying with him.

This was the first time a man had come after her

and brought her back. The first time a man hadn't walked away from her, or simply let her walk away.

She knew better than to read too much into it, but she felt her heart beat a little faster.

Six

The getaway was simple. Gui, Sheri and Tristan left together via Tristan's dark-windowed Mercedes sedan, which the housekeeper drove to the private airport where the Seconds corporate jet waited for them. They had decided that Sheri would accompany Tristan to Paris and then back to Manhattan instead of getting on the commercial flight straight back to New York that he'd booked for her return.

She'd lost that wounded-doe look and smiled at him whenever he looked at her—which wasn't as often as he would have liked, but ignoring her was the only way he could even pretend to himself that he wasn't starting to care for her.

In that moment when they'd heard her scream, he'd felt fear for another person for the first time in eight years. And the fact that he'd wanted to first protect her and then rip apart the photographers who had threatened her, had been a warning Tristan couldn't ignore.

Despite the fact that he knew Gui was right and the only way to protect Sheri was to keep her by his side, another part of him—the man who'd experienced the crushing blow of losing the only woman he'd ever loved—wanted her far away from him.

"Have you been to Paris before?" Gui asked Sheri.

"No, never. This trip to Mykonos was the first time I've been out of the U.S."

"You should travel more," Gui said. "Tristan, you should make sure that Sheri has the opportunity to see the world. Do you know she still lives in the same brownstone that she was raised in?"

Since he wasn't deaf and the corporate jet wasn't a jumbo one, he'd heard the details of her life as Gui pried into her past. He knew it was Gui's way, but he hated the attention that his friend was giving to Sheri. And hated even more the way she soaked it up. She was hungry for a man to talk to her.

"I heard."

"It's in Brooklyn."

"Thanks, Gui. I know where my assistant lives," he said.

Sheri flushed and he saw her sink deeper into her chair. He'd crossed a line with that comment. He didn't need to put her back into the employee role at this moment.

Gui gave him a sharp look and turned back to Sheri, telling her about his latest escapade with one of his cousins who was at the Spanish royal court.

She laughed, but the sound was hollow and he knew he'd done that. Taken away her joy by being a complete ass. He should apologize but, when she was ignoring him, he knew that they were both moving apart. The way they needed to.

But dammit to hell, if Gui didn't move away from her, he was going to leap across the aisle and strangle his friend. "Sheri, when you have a moment I'd like to discuss a few things with you."

"What about?"

"Work. Our delay in returning to the office will mean rescheduling some appointments."

"Of course. I didn't bring my laptop with me...."

"You can log in on mine," he said.

"Surely that can wait," Gui said.

Sheri patted Gui on the arm. "No, it can't. I don't mind working. It'll give me something to occupy my mind."

Sheri moved across the aisle so that she was sitting in one of the captain's chairs and she turned it to face him. He turned his laptop around on the built-in desk. She leaned forward, a lock of her hair slipping free and brushing against her face.

She concentrated on typing her log-in to the network and then her password.

He leaned back in his leather chair and watched her work. Since this was the corporate jet owned by Seconds, there were three distinct areas. Gui's area, where Sheri had been sitting, was decorated in a classic style very much befitting an aristocrat. There was something quite traditional about Gui underneath his rebel exterior.

Christos's area was modern and sleek. Eschewing anything traditional due to a severe disagreement with his father when he was eighteen, Christos always chose things that wouldn't fit the traditional Greek way of life that his father, Ari, wanted for him.

Tristan's area was a blend of modern and classical. His desk had been handed down to him by his grandfather. It was old, though well polished, and except for two marks, looked to be in perfect condition. There was a small ink stain near the hole where an inkwell was once kept, and under the blotter was a series of initials. Each Sabina who inherited it added theirs to the line.

For all that he was a second son, he wasn't like Christos, who hated his family's traditions. He liked knowing his place in the Sabina line. But then, he had sisters and a large pool of cousins. Christos had recently lost his only brother in a plane crash.

"When do you anticipate being back in Manhattan? You have two video conferences scheduled this week. Rene could handle them in your place."

"I saw those e-mails, too. I think we need to get Maurice on the phone to talk through the book for *Global Traveler*. The new layout is supposed to start in the next issue, and I'm still not satisfied with the changes."

Sheri typed as he talked. He knew she was jotting down notes. He did like how efficient she was. Even before they'd been lovers, he'd liked watching her work. Her fingers were long and elegant. He would have said they were the most attractive part of her, before he'd seen her last night.

Her body was exquisitely formed with generous curves, but not overblown. And she'd been—

"Tristan?"

"Hmm?"

"I asked if a conference call will be fine? We can get the book scanned into a PDF and have it available this afternoon."

"Yes, that is fine," he said, and turned his attention to work. It was the one safe thing they had between them, and he knew that, when they landed at Le Bourget airport in Paris, he'd once more be focusing on the woman and not his executive assistant.

Tristan's sister Blanche waited for them in the chauffeur-driven Mercedes at the airport. Sheri immediately wanted to hide back on the plane. But that was cowardly and she'd... Well, she wasn't going to do it, no matter how tempted she might be.

"*Bonjour,* Tristan," Blanche said, embracing him. She continued speaking in French, which Sheri couldn't follow at all when the speaker was talking as quickly as Blanche was.

It was clear from her tone that she was upset with Tristan and reading him the riot act. Sheri stood in the shadows and watched the two interact. She saw the affection beneath the lecture.

And Tristan smiled down at his sister indulgently. Sheri watched the two of them longingly. She'd always wanted a big family. Not necessarily blood relatives, but a network of people who cared deeply for her and let her do the same for them. It was clear that Tristan had that.

Watching him with Gui and Christos over the last week had given her a glimpse into that world. Seeing him with his sister added another dimension.

"Why are you hiding over here?" Tristan asked, coming back to get her. "Blanche wants to meet you."

She took a deep breath. "I wasn't hiding. I wanted to give you a moment alone with your sister."

"I appreciate that."

"It looked like she was lecturing you. I didn't think you'd tolerate that from anyone," Sheri said, without really thinking.

Tristan smiled, and for the first time she realized that he usually had a practiced smile for business, because this one lit up his eyes. He loved his family, she thought. She couldn't help smiling back at him.

"She's eleven months older than I am and thinks she can boss me around."

"Not many people can do that because of your arrogant attitude."

"Arrogant?"

"Um…I think you know what I mean," she said, blushing a little because she'd never meant to say that out loud.

"I really do not know. Explain it to me."

She shook her. "I'm not myself today. I didn't mean to say that."

Tristan tucked a loose strand of her hair behind her ear. She tried not to react to his touch. But everything feminine in her came to attention. She almost sighed, but that would have been too revealing. So instead she took a deep breath.

"Looks like she does a fairly good job at it. Bossing you around that is," Sheri said.

"Well, she is not the only one," Tristan said, arching one eyebrow at her as he led her across the tarmac toward the waiting car.

"I would never try to boss you around," she said.

"I might let you in bed," he said, and they were at Blanche's side before she could respond.

"Blanche, this is Sheri Donnelly. Sheri this is my sister, Blanche Sabina-Christophe."

Sheri held her hand out to the other woman but Blanche leaned forward and air-kissed her cheek. Sheri did the same but felt kind of silly. Blanche smiled kindly at her.

"Your name is familiar to me. Have we met before?"

"She works for me in the New York office," Tristan said.

Blanche's eyes narrowed as she glared up at Tristan. Sheri took a step back as the affable woman of just seconds before was replaced by someone who definitely resembled Tristan when he was angry.

"I don't think we've had the chance to meet before, Mrs. Sabina-Christophe."

"Please, call me Blanche."

Sheri nodded. There was renewed tension between brother and sister and she had no idea what to say to break it. As Tristan's assistant she was used to stepping in and smoothing over awkward situations but this…there was no way she could interfere.

"Um…I guess you saw the tabloids."

"*Oui*. The entire family is gathering to discuss it."

Sheri took a step backward, longing to hide back on the jet. Even more, she yearned for her small, comforting brownstone. The one place in the world that had always been her constant. The one place in the world where she felt safe.

"Can you give us a moment, Blanche?"

"Certainly."

"Why don't Blanche and I take the second car

and give you and Sheri some time alone on the drive to your parents' house?" Gui said.

"I need to talk to Tristan about some family business," Blanche said.

"I don't mind riding with Gui," Sheri said, thinking that would be the easiest solution.

"I would mind. Blanche can go with him. We need to talk."

Sheri realized that his indulgent attitude toward his sister only lasted for so long. The commanding man Tristan normally was had come back to the surface.

"Tristan—"

"Blanche, this is not open to discussion."

She shrugged in a way that Sheri thought was distinctly French and turned to Gui. "I suppose that will be fine. You must be on your best behavior, Gui."

He lifted Blanche's hand to his mouth and brushed his lips across the back. "With you that will be easy."

"I'd be flattered if I didn't know you were always trying to charm anyone female."

Gui laughed and said, "You always say the nicest things."

"Your ego can stand it."

"Indeed," Gui said, leading her away.

Tristan led Sheri to the car, and she slid inside.

She started to move across the seat to make room for him, but he closed the door behind her and walked around toward the other side. She sat there for a moment feeling as if she'd stepped into someone else's life. And realized that she wanted it.

Tristan wasn't sure that coming to Paris was the best idea he'd ever had. But he needed the resources of his family and he'd wanted to take Sheri to the safest place he could think of. The Sabina house on the outskirts of Paris was just that.

His *grandmère* had been a famous actress in Europe, and his *grandpère,* a director twenty years her senior. They'd had a scandalous love affair that had resulted in a marriage that lasted for fifty years, until his *grandpère's* death. And the paparazzi had hounded them all their lives.

Tristan's mother had grown up with the photographers following her and the world being interested in everything she did. Tristan and his siblings had done the same.

They were used to the attention, but there were times like this when he resented it.

"Are you okay?" Tristan asked, looking at Sheri.

She'd be so easy to care for. Hell, he already cared more for her than he should. But he had to keep his focus, his distance from her, because he knew that she was barely holding herself together and a full-blown affair with him wasn't going to help her.

"I'm fine," she said, but she was clutching her purse to her stomach and staring out the window.

"Sheri, look at me."

"Not now, Tristan."

"Yes, now."

She shook her head and turned her body away from his as if to emphasize her determination.

He simply took her chin in his hand and turned her toward him. She had that wounded look in her big doe eyes again and he felt the impact all the way to his cold and lonely heart. She kept her gaze fixed at his chest.

"What is wrong now?"

"Um…I work for you. Everyone in the world knows I slept with you. Figure it out."

He bit the inside of his cheek to keep from smiling. There was the sassy girl he knew. The one that he'd been attracted to and hadn't understood why.

But now it all made sense. There was a real fire and passion in Sheri that she kept deeply buried.

"What happens between us is our business, *ma petite*."

"That's easy for you to say. Guys will slap you on the back and say, go, you. But everyone will look at me and think…"

"Sheri, please look at me."

She turned to face him fully and lifted those beautiful brown eyes of hers to meet his gaze.

"You are never going to be able to control what anyone thinks about you but you can control how you feel about what happened. Do you regret becoming my lover?" he asked.

She nibbled her lower lip and then sighed. "No. I don't. Being in your arms was incredible."

"Then don't worry about the photos or the press or any of it."

She arched one eyebrow at him. "That'd be a little easier to do if I hadn't met that lot head-on this morning. It was a little scary."

"It is irritating. I will install you at my parents' house and then take care of the paparazzi."

"You keep saying that. And I don't like it."

"What don't you like?"

"You taking care of everything. I'm not some doormat. Despite how I might act at the office."

"You're borderline insubordinate at the office." He smiled to show that he was joking.

"Only borderline? I'll have to work on that," she

said, and he saw the spark of her personality peeking through the sadness that had engulfed her for most of the day.

He knew it was a mistake to want to cheer her up. To care so much about her happiness, and about seeing her smile, but he did. He wasn't going to be able to offer her anything else, so his protection and her happiness were it.

"I'm not above using discipline to keep you in line."

"Like what? You going to spank me?" She shook her head and covered her mouth with her hands. "I can't believe I said that."

Immediately he had a vivid image of her sweet, bare ass as she lay over his lap. He hardened, then shifted to relieve some of the pressure at his inseam.

She flushed, and he knew that he wasn't going to be able to keep his hands off her. He wanted her again. If he'd been able to distance himself in Mykonos, take her to the airport and put her on a commercial flight, it would have been different but now…he was going to have her again.

He needed to get her out of his system.

Seven

As her words echoed between them, Tristan leaned forward, took her face in both of his hands and kissed her. She closed her eyes and surrendered to the feelings he drew from her effortlessly. She'd been craving this for so long. It felt as if a lifetime had passed, instead of just hours, since he'd touched her like this.

She opened her mouth for his tongue, which teased hers. He ran it along the roof of her mouth and then drew back, catching her lower lip between his teeth and suckling her.

She shifted closer to him on the seat, needing more of him. Shivers of desire coursed through her body. She put her hands on his face, touched his jaw and then slid her fingers into his hair.

It was thick and silky. She tilted her head to the side and he drew her even closer to him as his mouth continued to explore hers.

He drew back from her and she opened her eyes, staring up at him. "I can't get enough of you," he said.

"Is that a bad thing?" she asked. Her lips were tingling from the contact with his.

"Of course not. I am French. We live for physical love."

"And romantic love?" she asked, because she knew deep inside that she was falling in love with him. The seeds had been planted long before she'd known him as anything other than an attractive man who was her boss.

"Romantic love…what about it, Sheri?"

"Do you believe in it, or just lust?"

"I believe that we all get a once-in-a-lifetime chance at romantic love."

"Once in a lifetime?" she asked. That sounded good to her. "I believe in that, too."

He gave her a little half smile. She thought about what she knew of Tristan. How he was rumored to still be mourning his deceased wife even though she'd been gone for a long time.

"Did you— Never mind."

"Go ahead and ask."

She knew she was prying, but after all they'd shared, and given the fact that she was vulnerable to Tristan in a way she'd tried to not let herself be to any man, she had to ask.

"Did you have that with your wife?"

He looked at her then, and the expression in his eyes made her realize there were layers to Tristan she might never understand. The pain in his eyes took her breath away.

"Yes."

She nodded. There really wasn't anything else to say. His one-word answer in that monotone told her everything she wanted to know about where this relationship was heading. Ha, she was kidding herself to call it a relationship. It was a one-night stand, except…he'd just kissed her like he wanted her again.

So she had to decide right now. Was she going to be an affair for him? Could she really deny herself Tristan just because he couldn't love her?

"Have you ever experienced that?" he asked her.

"Would I be here if I had?" she asked, careful

not to let on that she suspected he could be that once-in-a-lifetime love for her.

"I guess not," he said, stroking his finger down the side of her face and then down the length of her neck. "Why haven't you?"

She swallowed hard. "I don't know. I don't trust easily."

"But you trust me," he said. "You came to my bed last night."

"It wasn't easy," she said. "But you wanted me...."

"And you wanted me, too."

"Yes, I did."

"Did? And now you do not?" he asked. He traced the scoop neck of her blouse and then moved his fingertip lower, to the upper curve of her breast.

She shifted her shoulders and had to force herself not to follow his touch when he pulled his hand away.

"Do you still want me, *ma petite?*"

"You know I do. One night...it doesn't seem like enough time with you."

"What would be enough time?" he asked.

She doubted a lifetime would be, but she couldn't say that. So instead she shrugged.

He smiled down at her. "I want more time with

you. Are you willing to continue what we started last night?"

She thought about that. Her first instinct was to say yes. But what would that be like? Hell, she was going to be miserable when things ended between them anyway. Now or later…and later sounded much better than now. So…

"Yes."

He smiled at her. "Good."

"You are *so* arrogant."

"You say that as if it is a bad thing."

He leaned over and kissed her so deeply that she knew she'd made the right decision. Tristan might think all he had to offer her was lust but she sensed so much more swirling under the surface.

And he'd stayed, she thought, as she wrapped her arms around those broad shoulders of his and hugged him as close to her as she dared. She wanted to hold him even tighter, but she didn't, afraid he'd realize how much he meant to her. That might be the trigger that finally made him leave.

Rene waited for them under the portico at the side entrance of his parents' mansion. Tristan took one look at his older brother's face and knew that he was facing a long afternoon. And he also knew it was nothing that Sheri needed to be a part of.

His family was overbearing at the best of times. Today, with his face once again splashed on the pages of every gossip magazine, it would be even worse.

"You have two choices," he said, turning to Sheri as the car came to a stop. To the driver he called, "We need a minute, Tollerman, before we'll be getting out."

"Yes, sir."

Tristan curved his arm around Sheri's shoulders and drew her close to him.

"What are my choices?"

"I can have Tollerman take you to the Ritz and you can use the suite I keep there, but there is a chance that the paparazzi will be there."

"For me?"

"No. They wait there for a chance photo of anyone of interest. And I can call and ensure that you have security and can go in the back entrance."

"What's my other choice?" she asked.

"Come inside with me and sit by the pool while I deal with my family."

She sighed. "I'll stay with you."

"Good." He smiled at that. "We're ready now, Tollerman."

"Very well, sir."

The driver got out and opened Sheri's door first. As she slid out of the car, he noticed the way the fabric of her trousers pulled tight across the curves of her butt. The image of her across his lap flashed through his mind again. Dammit, he wasn't into anything kinky as a matter of routine, but he couldn't get the idea of spanking Sheri out of his head.

She glanced back at him just before the door closed and he realized she'd caught him staring. He rubbed his hand against his thigh and she giggled a little. He knew her thoughts were along the same line as his. That she'd found humor now made him feel good.

He climbed out of the car as Sheri came around to his side.

Rene pounced. "It's about time. We need to talk before you go inside."

"Blanche already delivered the news."

"Tristan—"

"Not now. Sheri, this is my brother, Rene."

She held out her right hand and wrapped her left arm around her own waist, something he noticed she did when she felt insecure. He didn't have to be a mind reader to tell that she felt vulnerable now.

It compounded his desire to make her safe. To take care of her. He was good at taking care of people, he thought. He didn't have to love her, but he could make love to her and take care of her until this storm blew over.

"*Enchanté,* Mademoiselle Donnelly. It's a pleasure to meet you in person."

"For me, too, Monsieur Sabina. Please call me Sheri."

"And I am Rene."

Tristan led her up the stairs away from his brother. He sensed she regretted saying she'd stay with him. He didn't give her a chance to change her mind, just ushered her into the house and found one of the downstairs maids.

"Nathalie, please escort Mademoiselle Donnelly to the pool area," he said in French.

"*Oui, monsieur.*"

"There's a cabana stocked with leisure clothing. I'll be a while, so you should eat lunch. Just tell Nathalie what you would like."

She glanced around the large foyer where Rene stood waiting for him and then she took his wrist and drew him aside. "Look," she said. "I think I've changed my mind about sitting by the pool."

"Too late."

"We're not at work. You can't just give orders and expect me to do what you say."

"Yes, I can. And I have. Go relax by the pool while I sort out my family."

"I don't like taking orders in my personal life."

"Too late. I'm a bossy kind of man, which you already know."

"Yes, but I thought—"

He bent and kissed her, because he knew Sheri would keep arguing and he needed to get her somewhere safe before Blanche and the rest of the family came out and started questioning him in front of her.

If he was going to protect her, he needed her safely tucked away.

He lifted his head, turned her toward Nathalie. "Go." He followed his command with a smack on her backside. She gave him a quick glance over her shoulder. "I will now, but this is the last time I'm going to be tucked away while you deal with a problem."

"We can discuss it the next time we're in this situation," he said, fairly confident that they'd never be in this situation again.

She shook her head, and he wondered if she regretted going with him last night. He watched her walk away, trying to make himself regret that he'd taken a nice young woman and put her in this situation, but he couldn't. There was something about Sheri that drew him. For safety's sake, he should back away, but he'd always lived for danger and this woman seemed like a challenge he could handle.

"An employee! Tristan, honestly, you've gone too far this time."

"Rene, it's not as it seems."

"Good luck explaining that to the board."

Tristan felt very much the wayward son as he leaned against the mantel in his father's den. It was funny to him that, outside of this room, he was considered to be a forceful man. Inside, he was always keenly aware that he was his father's son. And that he'd never lived up to the expectations Louis had for sons. Rene did it exceptionally well but he'd been the eldest and the expectations for him had been different than the expectations for Tristan, which were pretty much that he simply stayed out of trouble.

"This can't continue," his mother said.

"Maman, it's not as if I seek out this kind of publicity."

"We know that, Tris. But you have to admit your behavior is out of control," Blanche said.

"Out of control? I'm trying to have a normal life."

"We want you to settle down," his father said. "That's the only real solution to this problem. Until you do, the paparazzi aren't going to lose interest in you."

Tristan shrugged one shoulder. He wasn't marrying again, something he'd promised to Cecile on her deathbed. Their relationship had been so intense, even in those last moments when he'd held her fragile body in his arms and watched her slowly slip away from him.

"The press have always been interested in our family," he said.

"The rest of us don't do anything that gives them a reason to photograph us," Rene said.

"What are you getting at? I can't control their actions."

"That's right, you can hardly control your own," his father said.

"*Père,* I'm grown. I don't answer to you."

"Do you answer to Ms. Donnelly?" Blanche quietly interjected into what would have been a very heated argument between him and his father.

"Why do you ask?" Protecting Sheri had been on his mind since she'd screamed outside the villa on Mykonos. He'd brought her here thinking that together the entire Sabina family could help him keep her out of the glare of the spotlight, but he realized now that he didn't want to leave her in their care. Not that the option of doing that was open to him now.

"Because she's not used to being followed by tabloid photographers, and she works for us."

"Tristan, you slept with an *employee?*" his mother asked.

"Enough. I'm not discussing my personal life with any of you."

"This isn't personal. It's business."

"How do you figure, Rene?"

"If it involves someone who works for the Sabina Group, that does involve us. She's not some heiress used to the paparazzi and she would never have been exposed to them if not for Tristan," Rene said.

"I agree. We're going to have to do something. Maybe transfer her to the London office," Louis said.

"We're not transferring her anywhere. She's always lived in Brooklyn and I don't want her life disrupted," Tristan said.

"It's a little late for that," Blanche said.

Everyone joined in the discussion on what should be done with Sheri and how Tristan should have shown more sense, and he shook his head. He was tempted to grab Sheri and leave. Just walk away from his family and his position at Sabina Group, but he liked the magazine he'd started. And he wasn't a quitter. Never had been, even when the odds were stacked against him.

So he pushed away from the fireplace and waited until everyone stopped talking at once.

"Sheri isn't your concern, Rene."

"How do you figure?"

"She's my fiancée, so I'll be the one to look after her." The words came out of nowhere and stunned everyone into silence. He heard his mother gasp, and Blanche's expression—a cross between disbelief and shock—was comical.

"Fiancée? You're going to marry this girl?"

He felt trapped by circumstances and his own desires. He wanted Sheri and wasn't ready to let her go just yet. But he knew he had to do something to protect her from the tabloid press. As his fiancée, she'd be in the society pages for the right reasons.

He rubbed the back of his neck as he thought of the last time he'd told his family he was getting married. Cecile had been standing at his side, but otherwise the stunned disbelief of his family was exactly the same.

He tried to find the humor in it, but it was diffi-

cult. "Now that everything is settled about Mademoiselle Donnelly, I'm going to my townhome in Paris."

"Everything isn't settled, Tristan. Bring your
fiancée in here so we can all toast the new couple," Rene said.

"And I want to talk to her about planning a
party," Blanche said. "We can do it in conjunction
with the launch of our summer fashion guide. I
think that will be the best way to introduce her
properly to the world at large and as one of us,
don't you think?"

Tristan shook his head. "She doesn't have time
to plan a party. She's my assistant."

"Nonsense, Tris, she's your fiancée now, that
takes precedence."

"No, Blanche, it doesn't. You and Maman can
plan a party for us if you want to, but Sheri will
continue working for me."

"Why?"

"Because that is her desire. That's the reason
we've kept our engagement secret all this time."

Eight

Sheri had changed into a red-and-white maillot and a wraparound sarong. She sat in the dappled sunlight that filtered into the glass-enclosed pool. There was a sense of peace that reminded her of the quietness of her own small backyard garden in Brooklyn, although the indoor pool was heavily landscaped and looked like paradise, while her own garden was little more than a few fruit trees, bare now that it was the middle of February.

Aunt Millie had been a big believer that being

outside could soothe the soul as nothing else could. When Sheri had been upset by her father once again missing a birthday or scheduled visit, Aunt Millie would lead her to the backyard and tell her stories of fairy princesses who lived in the garden under Sheri's bedroom window.

She closed her eyes, reaching out with her mind to her aunt. She wished she could feel Millie's arms around her once again. She was so tired of being alone. Of facing every situation on her own.

She heard the sound of footsteps and glanced over her shoulder as Tristan approached. He looked grim, and she wondered if the paparazzi had followed them and were now camped out on his parents' doorstep.

She stood up. "Is something wrong?"

He shook his head. "Sit down."

She sank back down onto the lounge chair. It was thickly cushioned, probably more comfortable than the old mattress she slept on at home.

"What's up?"

"I've decided the best way to handle the paparazzi is to take charge of the situation."

She liked the sound of that. "Good. Running away seems cowardly to me."

He gave her a faint smile. "You never fail to

amaze me," he said, and for once that arrogant tone she associated with him wasn't there.

"How am I doing that?" She usually glided through life being dependable or invisible. Which, she realized, was why the photographers had shaken her. She'd never stood out from the people she worked with or dealt with on a daily basis. How could she handle the attention of the world?

"By being calm about the photographers and my family. A quick flight out of Greece to Paris hasn't seemed to upset you at all."

It was sweet of Tristan to say that, but she was anything but calm. "I guess we're going to pretend that moment at the airport where I almost bolted didn't happen. And the time when I started screaming in front of the photographers," she said in a teasing tone.

That startled a laugh out of him, and she felt better for it.

"*Exactly.* The solution I propose may sound a bit odd to you at first. But let me explain everything before you comment on it."

"Okay," she said, taking a deep breath. What was he going to say? Well, what could he say? *The board and I think you need to find a new job. And I want you to deny ever being with me.*

His touch on her shoulder startled her out of her thoughts and she looked up into those deep gray eyes of his. She loved his eyes, and had often imagined him looking at her just as he was right now.

"Breathe," he said.

"I am," she said, with a long exhale.

He took her hand in his and held it loosely in his grip. "You have such pretty hands."

Of course he'd notice her hands. Considering she wasn't beautiful like the women he normally surrounded himself with, her hands were probably the only thing he'd found good-looking about her.

He lifted one of them to his mouth and kissed the back of it, then tucked his fingers around it. She smiled at the way he did it…linking them together.

She felt a bit of calm steal over her. This didn't feel like the big brush-off. And she'd had enough experience with being shown the door that she'd know if a man was doing that to her.

In fact, her stomach wasn't a tight knot like it had been the day that her father had sat her down to talk. She realized suddenly that her dreams were still alive. All this time, she'd thought she was a cynic and a realist but, sitting in this beautiful solarium filled with the sound from the waterfall at the end of the pool and the scents of Eden around her, she was holding her breath not because she felt like something bad was about to happen, but because she anticipated something good.

Tristan made her feel like the kind of woman for whom a man would make a grand gesture to keep in his life. And in the car, he'd all but said he wanted to continue their affair. So what could this be about? What was he going to say to her now, in this paradise?

"So what did you come up with?"

"I want you to be my fiancée," he said.

Sheri was sure she'd misunderstood him, because she knew he wasn't the marrying kind, but she thought he'd said *be his fiancée.*

"What?"

"I want you to be my fiancée for the time being. Just until the furor of the press dies down."

She felt the blood rush from her face and closed her eyes. Of course, it was temporary. She had forgotten the one truth of her life—she was meant to be alone.

Sheri pulled away from him and got to her feet. Moving a few yards away, she wrapped one arm around her waist and then a few seconds later turned back to him, putting both hands on her hips.

"Why would I agree to that? That's a crazy so-lution. Who's going to care that we're engaged?"

"The Sabina Group board, for one. They wanted to transfer you to the London office where you could hide out until this blows over."

"Why wouldn't that work?"

"Because I need you in the New York office," he said. He wasn't giving her up. She was one of the only two assistants he'd ever had that didn't an-noy him and actually made him want to go into the office, Lucille being the other.

"I'm still not following why you came up with this solution," she said. She wasn't belliger-ent or demanding, which he would have brushed aside.

"The only thing that will get the press off your back is if we take control of what they are covering. A wedding is the kind of thing they eat up."

She tipped her head to the side and gave him a long, level stare. "So, we're getting married?"

"No, just planning a wedding."

She shook her head. "Do I seem that desper-ate to you?"

"No, you don't seem desperate."

"Well, then why do you think I'd settle for being your pretend fiancée?"

"Because you aren't going to be able to stay here at my parents' house the way I'd hoped. And your home in Brooklyn isn't going to offer you any protection from the paparazzi. They'll follow you from the second you leave until the moment you return. Are you ready to deal with that on your own?"

She shook her head and then turned away from him. He let her have a moment of privacy, but he could sense her weakening and he'd already decided this was best for both of them.

And he wasn't backing down. Sheri was going to be standing in his parents' den really soon, toasting their engagement with a smile that would convince the world that they were the real deal.

He went over to her, touching her shoulders. How he'd never noticed her before last night still amazed him. She had an incredible body. He lowered his head, dropping a soft nibbling kiss against the back of her neck. He ran his hands down her arms and drew her back against his body.

"I want what's best for you, *ma petite*," he said, unable to resist kissing her collarbone.

Her skin tasted faintly sweet, something he'd never noticed in a woman before. But she tasted good to him. And he brushed his tongue against her smooth skin to take a little more of that taste into his mouth.

She shivered in his arms, arching against him, tipping her head back against his shoulder. Her eyes were wide as she looked up at him. So very wide and vulnerable.

Her mouth trembled and he knew she was on the cusp of giving in to him. He leaned down and kissed her. Not softly, but with all the passion inside of him. He kissed her like a man who was hungry for his woman and wanted everything that she had to give.

He broke the kiss only when he needed to breathe and immediately came back to her again, sucking her lower lip into his mouth and drawing on it. She moaned and turned in his arms until he felt the curve of her breast brush his upper arm. Her nipple was hard; he felt it through the fabric of her maillot.

He felt a twinge of conscience at pushing her now. But in the end, he knew what he had to do to take care of her. This was all that was in his control.

"Tristan?"

"Hmm?"

"I... Why don't you want to really marry me?" she asked, her voice so soft it was hardly a whisper.

He closed his own eyes. "I told you I had my once-in-a-lifetime love, remember?"

"Yes, of course I do. But what has that got to do with marriage?"

Tristan turned her in his arms and tucked her up close to his body, trying not to remember how perfectly they'd fit together when making love despite the differences in their heights. Once he'd been buried hilt-deep in her body, he'd felt the perfection of it.

He drew her back into his arms, lowering his head once more, wanting to take her mouth and stop her questions.

But she pulled away. "No more. I want you, but I want answers, too. I don't understand why you won't really marry me."

"It is not you," he said, the words spilling out. "I will never marry again."

"Then why pretend to be engaged?"

He pushed his hands through his hair and turned his back on her. He couldn't look at her and lie. When she'd said she couldn't lie to him, in the office a few short weeks ago, he'd had no idea what she felt like. Now he did.

And he wasn't giving her up. He hadn't gotten Sheri Donnelly out of his system yet and he wasn't going to let her go until he did.

"It's the only way I can protect you the way I want to, *ma petite*."

"Why do I need protecting?"

"Because this is my world and I seduced you without thinking of the consequences."

"You didn't force me to sleep with you," she said, cheeky tone in place.

"I know that, Sheri. But you weren't aware of what it is like to be hounded by the press and I should have taken steps to protect you and your identity from them."

Even if she'd known how things would turn out this morning, Sheri doubted that she would have not gone with Tristan last night. Even now, sitting in a well-appointed formal living room surrounded by the entire Sabina family, she didn't regret her decision.

Tristan sat next to her, his arm resting casually over her shoulders. He toyed with her hair, something he did a lot. Sitting there she felt a sense of rightness all the way to her soul and she knew she'd said yes to his outrageous proposal for one reason and one reason alone. She was going to find a way to make Tristan Sabina fall in love with her.

She was going to do everything in her power to keep this man who'd stayed. And she was coming to realize that Tristan gave her clues all the time about what it was that he enjoyed about her.

If she paid attention, she could be what he needed her to be for him to fall in love with her. It didn't have to be the all-encompassing love that he'd had with his late wife. She'd be satisfied with just some kind of deep caring from him.

She settled into the curve of his body as Rene lifted his champagne flute and said something in French that she couldn't understand. Tristan squeezed her shoulder and lifted his own flute. So she did the same, taking a delicate sip of the delicious French sparkling wine.

Tristan leaned closer to Sheri and whispered directly in her ear. "Rene said that he wishes us happiness and laughter all the days of our lives."

She smiled up at him. "Well, I want that, too."

Tristan's eyes narrowed a bit but he dropped a quick kiss on her nose. She realized that he was going to fight her the entire time. Try to keep her in the role of pretend fiancée. And the only way she was going to get him to think of her as anything else was to make him need her.

He needed her body, but was sex enough? Could she hold him with sex when she'd never really tried to keep any of her previous lovers…? Okay, there hadn't been that many, but she had to look at it from a historical perspective.

Blanche stood up next. Tristan's sister made Lucille look like a country bumpkin. She was simply elegant and sophisticated. She spoke in a sweet tone, smiling indulgently toward Tristan.

Again the toast was in French. Tristan didn't lift his glass this time. Instead he put it on the table and stood up, leaving the room without a comment.

Sheri felt awkward. "I'm sorry, my French isn't good enough to know what you said."

Blanche shook her head. "I just said that we were happy to see him moving past the pain of heartache and moving into a new love."

But the way they were all staring at her, she realized they knew what she'd known all along. That Tristan wasn't in love with her. It was fine for the two of them to know that lust was all they had between them. But his family…

"I'm not the love of his life," she said.

"I'm not so sure about that, Sheri. You're the first woman he's brought to meet us in eight years."

Sheri took small comfort in that. "Will you please excuse me?"

"Of course. If you are looking for Tristan, try the third floor. Fourth door on the left."

She left the room without another word. Walking slowly through the house, she was reminded again that there was a huge difference between her and Tristan. This one—the material things—didn't seem as big a deal as their difference in willingness to love.

Tristan was such a dominant, arrogant man, she had a hard time imagining that he was afraid of anything, especially falling in love again.

But those rumors about his first marriage... about his first wife... She needed to find out exactly what she was up against.

She climbed the curving staircase, looking at the huge portraits hung on the walls. Pictures of men who resembled Tristan, and some portraits of people who were vaguely familiar to her. His famous grandparents, she thought.

He'd grown up surrounded by a rich history, whereas she had only what she took with her. Aunt

Millie's warm memory and the cold emptiness of her father's desertion.

She got to the third floor. At the landing there was an upholstered chaise centered under a dominant portrait of the Sabina siblings when they were younger...probably late teens, she thought.

Blanche was seated in the center and Rene and Tristan stood on either side of her. Blanche was elegant even as a teenager, smiling beguilingly out of the portrait. Rene was serious and even then looked as if he were all business. And Tristan. Her heart caught in her throat. He was laughing, very much the rebel in his casual rock T-shirt, whereas his siblings were dressed to the nines.

She had never seen an expression like that on Tristan's face and she thought that this is the part of him that died when his wife did.

She reached out to touch his face, letting her fingers hover over the curve of his mouth. It felt like what she'd done so many times in her apartment late at night. Lusting after a man she couldn't have.

And now that she had the Tristan she'd thought she wanted, she realized he only was giving her half of himself. The part he thought she'd accept without question.

And she knew now she wanted more. She was

falling in love with Tristan Sabina, and she wasn't going to be satisfied with merely keeping him from leaving.

She needed him to fall in love with her. Not just to care for her, but really fall head over heels in love. She turned to walk down the hall and saw the gilt-framed mirror and the reflection of the woman there.

She was going to have to make some serious changes if she was going to win Tristan's love.

Nine

Two weeks later, Sheri wasn't sure who she was anymore. Despite the fact that Tristan wanted their lives to remain the same, they had been changed by the "engagement." Blanche had even taken her shopping before allowing her to leave Paris. And Sheri had enjoyed her time with Blanche.

She found herself interested in clothing for the very first time. Standing in front of her closet in the brownstone in Brooklyn, she realized that it might be a bit small. It never had been before.

But then, she'd never had a closet full of outfits

for every type of event known to man. She'd turned into a socialite without even trying. She was exhausted, because Tristan had been extremely serious when he said that he still wanted her to work for him.

Her phone rang while she was in the middle of getting dressed in a Chanel linen-and-cashmere strip tunic that ended well above her knees, showing off her trim calves and ankles. She'd never really thought about her body, but Tristan's lovemaking and comments left no doubt that he liked hers. Her legs were slim because she'd always lived in the city and walked everywhere.

"Hello?"

She was getting better at accessorizing, but had been keeping the outfits put together the way Blanche had arranged them for her. Trying to make Tristan fall in love with her, trying to remember how to be fashionable and avoiding the paparazzi were a lot to add to her life. Most of the time she felt as if she was juggling and dropping most of the balls.

"*Bonjour, ma petite.* I'm downstairs in the car waiting for you."

"Good morning, Tristan. I'm almost ready."

Propping the phone between her ear and shoulder, she paired the tunic dress with a pair of lizard-

and-lambskin sandals and a calf-skin belt in white with a distinctive Chanel belt buckle. She had a chunky bracelet that she put on her right arm and then she carefully opened the box with the diamond watch that Tristan's parents had given her as an engagement present. They'd had her initials and the date of their engagement—the date she and Tristan had made up—engraved on the back.

"This would be a lot easier if you'd just move in with me."

"No, it wouldn't."

"Why wouldn't it?"

"Because then I'd have to move out again when the engagement was over. This way, I'll never have lived in your house."

"Or slept in my bed for an entire night," he said.

She always came back home after they made love at his apartment. And he never stayed the night at her place. She was doing everything she could to insulate herself against the pain of heartbreak, but she had the feeling that no matter what she did, it was still going to hurt her if he left.

"Well…"

"Well, what? Why are you so stubborn about this one thing?"

"Because I'm your pretend fiancée, Tristan. If

I were really your woman and you were going to claim me in front of the world, then I'd be living with you in a heartbeat."

He said nothing, as she'd suspected he would. "I'll be down in a minute."

She hung up the phone and turned back to the mirror. Her dark brown hair now had highlights and she knew how to put on makeup so that she looked like all the other women who had always surrounded Tristan. A part of her was amazed at how she looked, another part disgusted. She was changing every part of herself for a man who was her *pretend* fiancé, and she was no closer to figuring out how to make him fall in love with her.

She stared down at the engagement ring on her left hand. Tristan had wanted something big and flashy but she'd stubbornly refused. If he really loved her and was buying her a ring that symbolized his love, she would have bowed to his wishes, but he'd been buying the ring for others to see and she had dug in her heels.

She liked the understated platinum ring she had on. It fit her hand and her finger. And unlike a more costly ring, it didn't make her feel as if she'd sold herself to Tristan.

The clothes she knew she'd donate to Dress

for Success when she was done pretending to be his fiancée—if she didn't turn the pretend part into reality.

"Why did you hang up on me?"

She yelped and spun around. Tristan stood there, gorgeous as always. "Why are you in my house?"

"You gave me a key, remember? I am your fiancé."

She made a face at him in the mirror. "Just for pretend."

"Sheri."

He said her name in a stern tone that told her she was pushing too hard. But she didn't want to back down. She was tired of pretending, and the only way for that to stop was for Tristan to see her as more than a lover and an assistant. She was pretty sure that's all he saw when he looked at her.

"What?"

"What is the matter with you this morning?"

She shrugged. If he'd demanded an answer or kept pushing her, she could have gotten angry and then used her anger to keep the truth at bay.

"Answer me. Please."

"No."

She reached for a pair of platinum bangle earrings and slipped them into her ears. Tristan came up behind her, rested his hands on her shoulders and leaned in low so that his gaze met hers in the mirror.

"What is wrong?"

She bit her lower lip, afraid of saying too much. But suddenly she realized that the changes she made were all superficial and deep inside she was the woman she'd always been. And that woman wanted more.

"I don't want to be your fake fiancée. And frankly, I can't understand why this isn't real."

Tristan would be damned if he was going to have this conversation with her. He'd been dodging the same questions from Gui, who had warned him that toying with a woman's emotions was only going to lead to trouble. And Christos, who didn't know the engagement wasn't real and thought that he had made a great decision. Since Christos's marriage to Ava, the man thought all anyone needed to be happy was a wife.

But Tristan knew better. He wasn't toying with Sheri's emotions, and he sure as hell wasn't going to really marry her. He knew himself well enough to know that there were only certain things he could control. And surprisingly Sheri was one of them.

He bent his head to nibble on her neck in the spot he knew was sensitive. She undulated under his hands and reached back to put her arms around his neck, turning her head to the side until their lips met.

He hated not waking up with her every morning. He suspected that was why he still wasn't ready to move on from her. He had yet to spend an entire night with her, save for that first one on Mykonos. And he hadn't appreciated it then.

"I thought you were in a hurry this morning," she said, turning in his arms.

"Just to see you." Her dresser surface was clear except for a small jewelry box. "Are you wearing panties?"

"Yes," she said. "I tend to wear them when I'm going to work."

"Take them off."

"Ask me nicely," she said.

And Tristan leaned down to take her mouth with his, kissing her slowly, thoroughly. He caught her earlobe between his teeth and breathed into her ear as he said, "Please."

She shivered delicately, her hands clenching on his shoulders before she stepped back half an inch. "Okay."

She tugged the short hemline of her dress higher

and lowered a pair of whisper-thin white cotton panties. She balanced herself by putting one hand behind her on the dresser as she stepped out of her underpants.

The movement thrust her breasts forward. The high, round neck of her tunic didn't show nearly enough of her chest for him. He reached for the belt at her waist and unhooked it, letting it fall to the floor.

He lifted her up on top of the dresser and pushed her tunic dress to her waist. She parted her legs and he groaned her name. Blood rushed through his veins, pooling in his groin.

She continued smiling up at him as she leaned back on her elbows. "Was this what you had in mind?"

"Almost," he said, pushing her dress even higher until her breasts were bared to his gaze. The bra she wore had thin lacy cups and he could see the distended nipples peeking through the lace. He leaned down and licked them both.

Her legs shifted restlessly around his hips. Though it had been just last night, it felt like an eternity since he'd last held her in his arms.

He'd been aroused since he'd entered her house. She reached up and pulled his head down to hers. Her mouth opened under his and he told himself to take it slow, but slow wasn't in his programming with this woman. She was pure feminine temptation and he had her in his arms. He slid his hands down her back, finding the clasp of her bra and undoing it.

He grasped her buttocks, pulling her forward until he was pressed against her feminine mound. He felt the humid warmth at her center through the fabric of his pants and reached between them to caress her. She shifted more fully into him.

The fabric of her dress, bunched under her arms, just covered her breasts as she breathed heavily. He saw the hint of the rosy flesh of her nipples and lowered his head, using his teeth to pull the loosened fabric away from her skin. He ran the tip of one fingertip around her aroused flesh. She trembled in his arms.

Lowering his head he took one of her nipples in his mouth and suckled her. She held him to her with a strength that surprised him, but shouldn't have.

Her fingers drifted down his back and then slid around front to work open the buttons of his shirt. He growled deep in his throat when she leaned forward to brush kisses against his chest.

She licked and nibbled and made him feel like her plaything. He wanted to let her have her way with him, but there was no room here, no time for seduction or extended lovemaking.

He pulled her to him and lifted her slightly so that her nipples brushed his chest. Holding her carefully, he rotated his shoulders and rubbed against her. Blood roared in his ears. He was so hard, so full right now that he needed to be inside of her body.

He caressed her creamy thighs. God, she was soft. She moaned as he neared her center and then sighed when he brushed his fingertips across the entrance to her body.

The area was warm and wet. He slipped one finger into her and hesitated for a second, looking down into her eyes.

She bit down on her lower lip and he felt the minute movements of her hips as she tried to move his touch where she needed it.

He was beyond teasing her or prolonging anything. He needed her *now*. He swept her dress over her head and tossed it on the floor. She shrugged out of her bra and he lifted her off the dresser, turning her to face its mirror.

"What are you doing?" she asked, looking over her shoulder at him.

"I want you to watch us as I make love to you."

She murmured something he didn't catch. "Bend over slightly, *ma petite.*"

She did as he asked, her eyes watching his in the mirror. "Take your shirt off, please. I want to see your chest."

He smiled at her as he shrugged off the shirt she'd unbuttoned. His tie was tangled in the collar, but he managed to get them both off. He took out the condom he'd put in his pocket this morning and donned it quickly.

"Hold on and keep your eyes on mine in the mirror."

"Yes," she said.

He covered her with his body. Their naked loins pressed together and he shook under the impact.

He cupped her breasts in his hands then slipped one hand down her body, finding her wet and ready. He adjusted his stance, and then entered her with one long, hard stroke.

She moaned his name, still holding his gaze. He bit softly at her neck and felt the reaction all the way to his toes when she squirmed in his arms and thrust her hips back toward him.

A tingling started in the base of his spine and he knew his climax was close. She writhed more frantically in his arms and he moved deep with each stroke. Breathing out through his mouth, he tried to hold back the inevitable. He slid one hand down her abdomen, through the slick folds of her sex, finding her center. He circled that aroused bit of flesh then scraped it very carefully with his nail. She screamed his name and tightened around him. Tristan pulled one hand from her body and locked his fingers on the dresser over her small hand, then penetrated her as deeply as he could. Biting down on the back of her neck, he came long and hard.

Their eyes met again in the mirror and he knew that he wasn't going to find a way to live without her while he kept making love to her. And that meant he needed to come up with another plan. Something that didn't involve her being his pretend fiancée.

Ten

Two weeks later Sheri was still no closer to getting the answers she wanted from Tristan. But plans for the engagement party were going forward. The Paris branch of the Sabina Group was prepared to launch a new magazine on weddings and was using their engagement party as the first big glamorous event they'd cover. She'd promised Tristan that she'd stay with him until the engagement party was over.

A part of her worried that what she'd found with him was going to end too soon. Another part was afraid that it wouldn't end soon enough.

The one thing she didn't doubt was that she was in love with Tristan.

"Sheri, have Maurice come to my office in ten minutes."

"He's going to want to know what you need to see him about."

Tristan glanced up from the folder in his hands. "I'm going to fly your suggestion for the Travelogue column at the back. See if we can use celebrities instead of travel writers."

"Really? It was just an idea to boost readership."

"I know. I like it. I'll make sure that Maurice knows you came up with it."

She smiled. "I don't care about that."

Tristan leaned one hip against the side of her desk. "What do you care about?"

"World peace," she said, completely deadpan. She didn't want to have a serious discussion at work, but this was the only time when Tristan really opened up to her. It was almost as if he knew she'd only let things go so far in the office.

"*Ma petite,* are you going to leave me for a beauty pageant?"

"Not my scene."

"I know. This is your scene, isn't it?"

She nodded. "Working with you suits me to a tee."

"Just working?"

"Well, we don't live together."

"And whose fault is that?" He sounded almost huffy.

"Yours."

"Mine? I asked you to move in with me."

"More like ordered." She smiled. Take that.

"It didn't do me a lot of good."

"You wouldn't want a woman who just said yes to your every whim." That she knew.

"Try me."

"Try you? How?"

"Move in with me. Stop making me take you back to Brooklyn every night."

"What would change if I did that?" She was so tempted to say yes. Had been since the first time he'd told her to move in with him.

He leaned in close. "We'd be together all the time."

"But just temporarily."

"Is that what's stopping you from saying yes?"

She wasn't going to answer that question. She'd have to reveal too much of herself, too many things she'd long kept hidden. She glanced down at her computer screen and clicked on the instant messenger button to summon Maurice. The sooner they had someone else in the office, the better it would be for her.

"Sheri?"

"Hmm…"

"Look at me."

She glanced up.

"I want to know why you haven't moved in with me. The truth this time."

She folded her hands together on her desk blotter and then pulled them apart. "It is the temporary thing."

"I don't understand how it's any different if you move in with me," he said.

Sheri pushed her chair back from the desk and got up, walking around so that he wasn't leaning over her. "The difference is I've never lived anywhere but that brownstone."

Tristan stood up from where he'd been leaning against the desk. "The brownstone is your home."

"Yes. It's my home. It's the one constant I've had in my life since I was eight, when my mother died and my father dumped me at my aunt's, and, as you pointed out, what we've got going is only temporary."

Tristan didn't say anything else and Sheri wanted to curse at herself for letting the conversation get so personal. She really tried to be cool and breezy whenever she talked to him. Always tried so hard to keep her emotions bottled up and a secret from him.

"Is that it?"

"No…I'm also afraid that, if I move in with you, I'll start to buy in to the fantasy you've written for us. I might start to really believe that I'm your fiancée, and that would be devastating for me when you leave."

"All relationships end."

"How do you figure?"

"Even the strongest and most loving relationships end with death. So no matter what, everything is temporary."

"Tristan, that's sad."

"What is?"

"That you view life that way."

"It's realistic, Sheri. Hell, if you were to admit it, you see things the same way."

She shook her head. "No, I don't."

"Even though you won't leave your little brownstone?" he asked.

"That's different. I don't see relationships as temporary. I see them as unbalanced."

"I'm not following."

Sheri crossed her arms over her chest and stared at Tristan. His eyes were misty gray today because of the shirt he had on. He was so handsome, sometimes she worried that he'd wake up to the fact that there were a million gorgeous women in the world who'd gladly be his pretend fiancée and do whatever he asked of them.

"My reality and that brownstone are tied together. I see relationships as unbalanced because I've always been the one to care more than everyone else. And in the end, they've all left me behind."

Tristan didn't say anything and she felt like an idiot for revealing what she had.

"I'm going to run down and get Maurice."

She walked out of the office and down the hall, trying to pretend that nothing had changed, but knowing that everything had.

At the end of the day Tristan was tired. Sheri had made excuses to be away from her desk for most of the afternoon and he'd let her. There was work to do and he didn't need the distraction that she presented.

But in the back of his mind all he thought about was what she'd said about people leaving.

He thought in terms of temporary because his life had always been in constant change. The only thing he really counted on was his friendship with Gui and Christos.

And even that was changing, with Christos's marriage. He was happy for his friend, but at the same time concerned for him. Christos had never allowed himself to love a woman before, not the way he was in love with Ava. Tristan hoped they had a lifetime together, but his experience had taught him that they probably wouldn't.

There was a knock on his door.

"Enter."

The door opened to reveal Sheri. "I need your signature on these papers before I leave for the night."

She was all business. Until this afternoon, he hadn't realized how much of her personality she hid when she was in the office. It was only because of the last three weeks, when he'd seen so much more of her, that he now knew that.

She handed him a folder and he opened it up. He glanced at the papers and realized he wasn't reading them, so he closed the folder and pushed it aside.

"Please have a seat, Sheri."

"Is something wrong?"

"Yes. I have decided that I can't allow you to

continue living in Brooklyn. I have arranged for you to move into my place immediately."

She shook her head. "We've had this discussion."

"Exactly the problem. You need to be living with me." The engagement was working exactly as he'd hoped it would. The tabloid press was being very kind to Sheri and everyone he knew was excited for him. For the first time since Cecile had died, he felt as if his life was on the right path. He wasn't just running and trying to keep distance between himself and his life. And Sheri had given that to him.

And their conversation earlier had made him realize that he hadn't done the same for her. And that was not acceptable to him. Though he would never admit it, he liked the feelings she evoked in him. He knew they couldn't be love, because they felt nothing like the emotions he'd had for Cecile. But he did care for Sheri, and her happiness was important to him.

She nibbled on her lower lip. "What did I say that made you think that I'd agree to this?"

"It was what you did not say. Our engagement has given you a chance to change things about yourself. And I realized today that they were all surface changes. You need to move out of that brownstone if you are ever going to see yourself in a different light."

"Tristan—"

"No, listen to me. I know what it is like to be stuck in one place."

"That's a complete lie. You never stand still. How could you possibly know what I'm like?"

"That's precisely why I know. I have been always focused on the future to keep from dwelling on the past. Whereas you just stay there, stuck in time."

"I'm not sure you're qualified to be talking to me like this."

"Qualified?"

"Yes, qualified. You don't really know me all that well."

"I know you intimately, *ma petite*."

"So did two other men and they didn't have a clue about what made me tick."

He hated the thought of anyone else having been with her. She was *his*. He didn't know exactly when he'd started thinking of her in those terms. But he did now. He wanted to tell her that he'd be the last man to know her intimately.

Where the hell had that thought come from?

"Those men weren't me. And I'm not taking no for an answer on this."

She stood up and walked over to him. She pushed her finger into his chest. "You're being a bully."

"No, I'm not. I'm being a man and taking charge."

"This is the twenty-first century, in case you'd forgotten. A time of compromise and 'working things out.' Women don't need a man to take charge," she said. The flash of temper in those big brown eyes of hers made him hard.

He was so tempted to lean down and kiss her. But she lifted her hand and put two fingers over his lips. "No, Tristan."

"No?"

"Don't kiss me, because then we'll be making love and I'll find myself living with you."

"I do not see the problem. You like making love with me, and you are going to be living with me either way."

She shook her head. "I don't want to live you."

"Give me one good reason why."

She wrapped her arms around her waist and took two steps back from him. "I…well, let me just say that I have a really good reason and leave it at that."

He crossed his arms over his chest and arched one eyebrow at her. "That might work if you had plied me with sex, but since you declined…I'm feeling stubborn."

She just stood there, and he wondered if he was pushing too hard. Why was this so important to him? He wasn't one hundred percent sure, but he guessed he wanted everything that Sheri had to give. She gave so willingly of her body, but she kept a tight rein on her soul. On the secrets that she guarded for herself. And he hated that there was a part of her that he didn't know. He wanted to know everything about her. He wanted to possess her completely.

"Tell me."

This had been the longest day of her life. And the most stressful. She had no idea what was going on with Tristan, not that she ever really had. She only knew that if he wanted to know what was inside her head, then they were both in trouble.

Tell me.

He wasn't asking nicely, he was demanding. And when it came to Tristan, she had absolutely no willpower. She wanted him to know her secrets because she loved him. Because no matter what her mind tried to tell her heart...her heart still believed that if he knew all her secrets, he'd fall for her, too.

Which was so stupid. He was the man who'd told her that all relationships were temporary. That all relationships ended. And heck, she knew that. Everyone she'd ever cared about was gone. Even Aunt Millie, through death, just as Tristan said. Though that's where she and Tristan differed. She knew the difference of having lived a life with someone you loved in it and having that person taken from you in death, versus having someone leave you because they couldn't love you.

"Why is it important to you? Why do you care?"

"Because I'm not the type of man who would let my fiancée live in another house. I would want her in my bed every night."

"You'd want *her* in your bed every night?" she asked.

"I want *you* in my bed every night. I want to wake up in the morning and see your face."

Suddenly Sheri wasn't sure what she knew any-more. Was Tristan simply afraid to admit his feelings for her? She knew he wanted her. No man had made love to her as often as he had. No man had ever said the things he did to her, whispering in her ear about how sexy she was and how much he wanted her.

But a part of her was afraid to believe it. She simply wasn't the kind of girl who inspired that feeling in a man like Tristan. Yet now, here he was, saying he wanted to wake up with her every morning and… "Tristan, I want that, too."

"Then why won't you move in?"

She looked at him. Just stared at the face that had graced the cover of more magazines than she'd ever dreamed of. And realized that at some point in time, he'd become so real to her. The Photoshopped perfection of those magazine photos wasn't the man she loved. *This* was the man she loved.

The man with a small scar under his left eye. And five-o'clock shadow on his jaw. The man who looked at her with exasperation at times, but always with honest emotion. Even if she couldn't always identify that emotion.

The man she loved.

"I haven't wanted to move in with you, because I love you, Tristan."

He took a step back. His arms fell from his chest and he looked at her as if she'd surprised him.

What had he expected?

"Should I not have said that?"

He shook his head. Then rubbed a hand over his forehead. "I was not expecting that."

"You weren't? Everyone knows how I feel about you."

Sheri felt so incredibly vulnerable right now.

She wrapped both arms around herself, holding herself as tightly as she could.

"Everyone?"

"Well, Ava noticed, and she hardly knows me at all. I'm pretty sure Lucille knows. She picked up on it the first time we spoke on the phone. Even your friend Gui knows. And I didn't have to tell him, either, he just guessed."

She didn't expect Tristan to love her back. Oh, man, what if that was what he was afraid of? "I don't expect you to love me."

He shook his head. "I don't believe in more than one love in a lifetime."

"I know that. I think that's part of the reason I love you so much. I want to fill up that emptiness you have."

Tristan walked over to her then. He took her shoulders in his hands and drew her toward him. His mouth came down on hers, heavy. He kissed her so deeply and with so much passion she couldn't help but respond.

She wrapped her arms around his shoulders and simply held on to him. He was in complete control and he made Lucille forget everything. But she felt so much more now. It was as if, in admitting her love for him, she was finally free to let go of all the barriers she'd been keeping between them.

His tongue brushed hers and she moaned deep in her throat as shivers of awareness spread down her body. She moved closer to him. Needed to feel his body pressed up against hers.

Tristan lifted his head. "Thank you for loving me."

She couldn't help but smile at the polite way he said that. "You're welcome."

He brushed a strand of hair from her face and stared down at her with such seriousness that she felt a pang deep inside.

"There isn't a lack of love in my life, *ma petite.* There is a burned-out hole where my heart used to be, and I'm afraid no amount of love will ever bring it back."

Eleven

"I'm home," Tristan said as he walked into his apartment a little after ten o'clock one week later. He'd had a late dinner meeting and, for the first time since Cecile's death, he was coming home late not to servants and an empty house but to someone.

Sheri came down the hallway with a book in one hand and a pair of reading glasses on. She smiled at him. "How was it?"

"Not too bad. I think we will be launching a cooking magazine in the early fall next year."

"Good. I think that's great. Do you have any meetings you're going to need me to set up?"

"Yes, but I do not want to talk about that tonight."

Her smile turned suggestive. "What do you want to talk about then?"

"My woman."

"*Your* woman?"

She was sassing him and he had to admit he enjoyed it. He'd been unsure what living with Sheri would be like, but after the first night he'd realized that he made a good decision. He'd made love to Sheri twice last night, and then again in the morning before they'd left for work.

Having breakfast and then heading into the office together underscored to him what a great companion Sheri was. She suited his life perfectly. And the fact that she loved him made it all the sweeter.

"Were you waiting up?"

"Sort of."

"Why?"

She shrugged and he was starting to realize that's what she did when she didn't want to answer. It was her way of not lying about anything, of hiding when she felt that answering would leave her vulnerable.

"Will you come into the kitchen with me?" he

asked, shrugging out of his jacket. He hung it in the hall closet and then loosened his tie.

"Yes," she said. "Are you hungry? Mrs. Ranney made a pie."

His New York housekeeper was a whiz in the kitchen.

"Did you have any?" he asked, following her down the short hallway into the kitchen.

"No. I wasn't hungry earlier."

"Will you have a piece with me?"

"Maybe a small slice. I try not to eat after seven."

"Why?"

"Because unlike you, I don't work out every day."

"You could," he said, settling at the breakfast bar while Sheri moved around the kitchen. She found plates and cut them both a piece of pie. She was more at ease in his house than he was.

"You don't need to work out, *ma petite.* You look lovely as you are."

She arched one eyebrow at him. "Really?"

"Honestly. You have a sexy little body that I can't get enough of."

She blushed and smiled at him. "Then I should keep doing what I've been doing, and that's not eating late at night."

"Milk, coffee or some kind of after-dinner drink?"

She leaned over the breakfast bar to slide his plate in front of him. He took her chin in his hand and kissed her long and slow. Now he felt as if he was home. The home he found in her eyes and in her arms.

She pulled back, looking bemused, and he smiled inside. He loved that she was so guileless about how attractive she was and about the effect she had on him.

She turned away, grabbing a napkin and fork for him. "Did you want a drink?"

"Yes. Milk, please."

She poured him a glass and then brought her plate around to his side of the counter and sat down next to him.

He realized he wasn't interested in food. He'd forgotten what it was like to have a woman in his home. To have a woman take care of him.

"Mrs. Ranney said that strawberry-rhubarb was your favorite."

"It used to be."

"Do you want me to get you something else?" she asked.

"Yes."

She started to hop off her stool, and he lifted her up and settled her on his lap. "What are you doing?"

"Having something sweet."

"I didn't realize I was sweet."

"You're tongue is sharp, but your kisses, *ma petite,* they are very sweet."

"So are yours," she said. She wrapped her arms around his shoulders and held him close. "I missed you tonight. Your apartment is so big. I felt very lonely without you."

Lonely. That was a word he'd learned to ignore for a long time.

He thought about the future, and for the first time he realized he was *looking* at the future. One that he wanted with Sheri. Not as his wife, because he'd already given his name to the one woman who'd owned his heart.

But he did want her to stay with him. Wanted Sheri to be in his life, and not just at work.

"You're staring at me," she said. "Why?"

"Because I like the way you look at me."

"Ah, ego. I should have known."

He just shook his head. Then kissed her one more time, because he couldn't resist her mouth when it was this close.

He lifted her in his arms and carried her down the hall to his bedroom. Laying her in the center of his bed, he came down over her, bracing his weight on his forearms so that there was a small gap between their bodies.

"I want you to live with me."

"I am living with you," she said.

"I mean, even after the engagement party and my family goes home."

"Am I here for them?" she asked.

"No, *ma petite*. You are here for me, and I'm asking you to stay."

Sheri held her breath as Tristan lowered himself over her. She would never say it out loud, but she loved the feel of him on top of her. It made their relationship real when, after they made love, she'd wrap her arms and legs around him and just hold him, pretending she never had to let go.

But now, she thought, she might not have to let go. She didn't know what he meant by asking her to stay, but it sounded positive. She couldn't believe she'd waited so long to move in with him. Granted it had only been for a little over a week. But their lives had meshed together.

She liked living with him. For the first time in her entire life, she felt like she was in the place where she was meant to be with the man to whom she belonged.

"What do you mean?"

"That I want you to stay with me, and not just as my temporary fiancée. I want this to be permanent."

She felt a rush of joy and she tipped her head back, blinking so he wouldn't see the tears in her eyes. She took a deep breath and felt the gentle stroking of his finger against the side of her cheek.

"So what do you think?"

Her gaze met his and she tried to read the emotions there, but as always she had no idea what he was feeling. But she knew what *she* felt. She loved this man. She wanted nothing more than to say she was his and live the rest of her life with him.

"I think yes. I'd love to spend the rest of my life with you."

He gave her a tight smile and kissed her. "Great."

"Great? That's all you can say?"

"It seemed more appropriate than 'get naked.'"

She laughed and hugged him tightly to her. "Get naked would work."

"Really?"

"Yes!"

He laughed then, and she felt a sense of rightness deep down in her soul. In that empty part that had been hollow since her father had left all those long years ago.

He started to unbutton her blouse and she put her hands in his thick hair, rubbing the back of his scalp as he undressed her. She thought of the wedding plans she'd put off making, because planning a wedding she wasn't going to follow through with had seemed like torture. But now she could stop putting off Blanche and really start thinking about the kind of bride she'd be.

"When do you want to get married? I know we'd been putting off picking a date because of the pretense, but now that we're going through with it things are different."

Tristan stopped unbuttoning her blouse and lifted himself off of her body. "Married?"

"Isn't that what you meant, Tristan? If we're going to live together permanently..."

He pushed completely off her and sat on the edge of the bed, his back to her. And she realized he hadn't meant marriage. "What were you thinking?"

"That we'd live together," he answered.

"What's the difference in living together and being married?" she asked. "Everyone already thinks we're engaged."

"I don't give a damn what everyone thinks. We both know that we aren't really engaged," he said, glancing over his shoulder at her.

She shook her head, fiddling with the ring he'd given her, and realized that her shirt was unbuttoned and she was still laying in the middle of his bed. She sat up and quickly refastened her shirt.

"I don't know what to think anymore," she said, climbing off the king-size bed. "I never know what to expect from you, Tristan."

"I do not understand," he said.

And for the first time, she realized that he really didn't understand what she was talking about. Because Tristan was always looking out for himself. For his own desires, his own safety. She had been thinking that because he showered her with attention and gifts, he was caring for her.

"I love you. Do you remember that?"

He stood up and walked over to her. He touched her so softly, tracing the lines of her face with his fingertip. "I do remember it. Hearing you say you love me is something that I think about a lot."

"And…?"

"And that's why I want us to continue living together."

She staggered back away from him. "Did you ask me because you feel sorry for me?"

He shook his head. "I asked because I'm tired

of being alone. And you bring something to my life that I never thought to find again."

"Love," she said. "I bring love to your life."

"No, you bring that to yourself. To me you bring companionship and friendship…an end to the loneliness I've felt when I'm around other couples."

She didn't know what to say. Because she had the feeling that he'd asked her to live with him out of pity. She realized for the first time that her father had done her a huge favor by leaving. Because Tristan staying with her out of guilt or pity made her feel worse than being left behind.

"What are you going to do?" Tristan asked Sheri. He could tell that things weren't going the way he wanted them to. If there were a way for him to go back ten minutes, he would have kept his mouth shut.

"I don't know what I'm going to do. Obviously I gave you my word that I'd stay with you until the party and that's…in two days, right? So after the party I'll move back to the brownstone."

He knew he shouldn't be mad at Sheri. But he was. If she wasn't so stuck in her bourgeois American idea of what a relationship should be, then he'd have everything he wanted. "Running back to your favorite hiding place?"

"I'm not running," she said, crossing her arms around her waist and staring up at him with those big wounded doe eyes.

But this time he didn't let the eyes affect him. He knew better. She was as manipulative as the other women he'd dated. The ones that had always wanted to be Mrs. Tristan Sabina and had schemed to get there. Sheri was the same, she just went about it differently. "It sure seems that way from where I'm standing. You said you loved me, and now that I won't marry you…you're going back to the same place you've always run to."

She dropped her arms and stalked over to him. "Well, you'd know all about running. Of course, you hide out in the public eye. Dating a bunch of different shallow women. Acting like nothing in life affects you."

Tristan couldn't argue with that. "What do you want from me?"

"I don't know."

"Don't hedge, Sheri. Tell me what you want. How can I make this right for you?"

She turned away and then glanced back at him. "You could love me."

He didn't know how to answer that. "I'm...I can't do that."

She nodded. "Then you have nothing I want."

She walked to the bedroom door and he realized that she was leaving. That she was going to walk out that door and he wasn't ready for her to go.

"Sheri."

"Yes?"

"I really want you to stay."

She looked back at him. "I want to. But for the first time in my life, I realize that I can't keep settling for the least bit of attention. You changed me over the last few weeks. Made me into a different woman. And the one constant through all of that is how much I love you.

"But tonight, I realized that loving you isn't enough for me, and it's not fair to you. You need something more. Something I can't give."

He didn't know what she was talking about, but could tell that it made a lot of sense to Sheri. "Are you leaving tonight?"

"No. I gave you my word I'd stay through our pretend engagement party."

"Very well. Thank you for that," he said, gathering his facade around him. He always knew how to put on a good face. And it wasn't like he really loved her. She was his *pretend* fiancée. "I'll sleep down the hall."

"Okay."

He walked out of his bedroom. In the wide, long hallway he heard her footsteps behind him. "Tristan."

He looked back.

"I thought you were different," she said, her voice sad and low but still audible.

"Different how?"

"I don't know, just different from the other men in my life."

"I am sure I am different."

"On the outside you are very different. But inside, you're the same."

"Same how?"

"Hollow and empty. Unwilling to let your guard down for a second and accept the gift of my love."

Her words were heartfelt, and to be honest, he did feel an ache deep inside at her words. He'd thought for a long time that he wasn't exactly the man he used to be.

"I have a full life. After you break our engagement I will be back to my busy schedule and the life that I have become accustomed to."

"That doesn't mean that you're happy."

He saw the tears in her wide brown eyes and

knew he was going to remember that look on her face for a long time.

"Happiness is a fool's notion."

"No, it's not. Unless you think it's foolish to take a risk. To put yourself on the line. And I know you don't, because you take risks every day in business. At the Sabina Group, and with the nightclubs you own with Gui and Christos. It's only in your personal life that you refuse to take a chance."

He pivoted on his heel and walked back to her. "Studying me in magazines and tabloid stories does not mean you know who I am and what makes me tick."

"No, it doesn't," she said. "What makes me an expert is having fallen in love with you. And living with you this week has shown me a man that few people really see. I do know the real you."

"Do you? Who is the real me?"

She took a deep breath and looked up at him. In her bare feet, he felt like he towered over her. "The real you. Are you sure you want to know?"

"I asked, did I not?"

"That's right. You did. Well, the real man I've seen, Tristan, is a coward. Someone who's felt a deep pain, and I'm not discounting that. But because of one loss, you've cut yourself off from ever loving again. And that seems cowardly to me."

Tristan didn't answer her, just walked away. And this time he wasn't coming back. He wasn't a coward, and he wasn't about to let Sheri Donnelly use those words to make him do something he knew he'd regret.

Twelve

Sheri left early and arrived at the office before Tristan. He called from the limo and asked her to join him going to the airport to pick up his family. She made an excuse about being too busy, and he let it go.

She knew she would have to see him again tomorrow night at their engagement gala, but until then she was hiding out. She had never had a broken heart before. She wished she could fall out of love with Tristan, but it simply wasn't that easy.

He'd been the embodiment of every romantic

fantasy she'd ever had. The lover she'd always wanted. He'd made her feel as if she was the sexiest woman alive, and the pleasure he'd evoked in her body was beyond even her wildest fantasies. And the way he'd taken care of her… The way she'd felt when she was with him…

Working and living with Tristan had made her believe she'd found the other half of her soul. That she'd brought things to his life that had been lacking, and he'd done the same for her.

She put her head on her desk and realized that she wasn't going to be able to stay on here at the Sabina Group. There was no way she could sit in this office every day and pretend that she wasn't still in love with Tristan.

It was well after six and she was still working. She was scheduled to meet Tristan and his family and friends at Del Posto for dinner at eight-thirty. After calling Tristan a coward, she couldn't stand him up.

Her phone rang.

"Sabina Group, this is Sheri."

"Sheri, this is Palmer at the security desk. There is a Count Guillermo de Cuaron y Bautista de la Cruz here to see you."

"To see *me?*"

"Yes."

Why was Gui here? "Please send him up."

"I will."

She hung up the phone and pulled her mirror out of the bottom drawer of her desk, thinking she should fix her makeup, then realized she hadn't put any on this morning. She'd reverted to the old Sheri. She needed the comfort of her big comfy clothes and her plain appearance. There was a lot to be said for not being noticed.

"Ms. Donnelly, I'd like a word with you." Gui strode into her office like he owned it. But he stopped in his path and put his hands on his hips, cursing succinctly under his breath. She caught about every other word, since his Spanish accent was fairly heavy. "What the hell is going on with you and Tristan?"

"I think you should ask him that question. I'm taking care of some last-minute things here at the office. I think we're all meeting at the restaurant for dinner."

He shook his head. "I already talked to him, at the airport. And I came over here to find out what has happened between the two of you."

"Ask him again."

"I thought the problem was you."

She glanced up at Gui and realized there was a bit of truth in what he'd said. "The problem *is* me."

Gui shook his head. "How is it you?"

"I want things from him that he can't give me."

"Love?"

"How'd you know?"

"Because I know Tristan, and that's the one thing he thinks he cannot offer you."

There was something about Gui that made her want to pour out her soul. Something so understanding in those hazel eyes of his. "I think it might be me. I'm not the kind of woman who inspires that in any man."

"Don't say that, Sheri. Tristan wasn't always the man you see before you today."

"He wasn't?"

"He was badly hurt when Cecile died. He used to be the most gregarious of all of us. So filled with a big joy for loving. And then when Cecile was diagnosed with cancer…he thought they'd beat it at first. He put his entire life on hold to stay by her side."

Sheri ached to hear his words, but they mirrored what she already knew. Tristan had told her himself that he couldn't love anymore. That he'd had his once in a lifetime. It was just her bad luck that she had found *her* forever-love in him.

"I know all that. I thought I could love him enough for both of us. But that was silly, and now we're both moving on."

"I'm not sure that you haven't changed him, Sheri. He's a different man today than he was at Christos's wedding, and that's thanks to you."

"I doubt that. I'm not the type of woman who can change a man's life."

Gui sat down on the corner of her desk. "Yes, you are. Don't give up on him yet. Will you give him one more chance?"

She shook her head. She couldn't bear the pain of losing him again.

The phone rang, but it was after hours so she let it go to voice mail. "Why do you care?"

"Because Tristan is one of my dearest friends and you've made him happier in the last few weeks than I've seen him in years."

She was afraid to believe him. But at the same time, she knew Gui wouldn't lie to her. "I'm afraid to take another chance on him. I just made up my mind that he wasn't going to stay with me."

"You strike me as a fighter, Sheri. Someone who wouldn't let the chance of a lifetime slip away."

She looked up at Gui and realized that he was right. She was letting go of Tristan too easily. She loved the man, and that wasn't going to change. Shouldn't she keep fighting for him?

Sheri's absence was palpable to Tristan as the day drew on. Blanche and Rene had a lot of questions about her, and the more he talked with his siblings about her, the more he realized how much he cared for her.

When they got back to his place, he waited for Sheri to come and greet them but she must still be at the office, hiding from him. He felt the emptiness in a new way. Echoing around him.

Gui had been shocked by how he looked. When Tristan had mentioned that the engagement was definitely off, Gui had left in disgust to run an errand. And Tristan realized that his plan to make Sheri his fake fiancée hadn't been well thought out. He'd never considered how he'd feel when she left his life.

Blanche had nothing but good things to say about Sheri and Tristan found himself laughing at the stories she told about shopping with the woman he'd been trying to keep out of his heart for the last few weeks. As he pictured her in his mind, he realized he hadn't done a very good job of it.

He loved her. How could he not have realized

what he was feeling for her? The only excuse he had was that it was different than the sweet and gentle love he'd had for his Cecile. With Sheri the love was bigger than he was, passionate. And that's what had him running scared.

Dammit, she had been right when she'd called him a coward. He had been running from her, because he'd been afraid to risk being hurt again.

Realizing that, he knew he had to make things right for her. Had to find a way to win her back before she had to face his friends and family tomorrow night at the engagement gala. He wanted it to be a real celebration, otherwise what was the point?

He called the office, but Sheri's phone went to voice mail. He hung up without leaving a message. He had no idea when she was going to show up, or even where she was. But he did know she'd come to the restaurant for dinner. Because she always kept her word.

And that was another reason he loved her. She wasn't fickle or shallow. She couldn't tell a lie to him. Her love would never leave him, or let him feel betrayed.

He knew he needed to do something to show Sheri that he was serious about her and that he wasn't running away any longer. And he knew it would take more than the hour he had until he was supposed to start meeting his friends and family at Del Posto. He went and found his mother.

"Maman?"

"*Oui,* Tristan."

"I need your help."

"With?"

"I've hurt the woman I love and I need to make a big gesture to make it up to her, but we have reservations at a restaurant across town."

"How can I help, *mon fils?*"

"Be my hostess while I take care of a few details here. And when Sheri arrives, keep her there."

"Where will you be?"

"Taking care of details," he said, kissing his mother on the forehead.

"Okay, I'll do this. Are you sure about this girl? You always swore love was no longer in the cards for you."

"*Oui, maman.* I am more than sure. She's reawakened a part of me I thought was dead."

His mother smiled at him and then hugged him tightly. "I'm so glad to hear it. A part of me has long wept for that deadness inside you."

After his family left for the restaurant, Tristan made several quick, demanding phone calls.

Knowing the kind of romantic person Sheri was, with her secret dreams of how love should be, he arranged for flowers to fill the apartment. He ordered the finest French champagne sent up from his wine cellar and then called his favorite jeweler for a necklace. When the flowers arrived, he decked out the balcony to resemble the one at his villa that night in Mykonos. Now he had every detail he could think of in place—except for Sheri.

His mobile rang. A quick glance at the caller ID window showed him it was Gui. "What's up, Gui?"

"Where are you?"

"My place. Why?"

"Because Sheri is at the restaurant turning heads, but she's asking where you are. You need to get down here."

"I'm on my way. Don't let her leave."

"I won't."

Tristan's driver had him across town in no time at all. He walked into the restaurant and stopped in his tracks. Sheri wasn't sitting quietly in a corner the way she had during many of the activities that week back on Mykonos. Instead, she was in the center of his family and friends, wearing a stylish dress and holding court. He couldn't move as his heart skipped a beat.

This was what he'd been afraid to let himself see. That Sheri was the other half of his soul and he needed her more than he'd ever expected to need any woman. If she left him… God, he couldn't even go there in hypothetical. He needed her.

How could he have thought he'd be able to survive without her in his life?

He walked up to her and all the words he'd rehearsed escaped him. He saw her flush as he looked at her. He wanted her and he was sure she knew the signs of his arousal well enough by now to tell that. But he wanted more than just her sexy little body. He also wanted the joy in her eyes, the witty, sassy mouth of hers. He wanted it all.

And he didn't want to tell her in front of the world. She deserved to hear about how he felt for her the first time in private. Where he could do a proper job of it.

"Tristan?"

"Hmm?"

"Are you okay?"

He shook his head. "I'm tired."

"Well, I'm sorry to hear that," she said.

"Don't you want to know why?"

She nibbled on her lower lip. "Okay, I'll ask. Why are you tired?"

"Because I've been running for too long."

"What have you been running from?"

"I've been running from you, *ma petite,* and that has to stop." He reached out and snagged her wrist. "Please excuse us," he said to his family.

"Not so fast. We want to hear more about this running you've been doing."

"Forget it, Rene. My private life is supposed to be private. Isn't that what you've been telling me?"

"Indeed," Rene said.

Christos and Ava stepped in between Rene and Tristan to say hello. They looked wonderful together, smiling and happy and…loving. Tristan clapped his hand on his friend's shoulder, thanking him for flying in and promising to see them the next day. Then he drew Sheri away from the crowd and toward the exit.

"Why are we leaving? You just arrived."

"I need to be alone with you."

Tristan didn't say much in the car ride from Del Posto to his apartment, but he held her hand the entire time, rubbing his thumb against her palm and bringing her hand to his mouth several times to kiss it.

She wondered if simply changing her attitude

had changed his, but she knew that couldn't be it. Something had happened to Tristan, too. He was acting so different. When they got to his apartment building, he held her hand all the way up in the elevator and then made her close her eyes when they got to the front door.

"Why?"

"Because I said so."

"And I'm going to do this why?" she asked, teasing him.

He lifted her off her feet and into his arms, kissing her hard. "Stop sassing me or I really will spank you."

She shook her head. "Tristan, what is going on with you?"

"I am in love."

Tears burned her eyes as those words came from his mouth. She didn't believe them. He'd been too adamant about not falling again. "Put me down."

"No."

"Tristan, I mean it."

"So do I."

He reached down, unlocked his front door and carried her over the threshold. He set her on her feet in the foyer. She was blinking, trying not to cry, but it wasn't working.

"I wanted to do this properly."

"Do what properly? You don't have to pretend to feel something for me you don't feel."

"I am not pretending, *ma petite.*"

She wasn't sure she believed him, but she knew he wouldn't lie to her. He never had.

"When did you realize you loved me?" she asked him.

"Today, when I was surrounded by my family. I did not realize how much you'd done with them. They were all telling me stories about you and I realized that no matter how hard I'd tried not to fall for you, I already had.

"I love you, Sheri. And it does scare me. Because as much as I thought that Cecile was my once-in-a-lifetime love, I have come to realize that love is also what I feel for you. I need you in my life."

She was afraid to believe him. "It's okay if you don't love me. I'm not going to walk away from you like I did last night. That was wrong—"

"You are not listening to me, *ma petite.* I love you. I am not going anywhere without you anymore. No running unless you are by my side."

She was still afraid to believe him but there was sincerity in his eyes that made her want to.

He must have read the hesitation on her face

because he leaned down and kissed her. And when he lifted his head he said, softly, "I am not going anywhere."

Those words she believed. No man had ever said them to her before. "Promise?"

"Yes, I do. What about you?"

"I'm not going anywhere, either. I'm staying by your side from now on."

"Why is that?"

"I love you, Tristan."

He smiled at her and lifted her off her feet. He carried her through his apartment out onto the balcony that offered a splendid view of the Manhattan skyline.

"You're already wearing my engagement ring, but I need to ask you again...Sheri Donnelly, my love, the woman who owns my heart, will you marry me?"

She looked up at him as he stood next to her on the balcony. Taking a deep breath, she leaned up and kissed him before pulling back. "Yes, Tristan, I will marry you."

He pulled her into his arms and made love to her, sealing the bond they'd just made with their bodies. And she knew she'd found the happiness she'd always thought would elude her. She and

Tristan had found something rare, the kind of love that touched few people's lives, and she felt blessed to have him as her own.

* * * * *

Wealth and power are nothing without love!
Don't miss Gui's story next month as
Katherine Garbera's SONS OF PRIVILEGE
mini-series continues with
The Spanish Aristocrat's Woman.
Available in March 2009 only from
Mills & Boon® Desire™.

Turn the page for a sneak preview of

Marrying for King's Millions
by Maureen Child,

an exciting new story available from
Mills & Boon® Desire™
in March 2009.

Marrying for King's Millions
by
Maureen Child

"No way. Sorry, Travis, I just can't marry you." Julie O'Hara leaned against the closed door and kept her voice pitched loud enough so that it would carry to the man on the other side.

Clearly, he heard her.

"Oh, yes you can," he said, and even through the door, his voice was all steely determination. "Now cut the dramatics and open the damn door."

Julie's head dropped back against the door and she rolled her eyes to look at the high, beamed ceiling. Sunlight slanted in through the windows across the room and the golden wash from the sun created shadows on the walls that looked eerily like the bars on a cell.

Coincidence?

She didn't think so.

This was a huge mistake. She knew it down to her bones. The bad feeling that had been taking root inside her for the last month had suddenly blossomed into big, black flowers. Ooh, there was an image.

"Travis, think about this for a minute."

"Not really the time for any more thinking, Julie," he said. "The guests are here, the minister's waiting and we *are* getting married."

Her stomach did a slow pitch and roll and she clenched her teeth together and took a few deep breaths through her nose. Didn't really help. How in the heck had she gotten herself into this? Julie's eyes flew open when Travis King's knuckles rapped on the door again and she looked around the room with a frantic gaze, futilely searching for an escape route.

But there wasn't one and she knew it. She was trapped in this plush guest room in Travis's castlelike house on the King Vineyard. Just like the rest of the house, it was gorgeous, elegant and so far away from her ordinary world she felt like a servant girl who'd sneaked into the mistress's room to try on her clothes. Bad, bad feeling. And it was all her own fault.

She'd walked into this stupid situation with her eyes wide open. "Idiot."

"Open the door, Julie...."

"It's bad luck to see the bride before the wedding," she said.

"Uh-huh. Don't think that matters so much in our case, so open up."

Our case.

Of course their case was special. Because this wasn't your ordinary, everyday wedding.

It had all seemed so simple a month ago, she thought and instantly remembered just how she'd gotten to this place in her life.

"I need a wife," Travis had said. "You need a future. It's perfect."

Julie had looked at him, sitting across from her in a red vinyl booth at Terri's Diner in the heart of downtown Birkfield, California. In a small town, the diner was the one place where everyone eventually showed up. Julie had practically grown up sliding across the red vinyl seats.

Her first date had brought her here. She'd nursed her first broken heart over four double-chocolate shakes. And now she was getting a marriage proposal here.

Shouldn't there be a plaque?

"It's not perfect," she argued, thinking that at least one of them had to be logical here. Travis had always been more impulsive than she—well, except for that one time when she'd married a man she thought loved her, only to find out too late that he hadn't. See where impulsiveness had gotten her?

Firmly, she said, "There's an easier solution, Travis. Just go find another distributor for your wines."

He shook his head, dark brown hair flopping across his forehead in a way that made her want to reach across the table and smooth it back for him. She resisted.

"Can't. Thomas Henry is the best and you know I never settle for less than the best."

True, he never had. Travis had grown up as a member of one of the wealthiest, most powerful families in the state. He'd long ago grown accustomed to being on top. Being number one. And there was nothing Travis cared for more than King Vineyards. Ever since taking it over from his late father, he'd put in the time and effort required to make King wines known all over California.

Now he'd set his sights on not only distribution countrywide, but also eventually international exports, as well. Apparently, Thomas Henry was key to Travis's plan for world domination.

"Okay, but you don't have to marry me to get him."

"No." He sat back in the booth seat with a disgusted scowl on his face. "I don't. I could marry one of Henry's hideous daughters instead. I told you, Julie. The guy's kind of eccentric. He's a self-made millionaire and now his big goal in life is to get his girls married. I'm single. Rich. Therefore, I'm prime husband material."

She smiled. "He can't force you to marry one of his daughters. This isn't the Middle Ages."

"I wouldn't put it past him to try." Travis smiled wryly. "But if I turn down his 'darlings,' he can—and will—refuse to handle my wines. I can't risk that. King Vineyards is poised for the next big step. Getting the distribution deal with Henry would put me on the right path. All I need to make it all happen is a temporary wife. If I'm already married, he won't be tossing his daughters at my feet, will he?"

"Why me?"

He grinned…and Travis smiling was pretty spectacular. She'd had a crush on him when she was a kid. But then, Travis was gorgeous, charming and his smile had been known to melt a woman's resistance at fifty feet. Good thing Julie was immune. All it had taken was marrying a jerk and being dumped. Just because she could admire Travis's smile didn't mean she was going to turn into a puddle of mush at his feet.

"A couple of reasons," he was saying and Julie listened up. "First, because we know each other and I know you need this, too. Second, because I trust you to stick to our agreement and not try to bleed me for extra cash."

She knew he was wary of most women because King men attracted gold diggers in greater numbers than the gold rush had back in the day. "But if I marry you, what makes me different from any of those other women? I'll still be marrying you for your money."

"Yeah, but on my terms," he said with a smile.

MILLS&BOON
Desire 2-in-1
On sale 20th February 2009

Marrying for King's Millions *by Maureen Child*

Travis needs a wife. Julie needs a fortune. But when her ex arrives at their door, it turns out their marriage of convenience might not be so binding after all.

The Spanish Aristocrat's Woman *by Katherine Garbera*

Kara was only supposed to play the count's lover for one day. But suddenly she's become a wife.

Boardrooms & a Billionaire Heir *by Paula Roe*

Holly had been blackmailed into spying on Sydney's most infamous corporate raider. Until he turned the tables and seduced her.

Jealousy & a Jewelled Proposition *by Yvonne Lindsay*

To avenge his family's name, Matt sets out to take over his biggest competitor...and realises his ex may be the perfect weapon for revenge.

Series – Diamonds Down Under

CEO's Marriage Seduction *by Anna DePalo*

It was the perfect plan. Wed her father's business protégé and have the baby she's been dreaming about...until scandal threatens Eva's marriage of convenience.

His Style of Seduction *by Roxanne St Claire*

Lily was hired to give millionaire Jackson a makeover. But she was the one in for the biggest change...in the bedroom.

Secrets always find a place to hide...

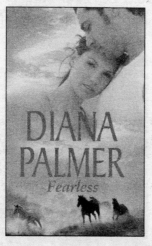

When DEA agent Rodrigo Ramirez finds undercover work at Gloryanne Barnes's nearby farm, Gloryanne's sweet innocence is too much temptation for him. Confused and bitter about love, Rodrigo's not sure if his reckless offer of marriage is just a means to completing his mission – or something more.

But as Gloryanne's bittersweet miracle and Rodrigo's double life collide, two people must decide if there's a chance for the future they both secretly desire.

Available 6th February 2009

M&B

FREE

2 BOOKS AND A SURPRISE GIFT!

We would like to take this opportunity to thank you for reading this Mills & Boon® book by offering you the chance to take TWO more specially selected 2-in-1 volumes from the Desire™ series absolutely FREE! We're also making this offer to introduce you to the benefits of the Mills & Boon® Book Club™—

- ★ **FREE home delivery**
- ★ **FREE gifts and competitions**
- ★ **FREE monthly Newsletter**
- ★ **Books available before they're in the shops**
- ★ **Exclusive Mills & Boon Book Club offers**

Accepting these FREE books and gift places you under no obligation to buy; you may cancel at any time, even after receiving your free shipment. Simply complete your details below and return the entire page to the address below. You don't even need a stamp!

YES! Please send me 2 free Desire volumes and a surprise gift. I understand that unless you hear from me, I will receive 3 superb new volumes every month for just £5.25 each, postage and packing free. I am under no obligation to purchase any books and may cancel my subscription at any time. The free books and gift will be mine to keep in any case.

D9ZEE

Ms/Mrs/Miss/Mr...Initials ....

BLOCK CAPITALS PLEASE

Surname ....

Address ....

....

....Postcode ....

Send this whole page to:

The Mills & Boon Book Club, FREEPOST CN81, Croydon, CR9 3WZ